What's wrong with you, Karthik?

What's wrong with you, Karthik?

SIDDHARTHA
VAIDYANATHAN

PICADOR INDIA

First published in 2020 by Picador India
an imprint of Pan Macmillan Publishing India Private Limited
707, Kailash Building,
26, K. G. Marg, New Delhi – 110 001
www.panmacmillan.co.in

Pan Macmillan, The Smithson, 6 Briset Street, London EC1M 5NR
Associated companies throughout the world
www.panmacmillan.com

ISBN 978-93-89109-50-4

1 3 5 7 9 8 6 4 2

Typeset in Aldine401 BT by R. Ajith Kumar, New Delhi
Printed and bound in India by
Replika Press Pvt. Ltd.

'... this was the great, abiding lesson of my boyhood: that I was in a world where it was not possible for me to be good.'

– George Orwell *Such, Such Were the Joys*

For Amma, Appa, and Akila,
for their unflinching support

PART ONE

1

Bingo

IT WAS A LITTLE AFTER six o'clock on a typical Bangalore summer morning. The air was crisp, the sky spotless and the sun cheerful, the sort of weather that my cousin in Madras dreamed of year round. I had recently told him that according to newspaper reports – and our neighbour uncle Mr Chacko, surely the only man in the country who took a greater delight in discussing the weather forecast than an Indian cricket win – there was clear evidence that Bangalore's summers were getting warmer and warmer. 'Get lost, Karthik,' he fumed over the phone, as if I had insulted his mother. Must have been bathed in sweat. So I let him be.

I was at Cook's Cricket Ground in the heart of the city, and part of a loose semi-circle of twenty boys waiting for catch practice to begin. We could have been fast asleep on this relaxed Friday morning in May, making the most of our summer holidays, if our parents hadn't woken us up and packed us off to Iqbal Sir's Sureshot Success cricket camp at an ungodly hour.

Sunil 'Zombie' Lobo, fourteen, was stationed at one end of the bracket, touching his shoes without bending his knees. I, recently turned twelve, stood an arm's length to his right, hands clasped behind my back.

Iqbal Sir, wearing a checked full-sleeve shirt folded up to his elbows over a pair of wrinkled khakis, was not yet ready for catch practice. He was busy instructing his assistant, Francis, on how to pitch the jute matting in the middle of the field. Sir spelled out the procedure in English and Kannada, and asked, 'Francis, everything clear?'

'Yessir, yessir,' nodded Francis, swirling his head as if it were a ball of clay about to be shaped over a potter's wheel.

'What yessir yessir?' barked Iqbal Sir, right thumb pointing up.

Francis knew he was to list out each step as he had heard it. He widened his eyes to dispel the lingering drowsiness in them.

'Sir, first I will nail down one side of the mat.'

'How many nails, man?'

'Three nails, sir.'

'You will nail the long side or short side?'

'Long side, sir.'

'You dumb owl,' Sir scowled, his hands on his head and face crumpled up. 'Why don't you go and admit yourself into NIMHANS?' (The iconic National Institute of Mental Health and Neurosciences was a mere ten minutes away by auto-rickshaw.)

Anil 'Big Dog' Suri found this uncontrollably funny.

Iqbal Sir turned around, eyes aflame behind square spectacles. He raised a bat over his head and ordered, 'Big Dog, shut your bloody mouth now.'

Big Dog pursed his lips.

Sir lowered his bat.

'Now run two laps before I break your head piece to piece.'

I stole a glance at Zombie.

I didn't know what to make of this fellow. Most of the boys at the camp were convinced he was a gone-case. He never smiled or frowned, didn't flinch when struck by a leather ball. During a game at the camp, when our mates had mobbed Big Dog after he claimed a wicket, Zombie had stayed put at mid-on, making sure his shirt was properly tucked in. A little later Zombie himself had taken a wicket and stood mid-pitch, arms folded over his chest. No one patted him on the back. No one gave him a high-five.

This morning Zombie Lobo's eyes were fixed on a lone clump of grass in a bald field, and his legs were occupied with squats and ankle rotations. I tried to chat with him when his windmilling arms slowed down. He ignored my 'hey' and swivelled his neck two-seventy degrees.

If there was anyone Zombie spoke to freely in the camp, it was me. He hadn't paid me attention at first but things changed when he gathered that I was younger than him and, more importantly, that I was hoping to get admitted into St George's Boys' High School, *his* school, which was 'without doubt the best in Bangalore'. From then on, our chats had fallen into two broad categories: i) Zombie's ravings about St George's; and ii) Zombie's frequent boasts about his gifts. In the short time I had known him, his parents had bought him a Slazenger cricket bat, a video-game set and a pair of roller skates. I didn't know where his parents worked but his velveteen cap, smart Nike shoes and a watch that glowed in the dark made it clear to me that they were rolling in cash.

My tennis shoes had faded from white to mottled grey after many a proper scrub with washing powder Nirma. My watch ran slow, so slow that I sometimes held it near my ear to check for tick-tocks. When Zombie spoke about his school and his gifts, I listened, alert. I didn't have all that much to say but even if I had come up with something deep, Zombie may not have taken note.

Still, I was hoping for a hint of excitement from Zombie when, seizing on a split second of eye contact, I broke the news about my admission to St George's Boys' High School. Now that was something, wasn't it? The school was the centre of Zombie's universe. Conversations about cricket bats invariably led to the recent exploits of the St George's cricket team. Small talk about Iqbal Sir grew into a review of the cricket coach at his school, who apparently knew 'how to get the best out of everyone'. So hung up was Zombie on St George's, and so convincingly had he made the case for its superiority, that my admission process had turned into a private mission to please him. At every stage, there lurked a chance to rise in his estimation and I told myself that by studying in Zombie's school I too could start to wear sleek shoes and jazzy watches.

Yesterday morning, anticipation bubbling over, my grandfather, father, mother and I had waited for the crucial phone call from St George's. I made sure to park myself near the telephone at nine o'clock, determined to keep my position until the call arrived. By ten, I was ripping out my fingernails and picking at the dead skin around them. Around eleven-thirty, I wrapped my arms around the telephone and, with my head resting on the table, nodded off. At one o'clock my father said that it would be best if we drove to the school to investigate. My mother, who was stretched out on the mosaic floor, a magazine in hand, shook her head with a stern 'uh hmm'. My grandfather assured the hall that it was only a matter of time before the phone would ring, but I had long given up, dreading the next meeting with Zombie at Sureshot, where no doubt he would air a laundry list of the possible reasons for my rejection. 'I guess your English wasn't up to the mark,' he would have declared with a superior air and lofty enunciation. 'Even one teeny-tiny mistake will cost you a spot at St George's, you know.'

The phone didn't ring till a little after two o'clock.

'Calling from SGBHS,' a lady announced in a singsong voice. 'This is S. Karthik's residence, correct?'

'Yes. Speaking. Hello.'

'Is there a parent or a guardian we can speak to? Your admission has been confirmed.'

'Oh, thank you,' I said, bobbing my head. 'Thank you so much.'

'Any parent or guardian there?'

'Yes. One minute. Thank you. Thanks a lot.'

I wanted to tell Zombie about this in its entire thrilling sequence but barely had I passed on the news when he stumped me with: 'Watch for the bingo.'

He mumbled it so fast I wasn't sure if he was talking to me or to himself. Nor could I immediately discern where one word ended and the next one began.

From the centre Iqbal Sir announced, 'Everyone take two arm's lengths,' firm and grumpy.

Big Dog was into the second lap of his punishment. Francis started to roll out the jute matting in the middle of the field.

Zombie took a quick step to his left. He spat on his stiff palms, rubbed them with purpose and lowered his hands in front of bent knees. So still was his pose, and so determined his set-up, I assumed he had decided to take his catching seriously from now. That would leave me the worst catcher among the twenty boys.

Iqbal Sir turned towards our half of the semi-circle and launched the first ball, at a comfortable height, to Zombie's left. Zombie got into a perfect position as the ball arrived. He grabbed at it rather than letting it come to him, as we had been taught, and fluffed it. Oohs and tchas flew around the semi-circle.

'Great start,' sniggered Iqbal Sir and waited for Zombie to look up, as if considering whether to shame him or excuse him. Zombie didn't pout, didn't stare at his palms as though holding them responsible, and didn't dare to glare at me. He retrieved the ball and under-armed it to Sir, stone face in place.

At eight o'clock, the practice session ended. Both of us botched a catch apiece, struggled to middle the ball during net practice and did little of note in the six-over match. As we walked off the ground leaving the stragglers behind – by which I mean the boys who would climb the city, district and state rungs of the cricketing ladder, boys whose mugshots would adorn the advertisement in the newspapers next summer: *Think you can be Sachin? Join Sureshot Success Cricket Camp and turn your dreams into reality* – as we walked away from those overachievers, Zombie spoke about his 'awesome' bat grip, his 'perfect' helmet and the batting gloves he was planning to buy that evening, all the while distracted by the bruise on my left elbow.

Examining it like it was a bullet wound, he said, 'What's wrong with you, Karthik? Diving like a madman. Not even in your dreams could you have taken that catch.'

I started to explain why I had dived full length to my left, but his driver pulled into the parking lot just then. He hurried off.

On the bus home, Zombie's four words turned into squirrels that nibbled at my brain. Gnaw, gnaw, gnaw. Ruining my afternoon nap, distracting me at evening prayers. 'Watch for the bingo.' What could that possibly mean? Maybe a 'bingo' was an artefact housed in a secret room in St George's, something that only a select few boys knew about. Or was it the party game that Mr Chacko brought out on New Year's Eve, when he regaled everyone with lines like 'made in heaven, sixty-seven' and 'two fat ladies, eighty-eight'? Perhaps it was a raffle that new students were expected to sell to raise money for the rest of the class. Or was it some group-bonding activity on the first day of every school year?

Brushing my teeth before bedtime, I began to suspect that it was none of those. So I settled on a plan: if Zombie brought it up again, I would ask him to explain. If not, it was best forgotten.

Nobody was as excited about my admission to St George's Boys' High School as my mother.

'He has had a great time at Sacred Valley,' she told our neighbour aunty Mrs Chacko, 'but we weren't sure ... we weren't sure if this style of education was preparing him for the real world.'

Mrs Chacko sat up in her chair and snapped her fingers, excited that my mother had finally seen the light.

'Yes, yes! Nice place and all that Sacred Valley, but so pricey and posh! And so far away from humanity. Absolutely no chance for Karthik to take part in the sports meets and lit fests in the city.'

'Good point,' my mother said, 'and the teachers were always saying he's doing well, he's doing great. Sometimes ... umm ... I felt they were saying all this just like that. You know ... I took Karthik to three temples today, offered thanks to the gods and the priests, circled the shrines hundred and eight times.'

Mrs Chacko was not in the least surprised. She knew how ardently my mother communicated with the gods. One rainy evening last year, when I was heavily delayed getting back from school, the one 'far away from humanity', my mother sent up a prayer that she would walk up the hill to the temple in Tirupati if I returned safe. My father and grandfather felt she had over-prayed. Mrs Chacko voiced her disapproval. 'Please don't mistake me,' she had said through a put-on whisper, 'but what if Karthik is, you know, kidnapped some day? Shouldn't you be saving these prayers for then?'

My mother was appalled. About a month later, she prepared enough food to last a week and embarked on the train journey to Tirupati, along with another one of our neighbour aunties, Mrs Nagaraj. Unlike Mrs Nagaraj's yoga-toned physique, my mother's bulky frame hadn't accounted for the twelve-kilometre trek uphill.

'Uh ho,' Mrs Chacko snorted when she saw my mother's sore knees and cracked soles. 'See, this is what happens. Not good. Not good at all. Health is most important, Kamala. Not as if we are getting younger, right?'

Now Mrs Chacko was fired up about my admission to SGBHS. 'You must make him properly ready for St George's, Kamala. It will be very different from Sacred Valley. I am telling you – very, very different.'

The same evening a checklist appeared on a square chit of paper, which my mother magnetically stuck to the fridge. This was to remind my father of the items to tick off over the next few days.

- Apply for K's bus pass
- Contact tailor for uniform (Rao & Rao Ph: 648177)
- Buy two pairs formal shoes and four pairs socks
- Ask school for list of textbooks and notebooks to buy. Buy brown paper to cover books
- Get K extra spectacles

Next she made another checklist, just for me.

- Cut hair in Excellent Salon
- Wash sports shoes
- Cover notebooks with brown paper (remind Appa to buy brown paper)
- Study first chapter of each textbook
- Memorize school song
- Practise handwriting
- Learn three new English words every day
- Take one tbsp Chyawanprash/morning and evening

There was something for everyone to worry about. The tailor's lateness caused plenty of headaches; the barber, as usual, bungled my haircut; and despite my diligent copy-filling, my handwriting just wouldn't look up. As if that wasn't enough, when I washed my shoes and left them out to dry, a downpour soaked them. It was unclear if my mother was sad, anxious, angry or frustrated by all this. So I assumed she was all of the above.

Iqbal Sir wasn't too fussed when the rains arrived, and wound up the camp in the final week of May. He had long ago identified the boys who had it in them to play for higher honours. The rest of us were wasting his time, good for little other than standing around and giggling as he roasted Francis in the mornings.

Zombie withdrew further into himself with each passing day. He wasn't comfortable talking about his school anymore, and once said that it would be two or three years before I could call myself a 'true blue Georgian'. He brushed off my admiring comment about his oversize batting gloves, which he had bought recently, and didn't say anything about his shiny new Adidas shoes.

One day, while he batted in the practice nets, a ball that rose awkwardly smashed into his left wrist and cracked his expensive watch – and even *he* couldn't stop his face from reddening when two boys congratulated Big Dog on his aim. From then on, Zombie didn't respond even to hi's and byes.

On the final day, minutes after Iqbal Sir had delivered a fiery speech and handed each of us an old cricket ball to take home – 'Remember, boys: hitting the ball builds confidence, being hit by the ball builds character' – I asked Zombie if we could meet up on the first morning of school.

'Eight-thirty near the main gate?'

Zombie ignored me.

'Eight forty-five?'

Again, no response.

'What happened, man? Is everything okay?'

Zombie slipped on his velveteen maroon cap and slung his kitbag over his shoulder. 'Dad's been transferred to Hyderabad, man,' he said, slitting my eyes with his gaze. 'Leaving in three days.'

Before I could make sense of what he had just hit me with, before I could bid him a proper goodbye, Zombie was gone.

St George's was to reopen on 7 June, a Monday, and I woke to a grey sky that wept non-stop, the raindrops tap-tapping the windowpane before gathering in a puddle on a cement path. The curtains may have been drawn wide open but I had to switch on the tube light to find my socks in the cupboard.

By the time I was done with my bath, the house was abuzz. The radio jingled, the pressure cooker hissed. My grandfather belted out prayer after prayer in the puja room, his manner so combative that it was unclear if he was imploring the gods or issuing threats. My mother, lording over the kitchen, screamed out orders every few minutes: 'Oil your hair, K', 'Don't forget to put a handkerchief in your pocket, please', 'Fill your water bottle before you leave, K'. Not to be left behind, my father kept asking if I had made sure to 'take everything' but, engrossed as he was in the morning newspaper, he didn't pick up my 'yeses'.

At seven forty-five, fifteen minutes before scheduled departure, I walked up to our full-size mirror to ensure everything was tip-top. Studying my reflection in the shiny glass, I adjusted my spectacles, tucked in my shirt, finger-combed my hair, fidgeted with my belt, re-tucked my shirt and re-set my hair. I wiggled my collar and loosened the belt before tightening it once again.

There was no need for this much tension. My dazzling white half-sleeve shirt was A-1; so perfectly had my mother ironed the sleeves the creases were arrows shot from my shoulder bones. My American khaki trousers glistened with confidence. The tailor may have stirred up panic with his multiple delays – 'Perfection takes time, sir,' he had shrugged when my father exploded with rage –

but nobody could fault the double-pleated piece whose stitch and fit were flawless. Holding the trousers in place was a jet-black belt whose buckle was polished to a twinkle. Plus, there was a delicate waft that rose from my new clothes, assuring me that everything was going to be okay.

A raspy slurp distracted me.

Having finished his morning puja, my amputee grandfather – 'right leg wronged, left leg still left' – had settled into his cane chair, his milky veshti and brand-new banian as bright and white as the thick strips of holy ash marked across his arms and forehead. My grandfather drank three cups of coffee a day, but it was the first two that usually dictated his mood. When the temperature, the 'degree', was exactly as he wished, as it was now, he let out a hearty 'umm' after each noisy sip. Blowing on the surface, he took great delight in rousing the vapours into a frenetic dance.

In the mornings, coffee time was also his workout time. After each sip, my grandfather rested the tumbler on the floor, sat upright in his chair and punched the air with his knotted left fist. He punched with his right fist and kicked his left leg at a diagonal, like a footballer sending in a corner. So furious were these kicks, so high their reach, it was a surprise his veshti didn't fly open.

Jab, jab, punt; jab, jab, punt

Jab, jab, punt; jab, jab, punt.

Ten sets completed, and coffee downed, my grandfather turned to the only window in the room, lowered his head towards the metallic grille and craned his neck heavenwards.

'Tcha,' he grimaced, crunching his dentures, coming to grips with the sky that shed many tears.

Irritated, he turned to one of his big sources of comfort when the outlook was gloomy: the oval pit of holy ash, the vibhuti, that sat in the windowsill.

'Come, Karthik,' he said, with a forefinger dipped in the pit, and marked a thick strip of ash on my forehead.

'See, grey sky, grey ash,' he said, pointing to my forehead.

'Will the sky change colour if I erase the vibhuti, Thatha?'

He raised his eyebrows, his eyeballs threatening their sockets.

'Will you dare to erase the vibhuti? Of all days today?'

'Just joking, Thatha.'

'Joking? Is this the time and place to joke about these things? What nonsense is this, Karthik? You need to stop acting like a child. You are in seventh standard now. Behave yourself.'

'Sorry, Thatha.'

'Today is your first day in a new school and here you are talking of erasing the vibhuti. Will Lord Ganesha accept that?'

'No, Thatha. Very sorry.'

'Wait, have you prayed to Lord Ganesha?'

'Yes, Thatha. I prayed before I put my shoes on.'

'You need to pray on your way to school too.'

'Okay, Thatha.'

'Now don't lose track of time. It's getting late.'

The hour hand neared the VIII. The minute hand flirted with the angled XI. The second hand continued its ruthless advance.

I raced to the hall, set to leave, but my grandfather's eldest son, my father, sat at the dining table, still absorbed in the *Hindu*, a newspaper that he often exclaimed was actually 'anti-Hindu'.

'Communist paper,' he growled, scanning the editorial page.

'Shall we leave, Appa?'

'The biggest problem with this country is that ...'

'Appa!'

He shook his head as if woken abruptly, wriggled his wrist and checked his watch. He glanced at the newspaper, then sized me up and zeroed in on my shoes.

'Not polished enough, Karthik,' he frowned, shaking his head.

My father's nails were uncut, his elbows scaly, his heels cracked and his hair rumpled. Tufts of hair peeked from his chest. None of this seemed to concern him.

'Fools run this country,' he thundered, returning to the paper.

Just half an hour earlier I had massaged the leather for five minutes, and my grandfather had inspected the shoes and said, 'Looks fine,' which, for a former army man like my grandfather, ranked somewhere between top-notch and mind-blowing.

It made little sense to repeat the whole routine. I dipped the brush in a cake of Cherry Blossom and, with my shoes still on, swiped against the leather. My father would have gone nuts had he seen this couldn't-care-less attempt but he was busy shouting at the communist editors of the *Hindu*. 'Such nonsense they publish these days.'

Up, down, up, down.

The shoe brush's molars pecked at my black socks.

Up, down, up, down.

Soon, bored of the mindless swishing with my right hand, I shifted the brush to my left hand. And it took three seconds for the steady swipes to turn into prods. The brush jiggled over the shoe and threatened to slip from my grasp. It was clear as glass that I had to slow down then and there but, driven by some lunatic impulse, I swished faster and faster, zigging and zagging brushstrokes from up to side to down to side to up ... until a crumb of Cherry Blossom polish flew onto my trousers' left cuff.

Smack.

Like a greedy fly on a bowl of payasam, the black bead of polish clung to the American khaki. I shook the cuff, ordering, then urging, then begging the speck to quietly collapse. But it refused to comply. Flustered, I carromed it with an index finger and – no no nooo! – smudged the khaki. Panic met fear met confusion. I applied a fingertip of saliva to the black smudge. It grew to the size of a five-paisa coin. By the time I came to my senses my brand-new uniform was beyond repair, and two thoughts hit me: i) there was no time to change into a new pair of trousers; and ii) if anyone at home happened to notice the smudge, I was finished.

My father, as was his daily habit, started to read the local news headlines aloud, out-shouting a radio advertisement for silk saris. 'Kidnappings on the rise.' 'Striking students burn bus on Mysore Road.' 'Robbery near Nandi Hills.' 'Two caught in ...'

'Aiyyo enough,' my mother screamed and turned the mixie to a high setting, no doubt agitated that her only child could run into kidnappers, robbers and bus-burners on his way back from school.

My father didn't push it. He turned to the obituary section and read softly, so softly that it sounded like he was mourning the dead. 'P. Manickavachakam. Retired AGM. BEL. Sad. Very sad. Latha Ramani. Wife of S. Ramani. Tcha. Not at all an age to die.'

'Polished, Appa,' I said, upbeat, maybe a little too much.

My father popped his face over the newspaper and squinted at my shoes. He couldn't see the smudge but just to be sure, I turned slightly left.

'Not enough, Karthik,' he said and disappeared behind the newspaper. 'How many times have I told you: your shoes are not polished until you can see your face reflected in the leather. Ask Thatha if you want. In the army you would have been punished for this. They would have made you hold a rifle over your head and run six laps around the field.'

This is how my father pushed me: not polished enough, not neat enough, not good enough. So mighty were his expectations, nothing was going to be enough.

Back to it. Up, down, up down.

The brush tamely skimmed the surface of my right shoe.

The cuckoo clock started to chirp out the time. My grandfather interrupted its tweets with a loud 'Kaaaarthik'.

'Eight o'clock,' my mother hollered, outdoing a feverish hiss from the pressure cooker. The lady on All India Radio reported the time, making it sound like a groundbreaking event. Now the whole country knew it was eight o'clock, and I hadn't left for school yet.

'Appa.'

'Such hopeless crossword clues,' my father announced, folding the newspaper in four and smashing the table as if to murder a cockroach. 'Go wait near the car. I'll come in a minute.'

'Okay, Pa. Bye, Thatha. Bye, Amma. I'm leaving now.'

'Leaving?' my grandfather yelled, his voice oiled with annoyance. 'How many times have I told you, Karthik? Never say you are leaving. Sounds as if you are going away forever.'

'Sorry Thatha. What I am saying is: I will go and return.'

'Say that again.'

'I will go to school and safely return, Thatha.'

'And don't forget to pray to Lord Ganesha on your way,' he roared, raising his voice so high that our neighbours might have paused to consider the command – though the Chackos, devout Catholics, would not have known the shlokas. Mrs Chacko assumed my grandfather screamed because he was going deaf. Actually, my grandfather jacked up the volume when he deemed something really important, and he was now hung up on Lord Ganesha because the elephant-headed wonder – remover of obstacles, provider of wisdom, and master of the arts and sciences – was the god of auspicious beginnings. There was no way I was going to start life at a new school without invoking His blessings.

I grabbed my black backpack, shot out of the side door and slid into the enclosed driveway. But I was still not out of earshot.

'You better not forget to pray, okay?'

The beige Maruti was sparkling from a wash. A plastic Lord Ganesha – holding a lotus in one hand, an axe in the second, a miniature laddoo in the third while blessing us with the fourth – sat on top of the speedometer, and my father, eyes shut, touched His feet and muttered a prayer. He adjusted the rearview mirror and pushed his seat back ... when he realized he had to adjust the mirror again. I positioned my bag to conceal the shoe polish smudge.

'One, two, three, go,' he said, pumping the accelerator before turning the key. The car chugged. It took a third key turn to excite the engine into a steady gurgle, which brought on a rapid prayer of thanks: '*Vakratundamahakayasuryakotisa*-mumble-*nirvignamkuru*-mumble-mumble-*sarvada*.' From inside the car stereo M.S. Subbulakshmi started her own prayer to Lord Ganesha and as we backed out of the driveway she had by way of accompaniment a background score: raindrops pelting the rooftop, wipers whining on the windshield.

'mudakaratha modakam sada vimukthi sadhakam ...'

The overnight rain had ruined many roads. Every time the wheels plunged into a crater my father sucked in air, but his patience ran out when a Luna-rider lost her balance and nearly toppled onto our car's hood. 'Some big minister has to die on these roads,' he shouted, emphasizing die. 'Only then will this hopeless city think of fixing them.'

I had occasionally hoped for such a tragedy myself. A big minister dying would mean we got a day off from school. And we were due, long due. In fact, I couldn't remember the last time my father had picked up the *Hindu* and announced some major death. 'Why can't some bigshot die on a Sunday afternoon, man?' my neighbour Chiku Chacko had asked on the eve of his final exams last year. 'Now that would be truly heavenly.'

'samasta loka shankaram nirastha dhaithya kunjaram ...'

Not even two seconds after we turned into Hosur Road, a red BTS bus blared out a lengthy honk and charged past on our left. 'The left! The left!' my father yelled. 'Why do all Bangalore bus drivers think it is their birthright to overtake on the left!' Splashing mud cakes onto our car, the bus came dangerously close to a cyclist, who in turn was trying to find a way between a teetering auto-rickshaw and an unruffled buffalo.

'Son of a widow,' my father squealed, rolling down his window and drowning out MS' soothing tune. 'Who the hell gave you your licence, you donkey? Have you gone mad? Have you informed your family to arrange for your funeral?'

The driver took a left and disappeared.

'mahaganesha pancharathnamadarena yoanvaham ...'

On seeing the bus escape, my father panted, puffed, slapped his forehead and gnashed his teeth. He pinched his nose and hurled a series of questions, questions for which he expected no response. 'Who will wash the car now? His father-in-law? Who will teach these fools to drive properly? No wonder so many people die on the roads every single day.'

Eventually, he gathered his breath and squinted in my direction but I turned away in the nick of time, surveying the scene outside the window. Seconds tick-ticked. This was the second time in a month when, with me in the passenger seat, my father had rolled down the window and screamed 'son of a widow' at a fellow driver. He knew my mother and grandfather would lose their minds if they found out about this, and, like any good father, he didn't want to be cursing in front of a twelve-year-old. Still, something told me he felt relieved to let off steam while driving, relieved to be able to gather all his frustrations and unload them onto the rash drivers of Bangalore in one furious blast, comfortable in the knowledge that

I wouldn't tattle. His swears were our secret, and he knew I knew that. So he let the words hover, silent, unsaid.

MS began a new prayer, this time to Lord Vishnu. My father kept his eye on the road. I distracted myself by reading signs on storefronts and memorizing number plates.

We stayed mute for ten minutes, all the way until we reached the parking lot outside St George's. There the engine stopped blub-blubbing and MS went quiet. I rolled down my window and took a sniff but there was not a whiff of rain in the air, only the sun pouring itself onto the cracked concrete. My father raised his hands to the sky as if talking to the gods. 'Raining at home, sunny here,' he said. 'This city has gone fully mad.'

I turned to him as I unlocked the door.

'All the best, Karthik.'

'Thanks, Pa.'

'You know which buses to take in the evening, right?'

'Yes, Pa.'

'If there is a problem give me a call at the office. You have coins?'

'Yes, Pa.'

'Good. See you, then.'

Holding my bag low to hide the smudge, I tumbled out.

'Oh god. What is this, Karthik?'

'Sorry, Pa,' I said regaining my balance.

'Is there any problem?'

'No, Pa. No problem.'

'Something bothering you?'

'No, Pa. All fine.'

'Listen Karthik. Sometimes I shout at these hopeless bus drivers. Okay? It's no big deal. Just forget whatever happened.'

'Yes, Pa.'

'And behave yourself in class. Don't get into trouble.'

'Okay, Pa.'

My father nodded a goodbye – raising his eyebrows, tilting his head – and shifted the gear stick into reverse. MS resumed her prayer. He took a sweeping turn, all set to zoom off. As I was about to turn to the main gate, the brakes squeaked.

No no no! My heart skipped a lub-dub. This was it. He had spotted the smudge in the mirror and was going to flame me in front of boys I did not know. He would smack my ears with acute topspin, and pinch my cheeks until they turned red. He would wet his fingers and frantically rub against the khaki ... but, to his horror, it would make things worse. Disgusted, he would rush me back home to change into a new pair of trousers and make me late for my very first day.

'Your hair is all over the place, Karthik,' he barked, leaning over the steering wheel and extracting a six-inch comb from his back pocket. 'Here, set it right.'

I walked up to the car and held out my hand, praying that he wouldn't look down at my trousers.

My father opened his mouth and enlarged his eyes. 'What is wrong with you, Karthik?'

'Pa?'

'Accepting things with your left hand? Really?'

'No, Pa. Sorry, Pa.'

I shoved my left hand behind my back and thrust out my right.

'Sometimes you forget all your manners, I tell you.'

'Sorry, Pa.'

'Hmm. Quick, quick. Make sure your hair is properly set.'

Turning to a side-view mirror, I parted my oily hair and ran my fingers over my scalp. Dandruff flakes thrived along the parting.

'Keep that comb now. Your hair is always messed up.'

'Okay, Pa.'

'And don't forget to pray to Lord Ganesha before class begins.'

'Yes, Pa.'

He restarted the car and drove off, hitting the main road before I could sneak the comb into my trouser pocket. The beige blob meshed with other vehicles, some of which were no doubt driven by mad sons-of-widows who should never have been given licences and who may well have informed their families to arrange for their funerals. I tracked him until I could no longer read the number plate. That's when I turned around to the main gate. At last, I had my school to myself.

2

7C

LEADING WITH MY RIGHT leg, as my mother had instructed, I stepped into the compound. The spikes on the gate had corroded. There stood a square marble pillar engraved with the founding year, the 1 faded but the 8, 5 and 7 holding out. I did a quick calculation to work out the school's age and estimated that 20,000 boys would have walked through the entrance. Among them, as per Zombie, were four state cricketers, one national cricketer, tens of professors across elite world institutions, hundreds of doctors, engineers, scientists, chartered accountants, bankers and lawyers, one popular newsreader, an up-and-coming film actor, a revered painter and a writer whose books were so sought after they were out of stock everywhere. Even one former governor. Would any of these chaps have been so careless as to mess up their trousers on their first day? The chances were slim.

The school's principal Father Richard Menezes came into view. There he was, standing in one corner of the quadrangle, monitoring those who passed by, his face and scalp clean-shaven, his rimless spectacles glinting and his bearing firm and poised. Angular sun rays bounced off his shimmering white cassock. Boys instinctively straightened up when they saw him. I hurriedly lowered my bag to cover my trouser smudge.

Two younger priests, their robes impressively bright but short of Father Menezes' dazzle, walked up to the principal. One hunched his shoulders as a mark of respect, the other bowed his head and offered the principal a 'Good morning, Father'. Father Menezes lightened the air with something witty, and the junior priests threw their heads back, as if under orders, and chuckled.

The principal led his colleagues to a nursery dotted with red and yellow roses, and waiting for them there was a man so lean that my mother would have concluded that he was uncared for as a child. This stick of a man had a black camera slung around his neck, and on seeing the three priests approach he adjusted his hair, rubbed his palms on either side of his hip, and offered Father Menezes a warm handshake. The principal ignored the outstretched hand and went on to take a spot between two rose plants. The two other priests quietly stood by Father Menezes' side. Clearly insulted, the photographer took his time adjusting the lens. He held up his right hand and raised his index finger like an umpire signalling an out, and it took the priests a few seconds to work out that it was time to smile.

The priest to Father Menezes' left beamed like a groom at a wedding reception. The priest to his right lent the moment a lukewarm grin. The principal, though, would not submit, not even when the photographer said, 'Father, three, two, one.' He shut his mouth and refused to soften his eyes for the camera.

'Smile please, Father.'

Father Menezes stiffened his jaw.

No one was admitted to St George's Boys' High School without a meeting with the principal and, my interview, for which my parents had been asked to come along, was scheduled for a Thursday morning. My father had requested a nine o'clock slot. My mother had insisted we visit the Ganesha temple on the way. And I, having tossed and turned in bed all night, couldn't stop thinking of Zombie's throwaway advice: 'Make sure you don't mess up. Otherwise you're in big trouble.'

We reached the school a few minutes early, which was what my mother needed to whip out a handkerchief, wipe the oiliness off my nose and cheeks, and dab them with talcum powder.

'His hair?' Appa said.

'It's fine,' my mother shrugged and refused the comb she was handed.

Had we been at home a tiff would have broken out but thankfully we were in the St George's parking lot. My father exhaled a gust. My mother invoked Lord Rama under her breath.

Father Menezes sat on a swivel chair behind a glass-topped table, a rectangular area that seemed so vast since it held so little: a tiny clock, a pen and a couple of glass paperweights holding down nothing. From the ceiling hung an intricate chandelier. Yet, the office was soaked in tube-light blue and decorated with framed certificates, plaques, shields and trophies – with a separate table for the silverware.

My father settled into one of the two stack chairs that faced the principal and my mother directed me to sit on the other. She adjusted her sari's pallu and positioned herself behind me, gently clasping the chair's shoulder. Father Menezes had a measured tone that suggested his words were perfectly in sync with his thoughts. It became obvious early on that he would do all the talking and we the listening.

Father Menezes started to lay out the plans for campus expansion and the frustrating roadblocks they had faced over the last few years. Assuming this was a two-way conversation, and trying to inject some jollity into the proceedings, my father added, 'Hope you have a *concrete* idea, Father.'

The principal snorted, unimpressed. It was no joking matter to deal with Bangalore's fickle weather and the ineptitude of the city development authority.

'Eventually,' he said, caressing the gold-crossed pendant that hung over his chest, 'it's all in the hands of the Lord.'

In his twenty-sixth year as principal of St George's, Father Menezes was expert in driving these 'interviews'. He had no trouble bouncing from topic to topic and needed only a fraction of a second to catch his breath – not over a full stop like many but rather over a comma. When my father found some semblance of rhythm, the principal cut him short and carried the discussion off in a different direction. Soon my father gave up, folding his arms and leaning back into his chair.

About ten minutes in, with us adequately subdued, Father Menezes wound down his speech, stood up and shook my father's right hand. 'Thank you for coming,' he said to my mother, and joined his palms as if in prayer. Delighted with the sophistication on display, she happily returned the namaste.

Next, the principal turned to me even as he continued to address my father: 'Now I would like a word with your son.'

Father Menezes' expression called to mind a doctor from a recent Tamil movie, and all he had to do to complete the scene was to remove his spectacles, utter a sober sorry and declare that I had six weeks to live. I searched for help, but my parents were more than happy to detach themselves from their only child and rush off to the exit.

Father Menezes returned to his seat. And I – trying to call up the definitions and formulae I had memorized – returned to mine.

'Stand up, Karthik,' he boomed, sprinkling spittle. My thighs smashed against the table's edge on their way up. Above him the chandelier quivered, its glass edges capable of splitting my head and bloodying his robe in a trice. Fortunately, it stayed in place.

'Did it even occur to you that your mother was standing the whole time that she was in here?'

'Father ...'

'And you took a seat as she stood by?'

'Sorry, Father.'

'How could you consider it, Karthik?'

'Sorry, Father.'

'What sort of behaviour is this?'

'Sorry, Father.'

'Listen to me, young man. I don't know where you got your manners but we insist on values here. We teach our boys etiquette and respect. We expect them to be gentlemen. I find it shocking that you sat down even as your mother – your *own* mother, a *lady* – stood behind you.'

If only Father Menezes had seen that it was my mother – my *own* mother – who had told me to take a seat.

'Very sorry, Father.'

'You may leave now. Expect a phone call early next week.'

'Sorry, Father.'

He glared at me over his rimless spectacles. I made my way out, humiliated, assured that I would never see him again.

Father Menezes thanked the photographer with a brief nod, waved at a mali who was tending to the lawn and marched across the quadrangle. His back was upright and his palms were folded into hammerheads. The junior priests stayed two steps behind him until the trio fused into a blur indoors.

The photographer walked to the main gate and, down on one knee, arched his back for long-range shots of the school's facade. I interlocked my fingers and took in the scene through the pinhole between my palms. The majestic structure, the square pillars, the chapel spire, the clean blue sky – everything was in the frame. A tongue click and I untangled the digital camera.

A tap on my shoulder.

Looming over me was an older boy with his hair set perfectly and uniform squeaky clean. A blue badge on his chest suggested he was a house captain or vice-captain, and the fountain pen clipped to his shirt pocket took me back to the time when my father's beloved Staedtler had blotched his white shirt before a major meeting.

'Is this how you polish your shoes?' the boy asked, two fingers pointing like a gun at my feet. 'Your pant is messed up, man.'

He was acting so polite, as if wary of my response. Had this been my father, he would have treated me the way my mother treated a ball of dough.

'If the princi or vice-princi sees this, you're dead meat.'

'Sorry.'

'I don't believe you have done this on the first day, man.'

'Sorry. It was really ...'

'I'm going to let you off this time. But you better watch it.'

'Sorry. Very sorry.'

'New boy?'

'Yes.'

'No wonder! Which year?'

'Seventh standard.'

'Section?'

'Sorry, I don't know.'

'Hmm. Enter that corridor – ya, you see those two boys, no? Just follow where they're going. Then take a right, go straight, and you'll reach a notice board. Search for your name in the seventh standard list and check your section. Won't be too hard.'

'Thanks a lot,' I said and broke into rapid strides, confused whether to be grateful or ashamed. It wasn't the boy's powers of observation that stumped me; after all, the school prospectus stated that only the 'crème de la crème' were considered for the roles of captain and vice-captain. Rather I was baffled by why he had let me off. Perhaps he was in a good mood on the first day of a new academic year. Or perhaps, years earlier, he had ruined his uniform and thought himself lucky to have been let off. That seemed the more convincing explanation.

Motoring across the main corridor, I saw that the school too was unprepared for the first day. Paint patches dotted hastily restored walls. Up on a wooden ladder, a uniformed peon cleared cobwebs with a long broom, supporting himself against a pillar so wide it would have been ideal for games of hide-and-seek.

Half the school seemed to have descended on the notice board, as if promised free Chocobars. Some boys stood in clusters of two or three, chit-chatting, mimicking, laughing. Others crowded the notice board to learn which section they had been allocated. Waiting for the crowd to clear, I stood apart.

I felt another pat on my shoulder, this time from a shorter boy. He wore no badge and carried no pen in his shirt pocket. His hair was so unruly I was tempted to hand him my comb.

'Hey,' I offered, expecting him to bring up the smudge.

'Hi. I'm Anoop. You?'

'Karthik. Nice to meet you.'

'Which year?'

'Seventh standard.'

'Oh, I'm also in seventh. Which section?'

'I need to check.'

'Umm. You were at the junior school, Karthik?'

'No.'

'Then?'

'Sacred Valley.'

'Oh, where is that?'

'It's far.'

'Oh. Then you better watch for the bingo.'

'What? You know Sunil? Zombie?'

'Zombie! What a name ...'

'Iqbal Sir's cricket camp.'

'What are you talking about, Karthik?'

'Sorry. I was just ...'

'Check your section fast.'

'I'll check now.'

Squeezing through the crush, I found the seventh standard list on the south-east corner of the notice board. My darting eyes located S. Karthik somewhere in the middle of the printed sheet. One B. Karthik sat above me. A Y. Karthik sat below. The column across my name said 7C, while the other two Karthiks were in 7A. Just to be doubly sure, I rechecked the list. Someone nudged my shoulder and asked me to 'get out of the way, bugger'. I scanned the notice board for any mention of the word 'bingo'. There was none. Wriggling out of the mass of warm bodies, I looked around for Anoop. He was gone.

The peon pointed me to the seventh standard block, angling his long broom towards the first floor and releasing a knot of dust over my head. I jogged past two corridors to reach a set of stairs, but just as I began the climb, three boys ran down like bulls chasing rags, coming within inches of knocking me over.

I yelped a 'sorry' and clung to a banister.

'Any more ash on your face and you'll look like a ghost,' the slowest of the three screeched, shaking with laughter as the other two crowed, 'It don't matter if you're black or white.'

'Sorry,' I said, raising my palms over my forehead, but they were too far out to care.

Shamefaced, I pulled out the water bottle from my bag, squeezed a jet onto my palm and rubbed off the holy ash from my forehead –

apologizing to my grandfather for letting him down. Two boys gave me strange looks as they walked past. 'He puked?' one asked.

How I would explain my bare forehead to my grandfather I had no idea. For now, my only concern was to rush up the stairs and speed past 7A and 7B towards the 7C entrance. Loud, jumbled noises spilled out of the classrooms. I took a deep breath, muttered a prayer to Lord Ganesha and hopped over the 7C threshold.

Here was the world I was set to inhabit. To my left a vast blackboard, a clean slate. Facing me, a teacher's table that held a boxful of white chalk as well as their arch-enemy – an Attila that could raze the chalk towers to powder – a green duster. To my right, worn wooden desks and benches, many of them ruined by compass scratches and sketch-pen marks. 'Ashok's big bum was here,' said one; 'DISHKIYAON,' said another. Some of these desks were so worn, so disfigured that a caterpillar crawling across their surface – weaving through craters, grooves and potholes – would be as miffed as drivers on Bangalore's roads.

Spears of sunlight had rushed in through the windows and carved six golden trapeziums on the mosaic floor. The classroom's back wall had endured seepage, and jutting out of a circular patch was a weather-beaten Jesus nailed to a wooden crucifix. There He was, limbs wiry, torso upright, watching over all of us and not in the least concerned that a ball of sunlight was splashed beside, and not above, His crown of thorns.

Clumps of boys stood around the classroom and chitchatted.

'You've become fat, da. Ate like a pig in the holidays?'

'How was Goa, man? Drooled over all the hot chicks?'

'Heard about Fatang? Dude got expelled for cheating in finals.'

A boy walked up and scanned my uniform. When someone addressed him as 'Paunchy', he turned to them, threw a wink and a thumbs up, and returned to me.

'New boy?' he asked, though he obviously knew the answer.

I nodded a yes, and held out my right hand for him to shake.

Paunchy took a step back, surprised.

I waited, hand firmly extended.

Paunchy's eyeballs swerved right, and following his line of sight I was led to a window that opened out to a jackfruit tree. On one of its branches sat a black drongo, which I identified from its forked tail – a tip I had learned on a bird-watching trip last year. Past the tree, past the compound wall, I saw vehicles jammed up on the main road, and from the faint honks and whirs, got an idea of the chaos that was playing out.

It was too late.

A lightning bolt shot through my waist. The leaves turned blurry, the road noises shut off and the drongo flew away. Or maybe I lost sight of it, I am not sure. My eyelids closed and my torso bent double. A stinging pain spread through my midriff and abdomen. With my breathing out of control and head topsy-turvy, my hands automatically grazed against my crotch.

'Welcome, new boy,' Paunchy announced. 'Welcome to the greatest school in the world.'

That's when I understood.

He had socked my penis with his knuckles, then opened his fist and squashed my nuts: punch, snatch, squeeze, release, all in one motion, like a soldier loading a rifle. Mission accomplished, he let out a whoop and joined the rest of the boys in a loud cackle.

A thousand chuckles filled the air just as my knees threatened to give way. Wobbling around, I was about to cling to a desk to regain my balance, but I stopped myself in the nick of time. This was not the moment to give up. I had to stay on my feet, had to be gutsy. Backing me up was a serene image of Lord Ganesha that flashed in my head, and I knew I had to pray to Him then and there. That was what everyone at home would have wanted, that was what would have made them proud. When I looked up, I saw the ceramic

Jesus still hanging from the back wall, His head resting on his right arm, His entire being unmoved by what He had just witnessed. Unbidden, I prayed to Him too.

'First bingo of the year,' someone clucked, handing Paunchy a high-five. The others stood around and giggled for what seemed like an hour ... until an electric bell screeched through the corridors, calling for morning assembly. Now it didn't matter to the boys if I were alive or dead; they rushed to the door like iron filings seeking a magnet. I had not used a prop to support myself, not dropped to my knees, not broken down. Nobody cared. The room hastily emptied out.

A deep breath, a prayer. Two more deep breaths, another prayer. In one split second I had gone from a new book whose pages gave off a delicious scent to a second-hand paperback, its pages yellowed, dog-eared and coffee-stained. No more an unknown, I had tags attached: the boy who was tricked, the boy with a weak dick and flimsy nuts, the boy who was dealt the year's first bingo.

With the morning assembly about to begin, I dropped my bag in a vacant spot in the last row and scrambled out of the 7C classroom. Limping down the stairs I rewound to Iqbal Sir's camp in May and the day when Zombie had warned me about the bingo. If only I had asked him to explain. At least I could have asked Anoop at the notice board fifteen minutes ago. Surely he could have warned me of the shock that lay in store.

Maybe. But maybe not. Perhaps a bingo was a rite of passage at St George's, the pain and shock a given. Who knows, maybe Paunchy had done me a favour by getting it out of the way so early. Just like that, the mystery had cleared up. Now that I had been cut down to size, I could try and blend into 7C, making new friends, and hopefully, over time, be wholeheartedly embraced. Joining my classmates at the morning assembly, I was relieved to have survived my first big test. I had come through without support. And, most importantly, I had not fallen.

3

Birthday Bumps

TUESDAY AND FRIDAY BROUGHT on more bingos, from different boys, each just as nasty as the other. Every day was rife with danger, especially during the forty-minute lunch breaks – ample time for these bullies to hound me and pummel my dick.

The fourth blow, a week on, was from a lump of a boy called Babloo, a fellow who would have taken great pleasure in burning ants with a magnifying glass. The moment he charged into the 7C classroom, midway through lunch break, I knew he would pin me to the rear wall – not too far from Jesus – and crush my penis. My bum crashed against the concrete, my spectacles lifted off my ears. Babloo grabbed my glasses and considered shattering them, but one look at his watch and, as if reminded of the ten others he had to bingo in twenty minutes, he rushed out.

Five of my classmates watched this scene. Two snickered before returning to their lunches. The others showed no interest. I nearly threw up in the corridor, swaying like a drunk, amazed that both Lord Ganesha and Jesus had allowed this to happen. Couldn't They have warned me about Babloo's design? Why had They permitted those five bodies to stand by and be of no help? Only when I reached a stairwell and gathered myself with deep breaths did it occur to me: that morning there had been no time to pray. I hadn't even prayed on my way to school. I had brought this upon myself.

Muttering prayer after prayer, seeking forgiveness, I hobbled down the stairs to the toilets – partly to relieve myself but mostly to be left alone. Not that the toilets were the most welcoming venue. Graffiti plastered the walls.

'Boobs, boobs, boobs'

'Dog sex>Goat sex'

'Cover her face, fire her base.'

Someone had traced a gigantic pair of breasts, then extended a line from each nipple and marked them 'Milk Booths'.

On the opposite wall was an inscription that said: 'Your a man only if its 4 inches'. A cigar dangled below the 4 to underline the point.

It's a wonder I didn't collapse when the piss stink hit me. The latch on a latrine door was broken. There were other doors with no latch. Clearly nobody cared for a guy's privacy at St George's.

Fed up, I got into one latrine and held the door shut with my left hand. I planted my feet on either side of the Indian-style commode, unzipped my pants and pulled down the elastic strap of my underwear. Piss gushed out at great speed, the rampant jet flying past the tiny, round bowl and wetting the floor beyond the commode. My arms and sides strained in a bizarre asana – torso twisted, legs wide apart, one hand holding the door, the other hand grasping my crotch – and it took some intense focus, and deep breaths, to hold this contorted pose until the job was done and I could shake off the final drops and feel whole.

'Rama-rama-rama,' I mumbled as I regained my footing and got to the delicate matter on hand: the state of my plumbing. Thankfully Babloo hadn't caused much damage to the apparatus down there. I wiggled the shaft up and down, left and right, and was happy to have it cooperate without any discomfort. I softly pinched the foreskin and – oh god no! – brought on a slight bulge. Ruffled, I put it back to sleep, curled up under my VIP Frenchie. I closed my eyes and patted myself for a job well done.

It was so much easier to think logically after a leak, after much of the anxiety had escaped in the jasmine stream. Of immediate concern was how I was going to cope when targeted with another bingo. Perhaps the trick was to not wear a belt and let my pants hang loose. Or maybe I could stiffen up the padding by putting on an extra pair of underwear. Dangerous ideas trickled in. I could carry a pebble in my pockets and smash the bullies' heads when they least suspected. Or I could conceal a blade in a cotton swab, with which I could slit anyone's wrist in a snap. Now that would teach those swines a proper lesson.

Loitering outside the toilets, each new scheme sparking off excitement, I started to relax. An older boy walked past, and turned into the urinals, pinching his nose, squinting his eyes. A minute later he walked out, composed, his face free of disgust.

Balancing out the toilet's odours was a riot of masalas escaping the teacher's refectory. Cardamom, clove, pepper and garlic, frolicking in the corridor outside, raising visions of a delightful meal. Lunch at the refectory was a big perk for our teachers, and some closed the fourth period early to get a head start. Especially on Fridays, like today, when they were served ice-cream.

The aromas briefly lifted my spirits. Until they reminded me of my lunch that had gone missing that morning, the theft having occurred during snack break when I had nipped out to refill my bottle at a water cooler. On my return, the six mint-chutney sandwiches that my mother had packed were gone. I searched for signs of my metallic lunchbox, trying to sniff out traces of mint. No luck. I looked around to see if anyone was giggling at my expense. Still no luck.

This was the second lunch I had lost in one week. Needled

by the mouthwatering smells from the refectory my heart was suddenly sick with the thought that in some corner of St George's, some blessed boy was stuffing his face with my mother's labour of love. Rascal. What would he have known of the pains she took each morning, planning out meals, shedding tears over onions and sneezing around peppery powders? Every night she asked, 'What does K want for lunch tomorrow?' and every evening she made sure to check if the lunch had been okay. 'Too salty? Too spicy?' 'It was great, Ma,' I would say without fail – an assumption on some days but a safe assumption nonetheless.

I wandered towards the football field and looked on as hundreds of boys darted about this way and that. The field was one giant unruly mess but that only seemed to add to the fun for those in the thick of things. Hand-tennis players weren't thrown off by fielders barging into them. A group that played marbles laughed when interrupted by footballers on the run. Scattered in the crowd were boys who whiled away their time, chatting, loafing or standing around, unmoved by the chaos around them.

A group was playing a game where one player pelted another with a hard rubber ball. The rules were simple: if you have possession of the ball, strike another player; if you don't have possession, save your skin. A strike earned you a point but the real aim, it appeared, was to inflict as much damage as possible. Hardly had I caught on to the rules when a groan rose above the din. One of the players was bent double, rubbing his chest, his face in a squirm. The boy who had thrown the missile pumped his fists and screeched, 'Got him!' Another player shouted to the injured boy to 'stop acting like a pansy, dickhead'. Enraged, he got to his feet, picked up the ball and flung it baseball-style, missing the nearest player by inches.

Games like these were unheard of at Sacred Valley – a school so distinct that I was a hero there. Yes, I, Karthik Subramanian – whom Georgians had already bracketed a 'scaredy-cat', a 'sissy' and 'chicken' – had been a role model at Sacred Valley. My speedy arithmetic calculations had left many open-mouthed, and I was established as an expert on countries and capitals the day I spelled out Ouagadougou on the blackboard. Over one Christmas break, I had read a book called *Famous Inventions and Inventors* and gone on to impress everyone with the story of James Watt and his hot kettle.

On the field there had been many memorable moments. I once struck a six in a game of tennis-ball cricket, launching the ball into a cluster of croton bushes. This was only expected: we were on an open basketball court, the straight boundary was less than a hundred feet away, and the bowler was floating dollies. Yet, everyone spoke about my smooth bat swing for about a month.

From as far back as I could recall, the boys in my class had treated me like a movie star. The girls too said many sweet things, like the time when Manisha was overheard telling Pallavi that I was one of the nicest people she knew. Naturally, coming as it did from the prettiest girl in class, it was safe to assume I was enchanted. There was even talk that Pallavi, whose father was a famous painter, agreed with Manisha!

That evening I went and gloated to Chiku Chacko, my neighbour, only to be informed that pretty girls call you a 'nice person' only when hot, dashing and sexy don't apply. He said 'nice boys' should give up on pretty girls and try and find some 'nice girls' instead. Here was Chiku Chacko doing what he was best at: convincing me that my little victories were actually crushing defeats.

Evidently some boys in my class were clueless. They believed the rumours and paired me with Manisha. They grinned when Manisha walked up, when she requested to borrow my notes and when she asked for help with homework. Thrilled with her requests, I gave Manisha whatever she wanted and then told the boys to stop making a big deal out of it, that she was just a 'good friend'.

All that was history. If my classmates at Sacred Valley had been around to watch the cricket trials at St George's, they would know that I wasn't even good enough to carry drinks for the senior team.

'Unbeaten for a week, fuckers,' cried the winner of the ball-pelting contest, extending his middle fingers upwards as he rushed to drink some water.

With two boys tied on five points, the game had neared a climax. One of the leaders, our resident Obelix, wound up to launch the ball ... except he stopped, turned left and let fly towards another player, getting the ball to sting his neck. In the mud, rubbing his nape, the felled boy went, 'Played, boss.'

Mr Suryaprakash, Director of Physical Education, came barrelling down the corridor. SP walked like an ex-policeman could be expected to, chest puffed out and arms smiting the motes that dared dance in his path.

I checked my shoes that had been trampled on earlier that morning. A stickler for discipline, SP had made a name for himself by busting boys with his surprise inspections. He was one teacher who didn't need a whip or a cane to make his point. His giant palms were more than enough to clobber the daylights out of those who strayed. Body tense, I rubbed my right shoe against my left sock.

'Good morning, sir,' I said as SP approached.

'Good morning? In which part of the world is it morning, silly fellow?'

'Sorry, sir. Good afternoon, sir.'

SP sniggered.

Walking past, he quickly turned back.

'Hang on, boy. Hang on.'

'Sir?'

'There's a bloody ink spot on the back of your shirt.'

'Sir.'

'Have you not seen this?' he demanded, tugging my sleeve.

'Uh, no, no, sir.'

'Stop lying now!'

'No, sir. I didn't know, sir.'

'Have your classmates been up to some mischief?'

'No, sir.'

'Look, boy, are you sure everything is okay?'

'Yes, sir. All okay, sir.'

'Are you new here?'

'Yes, sir.'

'Which class?'

'Seventh standard, sir. 7C.'

SP sized me up and shook his head, as if disgusted by every aspect of my appearance, from my unkempt hair down to my defaced shoes. He took a step forward and hunched close, close enough for his mouth to be within biting distance of my ear. I closed my eyes, hoping he would stop at one tight slap.

'Will you spray ink on yourself ever again?'

'No, sir.'

'Will you forget to polish your shoes ever again?'

'No, sir. Never, sir.'

'Hmm.'

'Very sorry, sir.'

'Now get back to class, quick.'

'Yes, sir.'

'And a bit of advice man to man,' he said in a low voice.

'Sir?'

'Your fly is open. Zip it up quick.'

I saw the rubber-ball pelters again a week later, when they took a break from their game and walked up to me. They asked my name, my class and section. Why had I shifted schools? Hearing that

Sacred Valley was co-ed, they wondered if I was going mad seeing 'boys, boys, boys' everywhere.

'Nothing like that,' I replied, uncertain, when one of the boys gripped my armpits and another grabbed my feet before the other four joined in to treat my backside to twelve blistering birthday bumps.

'I swear it's not my birthday,' I howled, sprawled in the mud.

'Of course it is,' our resident Obelix shot back. 'And maybe it will be your birthday tomorrow too. Ya, your fortieth birthday.'

It was hard to concentrate in class in the afternoon. I used my backpack as a cushion. I forced my thighs to take the bulk of my weight. After school, I limped to the bus stop. Sure enough, the bus pulled away when I was twenty metres out. Short of breath, I collapsed onto a bench and buried my head in my palms.

'Whatever happened to chivalry, men?' screeched a lady in a baggy skirt, wiggling a finger. I gave up my seat. She plonked down on the bench and placed her handbag a foot away, as if reserving that spot. I was tempted to snatch her handbag and empty its contents in the gutter, but I stopped myself just in time, when another bus came into view.

Back home, Thatha was getting ready to head out. Thankfully he didn't notice as I swapped my ravaged uniform for a T-shirt and pants, washed my face and set my hair. It was time for our weekly trip to the Ganesha temple two cross-streets away. Standing in front of the imposing idol – His head in a diamond-studded crown, His face and trunk bedecked with sandalwood paste, His lower body draped in a golden veshti – I vowed to circle the shrine a hundred and eight times if He put my life back on track. I slapped my cheeks during the show of aarti, touched the holy flame three times and applied generous amounts of holy ash on my forehead. Prostrating myself in front of the idol, I considered a vow to shave my head. This was a silly idea; no bully in St George's would let go of a chance to tear a baldie apart.

The physical attacks were only part of the problem; what stung more was how often I was ignored. None of my classmates drew me into conversation, none of them asked me to join their word games or chess matches, none of them requested to borrow my notes. Our Mathematics teacher didn't pick me when he called for boys to solve problems on the blackboard. No group of cricketers or footballers included me in their lunchtime games. My role at St George's was that of a punching bag: unnecessary for most part until the big boys wanted to have some fun.

Some nights the panic set in. Until now my dreams had been harmless affairs, some of them featuring animals in bizarre scenes, like cows playing football or dogs in a lemon-and-spoon race. Now I was flying off cliffs and colliding with buses. One night, three boys dipped my head in a lake and joked about how fast I ran out of breath. My arms flailed, my feet flapped. Dribbles of saliva gathered at my mouth even as my bladder threatened to explode. All that was left to do was send up a final prayer and surrender to the lake. My grandfather had once said that only the lucky ones die in their sleep, and for that I was thankful.

The instant I gave up, I woke with a jolt – palms tingling and clothes soiled. I looked around, taking in the nightly sounds: crickets chirping, a gecko's tik-tik, a stray dog howling in the distance. My grandfather was asleep in the bed opposite mine, wrapped in a cotton sheet from head to toe. In the adjacent room my father snored at his usual rhythm and my mother faced the other way, curled up, quiet, undisturbed. They would have been ready to lay down their lives if anyone tried to abduct me.

Relieved, I made my way to the bathroom. I wiped the sweat off my face and took a deep breath ... when it hit me: going back to sleep would mean running into the same ruffians again ... waiting at the same lake ... impatient to finish me off.

A few hours later, I woke with a pit in my stomach. If only my father could have opened the *Hindu* and declared a minister had died. Or, even better, if only he could have announced the onset of a fresh round of Cauvery riots. Two years earlier, the fight for the waters of the Cauvery river had led to nearly six months of no school – a dream sequence that ran: summer holidays, a break for possible riots, a brief spell of school, another break for possible riots, a lengthy break for the actual riots, Christmas holidays, and another break for possible riots as tension gripped the city. It was an unforgettable time.

My father had feverishly tracked the news, reading out snippets each morning: 'shop burnt', 'car smashed', 'cinema torn down', 'hundreds flee'.

Thousands and thousands of 'jobless idiots' were prowling the streets, waving the state flag, screaming slogans, beating up honest Tamil labourers and burning shops owned by god-fearing Tamilians, he had claimed.

My mother trembled. 'It's all going to be fine,' she said.

'Understood?'

'Yes, Ma.'

'But if someone stops you and asks for your full name, what are you going to say?'

I nodded, suggesting that I knew the answer.

'Don't go and blurt out Subramanian, okay? No final N. Subramania. Okay? Always say Subramania.'

Karthik Subramanian, the Tamilian, was in grave danger. Karthik Subramania, the homeboy, was safe in Bangalore. Karthik, of course, nobody could place. Every other boy, either side of the Cauvery divide, answered to that name.

Next she requested one of the neighbourhood uncles to make some free time each week to tutor me in Kannada. 'These sessions will make you better prepared for the entrance test at St George's,' she said. But that was a sham. She worried that, if caught in a riot, my half-baked Kannada would give me away.

When the Cauvery riots had shut our schools, my grandfather would wake me up before dawn, tune our radio to the Australian Broadcasting Corporation, and tilting his head towards the speakers, search for the sweet, woody sound of bat on ball. We held our breath when the fearsome Australian bowlers ran in, shook our heads when India's batsmen were beaten. When they struck fours, my grandfather would tap his thighs. How obsessed he was with Tendulkar. 'A cricketer so unique,' he said, his eyes agog, 'you will surely tell your grandkids about him.' Glued to his chair when 'shorty' batted, he threw in a prayer for him every few overs. And when the prodigy smashed bowlers twice his age, drawing oohs and aahs from the Australian crowds, my seventy-seven-year-old grandfather was seven again, waking the Chackos up with his shrieks.

All morning the radio played. Nobody rushed me to get ready. Even a former military man like my grandfather slacked off. As the day wore on, I often lazed in bed with a *Tinkle* or an *Amar Chitra Katha* comic. Sometimes it was *The Adventures of Tom Sawyer*, my grandfather's gift for my tenth birthday, a book I read at least once a week, play-acting like Tom, Joe, Huck or Sid as per my mood, imitating their accents, whistling when alone, and rummaging in our garden for buried treasures. I drew up a cricket match on the banks of the Mississippi where Tom and I opened the batting as men with Australian accents broadcast the game to my grandfather back home.

Day and night we bonded over cricket, my grandfather gushing about his favourite players, some whom he had only read about. Wes Hall, the towering Barbadian, apparently began his run-up at the boundary; M. L. Jaisimha effortlessly flicked balls from sixth stump to square leg; and the original Brylcreem boy, Denis Compton, swept so beautifully, he said, that bowlers were tempted to drift the ball onto his pads. Regardless of whether any of this was true, these memories filled him with immense happiness – which he passed on to me.

Now there were no riots, not even a hint. Everything was peaceful, my mother was thankful. Only I was sick and panicky. Had I broken down in school, the bullies would have taken it that they had won. Had I cried at home, my parents would have got a sniff of what was happening and straightaway complained to the principal. The ragging would have stopped but no one would have spoken to me thereafter. When you told on your classmates at St George's, you were as good as dead to them.

Which left me ... only the bus stops. So delayed were Bangalore's buses that I could cry my heart out as I waited, all the while ignoring passersby who took pity. Some asked if I was lost, some offered to call the police. A man on a Yezdi, his flowing mane sneaking out of his helmet, assumed I had run away from home. His pillion, who looked like an ageing diva pining for recognition, flashed a ten-rupee note and ordered me to 'take an auto and go home, son'. The man held out a toffee. Following my mother's dictum – 'strangers are kidnappers' – I refused it. 'Don't take so much tension, boy,' he said in a tender voice. 'The buses here have always been late.'

4

Stephen

THE FIRST MORNING OF every month my grandfather performed an hour-long puja. This was partly to thank the gods for the month gone by but mostly a plea for the month ahead. 'The tide will turn,' he said when he was done this time, as if foreseeing a defining event around the corner. He didn't specify how our lives were going to change; only gazed at the horizon and nodded sagely, pleased with what he saw in the future.

Not much changed in my world. My teachers continued to pay me no heed. My classmates launched paper pellets and chalk in my direction. I was forever on the lookout for chewing gum stuck to my bum. There were no bingos for a while but that made me even more panicky.

On the seventh day of July, a glum Wednesday, I returned to the classroom after morning assembly to find my lunchbox, water bottle, textbooks, notebooks and geometry instruments strewn near the back wall. My lunchbox was still shut, the curd rice and blotch of lime pickle intact but, my school prospectus, which my grandfather had asked me to take along 'just in case', lay open at the 'Dos and don'ts' page. I considered the odds of a monkey sneaking in through a window and triggering this chaos but with so many boys smirking at my misfortune, I set that thought aside.

Scanning the classroom, seeing how happy the boys were at my plight, ashamed at having to pick up my belongings in front of them, and tired of being taunted day in and day out, I was on the edge. I had put up with worse over the last month but to stare at the mess near the back wall was to see the last drop of my optimism vaporize. There was no point deluding myself. Each day only reaffirmed the reality: my life at St George's was never going to look up. Squatting at the classroom's rear, stacking my notebooks and textbooks, I sensed the prick of each boy's gaze, watching me, judging me, waiting for me to crack. The tears prepared to burst forth.

'Leave it there,' growled a voice in the vicinity.

I screwed up my eyes and swayed left, expecting a knockout blow in my nuts. Three seconds passed. Then five. The classroom noises mingled in a hush. I summoned the strength to open my eyes, and spotted a pair of black shoes standing by, ready to crush my fingers like they were cigarettes to be stubbed out. Three more tick-ticks went by. I looked up.

Towering above me was Stephen Mohanraj, the tallest boy in 7C and my neighbour on the last bench. Why he was standing there and ordering me to leave my belongings on the floor, I had no idea. Stephen was a bit of a mystery to everyone in 7C. He was repeating a year after failing every subject in the final exams. 'How is that humanly possible?' I had overheard one boy ask another during one of the breaks. 'How can anyone fail Moral Science? Or English Language?'

Stephen threw me a cold stare. 'I said, leave it there.'

We may have shared a bench but I hadn't ever spoken to Stephen. To my great relief, he hadn't spoken to me either. I had gone so far as to avoid eye contact, especially when I learned his voice had cracked. That made him an adult in my eyes, and I was clueless how to start a conversation with most adults, living as they did in their own world, bogged down by adult problems, excited about adult issues, pulling me up for doing something wrong – 'Act like a grown-up, Karthik' – and returning to their adult lives. Stephen had it in him to slot neatly into that world. He not only looked like an adult – being taller and stronger than everyone in 7C – but also acted like one – scoffing at the jokes that made many others laugh. And he had started to shave, oozing the same Old Spice scent that my father and grandfather gave off.

Now Stephen stood still, his brows tense, his hair slicked, his face pimple-free and fragrant. His eyes were still, dangerous, refusing to return my nervous blinks, and I couldn't help but notice his large feet or recall my neighbour Chiku Chacko saying this was the surest sign of a long penis. God knows how Chiku came up with these theories but even he would agree – and Chiku rarely agreed with me – that Stephen could silence a room full of girls by simply stepping in. The girls would have stopped whatever they were doing. They would have made light of his crude remarks and his leery stares, assuring themselves that he was merely showing interest. And no girl would have classed Stephen as a 'nice person'. No chance. He was too dashing, too hot, too sexy; charming enough for his every misstep to be forgiven.

I too was awed but nowhere as much as I was terrified of the damage Stephen could inflict. By looking past me for six weeks he had let the suspense simmer and now, with the whole class gathered, he could chop me up, toss me in a blender and turn me into juice. Finally, his time had come. Expecting the mother of all bingos, my hands hovered in front of my crotch.

Stephen jerked his head right, directing me to get back to my seat. The sign was quick, the message clear. I waited a few seconds before slowly walking towards the last bench.

With me out of the way, Stephen went about organizing my stationery. He squatted on his toes, yet was perfectly balanced, his torso erect, his arms limber, each graceful bodily movement conveying a supreme athletic ability. Gathering my textbooks, notebooks, prospectus and geometry box in one hand, he scooped up the lunchbox and water bottle with the other and stuffed the tissue-wrapped Marie biscuits in his shirt pocket. He got to his feet with my loot and, throwing his head back, ambled towards our desk. Nobody said a word; the silence was pin-drop. Stephen set the pile down in front of me.

Getting into his seat he fished the biscuits out, unwrapped them and, with his right leg crossed over his left, crunched one in half.

Son of a gun!

A less shell-shocked Karthik might have stood up and clapped. Or swung a fist pump. Or screeched a full-blooded 'Yeeeaaah', as if India had won the World Cup. At the very least I could have relayed my thanks with a grateful thumbs-up or head bob. All I managed was to turn around and quietly thank Jesus hanging from the back wall. In English. Then a quick prayer to Lord Ganesha in Sanskrit. Followed by an informal thanks in Tamil.

An anxious murmur spread around the room, carrying with it wonder and confusion. Was this meant to be Stephen's message for the prankster? Or had he acted out of concern for a new boy, since he too was new to 7C? Nothing was certain. Paunchy's mouth was open, his eyes flush with guilt. The boy next to him whistled a low ohhh. If only I could have taken Stephen on a walk around the room, picked out the boys who had assaulted me over the last month and got him to drill holes through their abdomens. Just thinking of the possibility had me beaming.

My classmates' response told me I was finally free. Bingos, birthday bumps, bubble gum on the bum: these were unlikely to return. Nobody would stain my uniform from now on. Nobody would dare steal my lunch. I didn't wear a badge over my pocket, wasn't elected house captain or vice-captain, but Stephen had granted me power. At the end of the first period, two boys walked up and introduced themselves. One even asked for help with Biology homework.

The next day, a Thursday, promised a fresh start to my life at St George's. I was woken not by an alarm clock that punctured the uneasy quiet after a torrid night or by a strident grandfatherly 'Rise and shine, Karthik!' but by a shaft of sunlight that crept in under the curtain. The bath water was heated to the precise degree. My mother applied just enough oil to set my hair. The Cherry Blossom polish infused my leather shoes with a deep glowing moisture and, for the first time in weeks, the bread slices popped out of the toaster crackling perfect.

By the time I reached school a burst of rain had soiled my hair and ruined my shoes. Two periods into the day and an angry sun got its revenge, banishing the clouds and setting St George's ablaze. Our classroom was a boiler, and sweat beads trickled from our foreheads to our cheeks to neck to chest and glued our shirts to our skins. Our Geography teacher Father Xavier asked two frontbenchers why they hadn't the common sense to 'open the windows and let the airforce in'. The boys did as instructed. Father Xavier wiped his face with a damp handkerchief and sniffed the air that made its way through the windows.

Father Xavier, or Fax for short, rarely detached a scowl from his pockmarked face. When anyone misbehaved, he took it as a personal insult. When he messed up, he turned it into someone else's fault. A month ago, he had introduced himself to class 7B with, 'I am Cochin from Xavier,' and gone on to whack two boys who laughed at this slip-up. Everything he said, we had to accept. Which explained why no one in 7C had anything good to say about Fax, especially after the Pigeon Lady incident.

The Pigeon Lady was a frail, bent, homeless person, who trudged in through the back gate after the final bell went off. She would settle down on a bench to chat with the flock of pigeons. She tossed them breads and puffed rice. And the pigeons hopped onto her shoulders and into her lap. This had reportedly been going on for years.

One evening, late in June, Fax had walked up to her and yelled, 'Out, out, out,' closing in like she was a stray to be shooed away. Pigeon Lady ignored him and continued to pamper the pigeons. An enraged Fax waylaid a hockey player, grabbed his stick and commanded her to get out or else ... 'Go to hell,' she screeched only for Fax to smack her on the shin. The story caught fire the next morning. There were rumours about a jail sentence, and Paunchy – who had borne the brunt of multiple beltings from Fax – went so far as to say he deserved to be hanged. Barely a few minutes before the morning assembly was to start, Fax emerged from the teacher's quarters onto the balcony of the chapel. First we saw his balding head and bespectacled face, then his wrinkled neck and faded cassock. And what a sight it was: him waving to the left, waving to the right, clearly expecting us to applaud his heroic act. All he got were hoots and boos but Fax countered with an angelic smile. 'The bugger has no shame, man,' said a boy behind me. 'Acting like he has won the Nobel Peace Prize.'

At the end of assembly, Fax disappeared into the teachers' quarters. Rumours continued to swirl but it was hard for us to gauge what was happening. Neither the principal nor the vice-principal put out a statement about the incident. The alumni association didn't kick up a fuss. The police didn't turn up to interview witnesses. And when, ten days later, Fax resumed classes, his colleagues acted as if nothing had happened.

As for Pigeon Lady, nobody seemed to know what became of her. Someone claimed he had seen her begging on M. G. Road; someone else suggested she had returned to her village. Boys stopped looking for her near the back gate and, according to the hockey players, the pigeons had shifted to the other end of the field to seek out their snacks. They hadn't returned to the bench where she usually sat. They had decided it was time to move on.

Now, fanning himself with the attendance register, Fax divided the blackboard into three columns and sternly announced, 'This table will appear in some test or exam at some point, so shut your silly mouths and take it down like obedient servants.'

Today's lesson: vegetation patterns in sub-Saharan Africa.

I copied down the table with a Hero fountain pen, an instrument that my grandfather held was 'a key to a student's success'. His formula for pens:

Bad student: ballpoint pen
Good student: microtip pen
Exceptional student: Hero fountain pen.

He hadn't accounted for a Hero to have an off day. Midway through copying the table, a blob of sweat dripped from my forehead and smudged the first entry. My right hand fumbled. The pen slipped from my grasp and – drat! – drizzled ink across the page. Thank heavens Fax wasn't on one of his routine walks around the room. One look at this inky mess and he would have flung my notebook out of the window.

Stephen sat to my left with not a trace of sweat on his face. Rather than worry himself with Fax's vegetation table he was signing different versions of his name with a Reynolds ballpoint. Three slanted Stephen Ms, two Stephen Mohanrajs, each underlined with two dots below, and two StephenM-squiggle-slash-dashes. They were all so easy to read, so smooth and cursive, a trickster would have had little trouble forging the sign.

Stephen saw me scanning his work. He turned the notebook to the last page, tore a chit, filled something in and nudged the crumpled pellet across the desk. Internal voices urged me to ignore this memo.

I opened the paper ball to read the message:

A.F.R.I.C.A – After Fucking Rest In Cool Areas

Stephen puckered his lips and raised his eyebrows, perhaps expecting me to scribble my response. I read the message again, this time slower, unsure of what he was trying to convey.

My eyes hovered longest on one word, for up until then I had only heard it spoken, never seen it spelled out. I had watched older boys contort their faces and curse during games of football, the sound of the swear so grating it raised visions of a delicate butterfly fuh crushed against a pointy granite uck. I had played tennis against a boy who let it slip after losing a long rally, which prompted our coach to shoot daggers at the boy's mother, and for her to turn away, ashamed. I had sat opposite my uncle when he toppled a tumbler of coffee and went 'ohfak', spurring my aunt to close her eyes and mumble a prayer. If someone were to go so far as to write out the word, I assumed it would be scribbled in anger, the seething nib singeing the paper.

Instead here it was, in marvellous cursive, tilting its head and fluttering its eyelashes. The loopy 'f', a pair of folded spectacles, leading to a tiny pail of a 'u', whose handle arced into a claw-shaped 'c' to set up a runway for take-off: a 'k' that flew high and looped back in a stunt that finished with a bulb traced at the base. Stephen's 'k' was a king on a morning stroll: head held high, body tilted forward, bestowing the 'fucking' with an air of majesty.

Fax turned around to take in the general mood of the classroom. I carefully shoved the chit in my pocket and submitted a hopeless apology to the gods before restarting the table afresh. Fax wiped his neck with his soggy handkerchief. 'You know what these classrooms need?' he said at the top of his voice. 'F for …? Yes, F for? Fans, man. Fans.'

The boy in front of me, Leo Pinto, tore a page from his notebook and went about folding it into a glider. The moment Fax returned to the blackboard, Leo blew through the tail's vent and launched the paper plane at a diagonal. About twenty boys watched it soar over the middle aisle before it swerved right and dipped towards S. Anoop's head. Snoop didn't notice at first; his curly mop was so bushy the glider stood at an incline for a few seconds, and it was only when he heard the snickering that he snatched the glider and slipped it under his desk. Leo and his pals jiggled with delight but just as Fax turned around, they put on their dead-serious looks. How they switched from jokey to thoughtful in a fraction of a second, I don't know.

Fax realized he was a split-second too late. As much as he would have wanted to seek out the gigglers and reduce them to tears, he knew the moment had passed. Thwarted, he turned around to complete the table, his writing as curvy as ribbon pakodas.

Stephen tapped our desk with his knuckles. I expected another chit to be flung at me, another continent expanded, but no, this time he was drawing my attention to something lying on his lap. And it took a few seconds for my head to make sense of what my eyes were seeing: a topless lady on the cover of a glossy magazine, her arms crossed into Vs, her navel exposed over unbuttoned jeans, her ruffled black hair falling on her neck, her skin the colour of Cadbury Dairy Milk, her face bathed in sunlight, her eyes closed, serene. What the heck! Why was Stephen on this mission to get me expelled from St George's?

'What do you think, Karthik?'

'She's sleeping?'

Stephen glared at me, like I was talking in Swahili. 'Sleeping?'

'Why are her eyes closed?'

'Jesus Christ. Why the fuck are you looking at her eyes?'

Confused, I returned to my notebook, promising to not look up until I was done copying Fax's table.

'Unbelievable,' went Stephen, shaking his head.

Fax asked if we had any questions. He read out the assignment for the week – 'Take this down, jobless fellows' – and warned that those who didn't get it done would be in 'deep, deep trouble'.

He then opened the register and rushed through attendance.

'Aakash Aggarwal.'

'Present, Father.'

'Abdul Rasool.'

'Yes, Father.'

'Abhishek S. R.'

'Yes, Father.'

Stephen folded the issue along the vertical, inflicting a sharp crease on her chocolatey skin, and shoved it into his bag.

'Still can't believe you were looking at her eyes, Karthik.'

Unsure of how to explain myself, I shut up, but those eyes had an irresistible appeal, more than her ample breasts and perfectly round navel, more than her sensuous nose and sinewy fingers. I couldn't believe that she had closed her eyes while the photographer had greedily clicked away. Was she not even slightly uneasy? Had she been forced to pose in this manner?

None of these questions bothered Stephen. He wasn't going to apologize to the lord for finding her ravishing. What he cared about, as he told Leo during the break, were her '6/10 bod, 7/10 boobs, and 8/10 figure'. She was a welcome distraction during class, but she also satisfied his ultimate fantasy: an older woman who could bully him to do her bidding, a 'sexy aunty' who could tease him and order him around before delivering the most pleasurable bingo of all.

5

Mugpot

FINALLY, AFTER SIX WEEKS of tossing about like a snail in a thunderstorm, I could venture out of my shell.

The 7C classroom comprised fifty-two of us, spread around six rows and three columns of rickety teak furniture. Cramped for room, on benches that barely fit three, many boys elbowed their bench-mates when taking notes. The aggressive ones slammed their neighbours' knees or barged into their shoulders. Occasionally, as long as our teachers' back was turned to the blackboard, some scoundrels let fly head butts.

The first two rows held the shortest boys and, determined to cash in on their proximity to the teachers, some frontbenchers put on their best impression in class. Like the fellow nicknamed Pocket Rocket, who had built a reputation as an ass-kisser. Our teachers had to simply turn to him; Pocket Rocket's head bobbed as if guided by a spring. This turned into a ritual during class and some teachers reciprocated with ardent nods of their own. One day Father Xavier asked, 'Do you fools take me for an idiot?' Pocket Rocket nodded as usual. Fax called him to the front of the class and clouted his butt with a foot-rule.

Pocket Rocket and his frontbencher pals stayed back in the classroom during the lunch breaks, and they were least fussed that

I too hung around and overheard all they discussed. I couldn't make sense of their jargon at first; it took time to figure out that 'stop woaling' meant 'stop making things up', that 'cop' and 'vice-cop' referred to the principal and vice-principal, and that you could be accused of playing 'pocket billiards' when walking around with your hands deep in your pockets. Gradually I learnt Pocket Rocket was a hardcore coin collector, that he hung out with his fourteen cousins on Sundays – 'church, then football, then lunch and more football' – and that he had a ten-year-old brother who was almost as tall as him. 'What are you going to do when he becomes taller than you, man?' asked Kulla, the shortest boy in 7C. 'No big deal, dude,' said Pocket Rocket with a shrug, signalling that he had thought hard about this. 'I'll make sure he tells everyone that I am the younger one.'

Two rows behind Pocket Rocket sat a chatterbox called Ammonia, nicknamed partly for his stinky farts but mostly for the hot air he spewed. Oh man, could this chap talk or what! I overheard him deliver a lengthy lecture about the Gulf War, including a reference to Teenage Mutant Ninja Turtles, before he held forth on why Karna is the greatest character in literature. His confidence was scary, his English impeccable and however trivial the topic, he was armed with strong opinions.

Not many in 7C took Ammonia seriously though. 'He is okay for a little while, da,' Pocket Rocket said, dismissive, 'but five, ten minutes of that yakyakyak and you want to punch him in the face. You know, Reddy and gang got so pissed off with him last year, they tied Ammonia's hands up and taped his mouth.'

'Oh damn. That's crazy. But how does he know so much?'

'He's mostly woaling, Karthik. Believe me. He once told me that if you swallow chewing gum, it will stay in your stomach for seven years. Proper woal. My pop laughed when I asked him.'

'He really said that?'

'Ya, man. Don't ever believe him. He keeps saying that there is research that shows that the taller you are the richer you will be. I told him to take his research and stuff it up his fat ass.'

Pocket Rocket's assessment began to make sense when I saw Ammonia at an inter-house debate. The topic: 'Television – a good influence?' And as excellent as his speech appeared, it was hard to work out if all his claims were indeed true.

'There is enough evidence to suggest that long hours of television viewing can result in obesity, eye problems and a disposition to violence among kids,' he said, pounding the lectern and nearly toppling the microphone. 'The research is out there, dear sirs, and it is time to take away the idiot box from impressionable teens.'

Pocket Rocket turned to me, his eyebrows raised. Kulla said Ammonia was 'gassing as usual'. But none of that seemed to matter to the judges. As one of them elaborated when announcing the results: 'The best debaters don't have stage fright. They don't ramble and they don't overshoot their time. They are forceful with their arguments. And they stay calm at the rebuttal.' Everyone knew who he was referring to. And sure enough, Ammonia was awarded the shiny first-place trophy.

The honour of sharing a bench with Ammonia went to Bugs and Soda, a bespectacled duo who were too preoccupied with *Trachtenberg Speed Mathematics* to take note of Ammonia's theories. Across the aisle sat Mangu and Baab, a chess-obsessed pair who often played rapid chess but were now in the middle of a weird experiment, limiting themselves to just one move a day. Seriously. They went through the snack and lunch breaks doing little but staring at the chessboard, and once the day's move was made – in slow motion – returned the board to a slot below the desk. I asked if I could play the winner. Sure, they said, but only when their game ended, in three months.

Pocket Rocket, Kulla, Ammonia, Bugs, Soda, Mangu, Baab: all were serious about coursework, but everyone in 7C agreed that no one could match the Maniacs – Aakash, Nitin and Tarun – when it came to tests and exams. These three were always on top of their game, whether it was how neatly they jotted down notes during classes or how particular they were about refilling their water bottles every two hours. Always the first to submit homework and assignments, they asked the best questions in class, questions that made it clear they had studied the relevant chapters in advance. During the breaks, they lost themselves in brainteasers, word games and trivia, and Pocket Rocket had no doubt that the Maniacs' vocabulary and general knowledge were in a different league. I happened to be around when Aakash told some boys about the aardvark – the first animal listed in the Oxford English Dictionary – and he was quick to point out that, like the aardvark, he too had a name that would lead all ordered lists. 'Hmm,' said Ammonia, eyes full of mischief. 'So you're basically saying you are the St George's equivalent of the African ground pig?' Aakash walked away, red-faced. 'Shut your gob, Ammonia,' Nitin said, and quickly followed Aakash.

I sat two rows behind the Maniacs, in the corner of the last row. Not because I was that tall but because on the first day of school, rattled by Paunchy's bingo, I had picked the only free seat, on the rightmost extreme. Nobody had asked me to move since. So I sat there, next to the tallest boy in class: Stephen.

Like Stephen, many of my fellow backbenchers had arrived at puberty. Metric, a tall, lithe chap who had captained the junior hockey team, was said to have 'a forest for armpits', and Leo didn't even want to imagine 'how hairy Metric was down there'. Next to Metric sat Musu and TP, lynchpins of the junior cricket team, with chests that showed signs of bulging and voices ready to crack. The real superstars of the last two rows were boys who excelled at arm-wrestling, where the build-up for bouts lasted days and shock victories assured instant fame. There were Pepsi and Five-Star bets on arm-wrestling matches and, occasionally, boys from 7A and 7B came to watch a big clash. When an upset loomed, excited spectators shrieked 'kill him', 'fuck his ass' and 'nail the bastard', pounding desks, pumping fists and howling with delight.

On an overcast July evening, walking across the field towards the back gate, I saw an older boy trap Kulla and twist his arms. He socked Kulla's penis with his knee and, digging into his bag, sprayed him with a bottle of ink. It was fair to assume the older boy had taunted Kulla about his shortness and that Kulla had hit back with an insult. Provoked, the big boy left Kulla writhing in the long-jump pit while he rushed off to the canteen. I had endured worse but to watch someone being manhandled this way …

Kulla looked around the field for help. Inevitably, his gaze met mine. I turned to the canteen to check on the bully. Realizing we were being monitored, Kulla got up, dusted sand off his trousers and made for the toilets. My first thought was to run after him, to spell out that I was on his side and his side alone, but with the older boy's eyes firmly fixed on me, I couldn't muster the guts.

Kulla offered to buy me a burger the next morning. This was his cry for help, hoping I could convince Stephen to come to his rescue. 'Not hungry, man,' I deadpanned. 'Maybe another time.'

Kulla wasn't the only one to get pally with me. Pocket Rocket offered Gems and Poppins from time to time, and showed me a fifty-paisa coin from 1972: 'a rare gem, issued to commemorate the twenty-fifth anniversary of independence'. The chess nuts asked about my favourite openings. The Maths buffs suggested I should buy a 386 or a 486 so that I could play the 'greatest game ever': *Prince of Persia*. I had no clue what these numbers meant – and had never heard of this game – but was certain that my father wasn't going to buy me a computer. He loved to quote a colleague at work who had once proclaimed: 'TVs are like cigarettes, VCRs are like alcohol and computers are like drugs.'

The only group still indifferent towards me were the Maniacs. There were no smiles, no hi's, no waves, not even when I made eye contact. This 'too-cool-for-school attitude', which Ammonia accused them of, didn't worry me. I assured myself they would come around if I asked sharp questions in class and submitted my assignments before they did.

Nothing was good enough. My keenness evoked no interest. Soon their unconcern was like a boil over my tongue – a minor irritation that had turned into a full-on annoyance.

My best chance to introduce myself was during the lunch breaks, when the Maniacs convened at the Pegasus fountain: a stone horse with forelegs raised, spouting water from its ears and nostrils. This was so popular a hangout I had heard about it from Zombie at the summer cricket camp. Zombie had raced paper boats at the fountain when at the junior school and had occasionally mounted the horse when no teacher was around. He had told me about the Pegasus Scandal from a year ago, when an eighth standard boy had introduced vermillion into the pipes, getting blood-red water to stream out of the horse's ears and nostrils. Hundreds of students had rushed to the spot to take in the gory sight, and so frenzied was the scene that many classes were discharged midway. The principal urgently set up a committee to investigate the matter. But the mystery had remained unresolved. No student had given the prankster away.

I chose a Friday afternoon to lurk in the shade of a gulmohar, waiting for the Maniacs to settle down for lunch. The sky a blue bedspread, was spotless, smooth; the sun, a yellow cushion, was at its zenith; a talkative sparrow trilled from the branches above; and the crystal-clear water swooshed with delight.

The Maniacs sat down on the granite ledge that circled Pegasus. Aakash washed his hands with water from his bottle. He spread out a green hand towel on the ledge and brought out his square ever-silver tiffin box. Nitin and Tarun did the same, before the three closed their eyes in prayer. Only then did they dig in.

Two bites into his cauliflower paratha, with each chunk carefully dipped into a blotch of pickle and a cup of curd, Aakash suggested that the group play Last-Letter Geography.

'Can I also play?' I asked, emerging from the shadows.

Aakash looked at me as if I had shredded his notebooks.

'Was just ... was just walking by ...'

'Oh. You've played this game before?'

'A few times, yes.'

He turned to his friends.

Nitin and Tarun sized me up, then turned to Aakash and shrugged. My presence wasn't going to affect the outcome anyway, they seemed to be saying, so how did it even matter.

'Alright,' said Aakash. 'But only countries, cities, states and towns. Okay? No localities within cities, no monuments and all. And ya, no rivers, no lakes, no mountains.'

'Got it.'

'And you can't use the same place twice. Okay? Like, you can't say Hyderabad twice because it's there both in India and Pakistan.'

'Okay.'

'Hmm. Let me start then. Angola.'

Arizona – Alabama – Armenia – Almora – Addis Ababa – Accra – Ankara – Agra – Acapulco – Oman – Nigeria – Asansol – Luxembourg – Ghent – Thimpu – Uruguay – Yemen – Nicaragua – Almaty – Yerevan – Nairobi – Indonesia ...

'Antwerp,' said Aakash, starting on his second paratha.

'Peru,' said Nitin.

'Ukraine,' said Tarun.

Which left me with 'e': a chance to knock their brains out. 'Essex,' I announced, stressing the x, looking around the group, triumphant. I had stumped my classmates at Sacred Valley with Essex, Sussex and Middlesex, and watched their jaws drop. Now it was Aakash's turn to surrender, and for me to mount Pegasus and fly off into the limitless blue. I had not only survived my first big test with the Maniacs; I had trounced them.

'Xinyi,' said Aakash, legs jiggling with glee. He said Xinyi was in the Guangdong province, and pointed out that he knew six other places with x, including one *not* in China. Gulping down water, he wiped his lips with the back of his palm. He may as well have bingoed me, so ruthlessly had he put me down.

The three of them continued as if nothing of note had happened. They brought out countries and cities I had never heard of, like Paramaribo, Lilongwe and Palau – which Tarun jokingly pronounced 'pulao' to confuse me. The worst part was being eliminated on 'q', since I had only recently read in the *North Star Quiz Book* that Quito was the capital city closest to the Equator.

It was hard to work out what the Maniacs had made of me. Did they think I was a worthy opponent? Or were they happy to have shown me my place? Either way, there was no use shadowing them and embarrassing myself. I would rather keep up with them academically and hope they recognized my worth.

This single-minded focus brought on nicknames like 'mugpot' and 'assignment freak'. Leo imitated how I nudged my spectacles up the bridge of my nose, and the way I bit my pen cap while solving problems. Musu started a rumour that I was secretly requesting our teachers for extra homework, that it was *me* who was responsible for everyone's heavy workload. Thankfully Paunchy squashed this lie with a loud 'fucking bullshit' and slammed Musu for spreading 'out-and-out lies'.

'Forget about these wasters, Karthik,' Paunchy said, walking up to my bench. 'You just carry on. These guys can go hang.'

Here was Paunchy, who had squashed my balls on day one and disregarded me for the next six weeks, acting all pally.

Unsettled, I stayed silent.

'So Karthik ... you are doing the Maths assignment now?'

'Ya, just finishing.'

'You think it will be possible to help me with that?'

'Sure. Which questions?'

'As in ... I am saying ... can you do my assignment for me?'

'The *whole* assignment?'

'It's just ten questions, man.'

'I know but that's just ...'

'It won't even take you an hour, dude.'

'But ...'

'Now you don't worry about anything, Karthik. Just do my assignment and I'll give you a solid treat in the canteen.'

'I'm sorry man, but...'

'Here,' he interrupted, pulling out a packet of Yummies chips from his pocket. 'This flavour is great. You should try it.'

Before I could weigh the pros and cons – or even return the tomato-flavoured Yummies – Paunchy walked out of 7C.

I looked around the classroom, hesitant. None of the boys who watched this exchange was surprised. 'Paunchy's dad is a bigshot surgeon, da,' Pocket Rocket explained, 'and he thinks he can get anything as long as he gives treats in the canteen.'

'So I should say no?'

'No question, Karthik. Give him an inch and he'll take a mile.'

I mulled over the offer crunching the tasty Yummies. Paunchy's assignment would take me forty-five minutes at most, and everyone knew that Father James didn't check these too closely. 'I think I'll just do the assignment for him and move on, man,' I said. Pocket Rocket looked at me like I had taken my clothes off.

Paunchy couldn't believe his luck the next day. He was possibly prepared for another round of negotiation, eager to tempt me with a higher bribe, but here I was, before morning assembly, handing him exactly what he had wanted.

'Thanks a million, dude,' he beamed, his excitement surging as he scanned the pages, 'but why is this so neat, bugger? Haven't you seen my handwriting? My mother always says it's like an ant dived into an ink bottle before running wild across the page.'

I blushed.

'And please, no fountain pen next time. Only microtip.'

'Next time?'

'What's the big deal, Karthik? It's not taking you much time anyway.'

'No, Paunchy, no. No way.'

'Okay, just one more Maths assignment. Please.'

'No chance.'

'Please, man. I beg you. Please, please, please!'

I didn't tell Pocket Rocket or anyone else about this. Aping Paunchy's largely illegible microtip scrawl, I rushed through the next Mathematics assignment and accepted a bottle of Pepsi as a reward. Paunchy didn't ask me for more help, only hoped that I would consider an assignment or two closer to the mid-terms.

The Pepsi, though, was a lapse in judgment on my part. Stephen knew something was afoot the moment he saw me walking from the canteen, sipping on the costliest item. 'So Karthik,' he hissed at the end of the first period after lunch, 'I hear you are the king of assignments.'

Nervous, I waited for more.

'Physics,' he said. 'By Monday.'

There was no 'please', no 'just this once, man'. Just the subject and the deadline.

My first instinct was to wave him off with an excuse, yet I gradually found the offer tempting. Here he was, finally acknowledging my worth. He could have asked any number of boys to assist him with his assignments but it was *me* whom he trusted. And coming to think of it, was this really that big a risk? Admitted, the chances of getting caught were higher with Physics but as long as I made sure to cover my tracks, these extra assignments would only ensure I was thoroughly prepared for my unit tests and exams. The Maniacs would be impressed with how hard I was slogging, as would everyone at home, especially my grandfather, who made it a point to regularly remind me about high-flying relatives, like his grandniece who earned a PhD in Chemistry at 'a prestigious university in America' and a grandnephew who placed thirty-eighth in an all-India engineering exam.

'You must finish in the top ten, Karthik,' he had said on hearing the news, seemingly jealous of the progress his cousins' children were making. 'I want your photo in the *Competition Success Review*.'

'I'll try my best, Thatha.'

'No try vie nothing. It has to happen. Okay?'

'Yes, Thatha.'

'You see, what I am saying is, this country has way too many people, Karthik. The population is exploding. It's a big curse, I tell you. Unless you are at the very top, you will be a nobody. And all these quotas and reservations make it so hard for people like us. These politicians will soon make sure we Brahmins have only one or two seats in each college. So you *have* to be at the very, very top. There is no other choice.'

'Yes, Thatha.'

'So listen carefully. If you come first in your unit tests, I will buy you a new shirt. If you come first in your mid-terms, I will get you a ticket for India's next match in Bangalore.'

'International match!'

'Of course, Karthik. You could be one of the forty thousand people at the Chinnaswamy Stadium. Imagine that!'

'That will be super, Thatha.'

My grandfather was already in match mode, visualizing the oohs and aahs that would ripple through the stands, the cheers for every Indian four or six, and the tension that would envelop the crowd if the game went to the final over. On top of all that, here was my chance to see the great Tendulkar in the flesh – which, in my grandfather's world, was the ultimate prize.

Dead set on making him proud, I promised myself:

- to cover the portions well ahead of my unit tests;
- to limit cricket with Chiku and friends to weekends only;
- to stay back in school and finish my assignments; and
- to wake up an hour early to prepare for the day's lessons.

Now, doing Stephen's assignments would fit in perfectly with my plans. It would help me gear up for my unit tests in September, but also serve as a gesture of appreciation for ending the bullying and turning my life around.

'Wow,' he went, eyes lit up when he saw my near-perfect imitation of his ballpoint cursive. 'Looks just like my handwriting.'

I turned around to ensure nobody else had heard him.

'Too good, Karthik. Too good.'

'It's fine, Stephen. No big deal.'

'You enjoy these assignments so much or what?'

'It's just ... I don't know ...'

'Your dick gets fully hard when you do them, right?'

I wasn't sure where to look.

'Just joking, fucker. Stop acting like you got run over by a bus.'

'What do you mean, man?'

'Nothing, dude. Forget about it. It's just funny how much you love doing these assignments. For me, it's a big bore.'

I couldn't explain myself, and anyway, Stephen wouldn't have understood where I was coming from, given that he needed to do so little to be noticed in 7C. Everyone was wowed by his physique and confidence. He was so awesome an arm wrestler, nobody dared challenge him to a bout. The seventh-standard push-up record was his for good. When Father Rosario caught him chewing gum in class and punished him by smashing his palms, the wooden foot rule had snapped in half.

As if his strength and athleticism weren't enough to cement his stardom, Stephen was armed with an endless supply of jokes. There were full forms for most countries – like JAPAN, which he expanded to Jumping and Pumping All Night, and CUBA: Caught Under Bra Area. To teach a girl arithmetic, one had to 'add her to a bed, subtract her clothes, divide her legs and start multiplying'. And he cooked up a story about a crime syndicate where the hero, I. P. Daly, rescued his sweetheart, Sheikh Mehboobi, from the scheming Kaikomere Ballsquashky.

Most of the backbenchers were drawn to Stephen like bees to a honeypot. His sleazy magazines were in demand, and boys were blown away by how Stephen spoke of women's body parts like they were items on a grocery list: analyzing juicy melons, red-hot apples and peeled oranges. They laughed along when he rated models on a scale of ten, like the time he said: 'She could be a nine but only if her guavas turn into mangoes.'

Since that muggy July afternoon, when he had tried to interest me in the topless model on the magazine cover, Stephen had taunted me about my initial reaction to the nude: looking past her shapely breasts and asking about her closed eyes.

'You had the Taj Mahal in front of you, man,' he reminded me again on a Monday morning, while we waited on the football field for the start of morning assembly.

'It was in the middle of class, Stephen.'

'So what, bugger? Still crazy that you were looking at her eyes.'

I looked away, though deep down I was not too perturbed by his friendly needling. These awkward chats, I told myself, were like Fevicol drops, icky and irritating at first but necessary to strengthen the bonds of our friendship.

We were soon joined by four of our classmates, reason enough for Stephen to grasp a goal's crossbar and rise for three pull-ups. An older boy approached and, to prove his superiority, swiftly did five pull-ups. Stephen responded with six, puffing out his biceps for everyone to see. The older boy did five, but just as he rose for the sixth, his hands slipped. A wave of ohshits and fuckinghells rippled around the goalpost. Stephen shook hands with the older boy and agreed to arm wrestle after the final bell.

There were still five minutes to go for the morning assembly. Metric cursed the charcoal-dome sky. Musu compared Stephen to the Olympic gymnast Vitaly Scherbo. Leo brought up Lorena Bobbitt, in the news for grabbing a knife and cutting off her husband's penis while he was asleep. Paunchy shook his head, disbelieving. Leo swore this was 'absolutely true'. Paunchy continued to shake his head with 'no way, man, no way'. Leo promised to cut off Paunchy's dick. 'Stop woaling,' said Paunchy, feigning a bingo. And on and on they went, issuing threat after threat, insulting each other's dicks, their mental faculties and their mothers. Soon they were blurting out whatever thoughts popped in their heads – thoughts that, like fireflies, lit up for a brief instant and just as quickly disappeared.

Stephen asked the two to shutthefuckup.

Leo agreed that this was a pointless argument, especially when there were far more important matters to discuss. The five of us turned to him, curious. 'The thing is ...' Leo began, hands in his pockets, and told us that he had jerked himself off fourteen times on Saturday. 'From eight in the morning till midnight, man. By the end it was so damn watery.' We waited to see if there was more. 'It pained so much I couldn't sleep all night, dude,' he grimaced, as if he had been forced into this strokeathon.

Paunchy bent double. 'Fourteen fackin' times!'

A grinning Stephen slapped Leo on the back with a 'no way, dude', even though he seemed to mean, 'way to go, dude'. The other three boys were out of control.

Leo soaked in the reactions and tittered like a three-year-old ... until his eyes met mine. That's when he let out a giant howl, and alerted Stephen and Paunchy. Everyone saw how shaken I was. And the laughter soared to a higher octave.

Stephen was the first to recover his composure. 'Hey Karthik, why so shocked, man? You haven't started shagging yet? Or waiting to read about it in a textbook?'

More cackles. More embarrassment.

Stephen didn't let up, repeating the question, his right hand tugging an invisible penis. 'Surely you have shagged at least once,' Paunchy asked, intrigued, even as he thrust out his pelvis.

I didn't know what to say. Everything had happened so fast when, five months ago, during a hot-water shower, a water jet had struck the tip of my shaft and sparked off a shock like none other. At once, I had known I was in forbidden territory, as I would have been if I had gobbled a boxful of chocolates or polished off a packet of chips. There was no way that something that felt so good could ever be acceptable. A few seconds later, another jet of water set off another shock and, before I knew it, I was caught between a mind that wished to stop and hands that wouldn't listen. The faster I yanked, the worse it got, but slowing down only deepened the pleasure and dialled up the guilt. Convinced there was no way out, I decided to get it over with. The climax was so terrific, the pleasure so electric, it left me feeling awful. Having hurtled onto the dark side, there was no going back. My family would never forgive me if they found out. No apology could make up for this disgusting act. Even the prayers I poured out rang hollow, and I couldn't look Lord Ganesha in the eye once I got out of the bathroom. He had explicitly ordered me to stop. And I had dared to disobey.

Stephen was still waiting for my response. I cursed Leo for being a 'terrible person' and walked away from the group, towards the toilets. The story spread like wildfire around the field. Hundreds of boys, who took it that I had never jerked off, shared a hearty chuckle. Leo, of course, laughed the loudest.

Our principal began the morning assembly with a prayer.

Our Father in heaven,
Holy be your name,
Your kingdom come,
Your will be done,
On earth as in heaven,
Give us today our daily bread,
Forgive us our sins,
As we forgive those who sin against us,
Do not bring us to the test,
But deliver us from evil,
Amen.

Stephen's question had a straightforward answer: yes, I had pleasured myself, three times to be exact. Each was a harrowing experience, soaking me in regret. But now it had been three months since my last time. Lord Ganesha had delivered an emphatic punishment via Paunchy's bingo on day one. And the next three weeks of bullying had only clarified His message. To atone for my sins and seek forgiveness, to make amends for these reckless experiments on my body, I had to give up all physical pleasure.

Additionally, in my quest to ace my tests and exams, it was vital to rid myself of all distractions. The deeper I immersed myself in coursework, the higher were the chances of watching India's next cricket match in Bangalore. Here was my chance to make my grandfather happy. And to experience a genuine pleasure out in the open, guilt-free: to watch Tendulkar's back-foot punch from close range, to see him tear bowlers to shreds, to hope for something unparalleled – and watch him fulfil that expectation – to sneak his autograph, maybe even shake his hand, to surrender to his aura and be swept along.

6

Remington

EARLY IN SEPTEMBER A rainstorm felled trees, toppled auto-rickshaws and sent stray dogs into hiding. Gigantic z's of lightning gashed the leaden skies. We lost power for two days and sat around in candlelight, battling mosquitoes with an electric racket. My father called the Electricity Board and shouted at whoever picked up. 'You fellows have made us powerless. Got it? Power. Less.' When he hung up, he boomed, 'We are truly back to the dark ages. Got it? Dark Ages.'

The storm gave way to a persistent pitter-patter. The power returned early on Saturday – the flickering tube light jolting me awake – but the window opened out to a scene so drab, I curled up under the velveteen razai and went back to dreaming about a football match.

'You can sleep all you want later in life, Karthik,' my grandfather hollered, jerking my ankles, preventing me from scoring a dreamy goal. 'Now it is time to rise and shine.'

'Just five more minutes, Thatha,' I begged, turning onto my stomach to bury my face under my soft pillow.

'Five more minutes? That is a whole minute longer than it took Roger Bannister to run a mile, Karthik. That is how much you can achieve in five minutes. You know, in five minutes ...'

Throwing off the pillow, I sat up.

'Karthik! Have you gone fully mad?'

'Sorry, Thatha.'

'Is this how you shock your body first thing in the morning?'

'No, Thatha. Very sorry.'

'First look at your palm lines. Yes, go ahead. Now thank Lord Ganesha for being kind enough to give you another day in this world. Yes, go on. Why are you whispering, Karthik? Pray loud and clear. Nobody will kill you! Okay. Now take three deep breaths. Inhaaaale. Exhaaaale. Hmm. Okay. Go and wash your face now. Gently. Don't splash water. Slow and steady.'

With two weeks to go for my unit tests, my grandfather had cellotaped a study schedule to the wall, at the perfect spot for me to notice it when I rose from bed. The weekday squares were choc-a-bloc, his teensy letters spilling over the borders; Saturdays were blank, to attend to backlogs; and Sunday mornings were reserved for a quiz, when he flipped through my textbooks and fired off questions. On the days I messed up, he demanded that I revise the relevant chapters in the afternoon. Otherwise I could join my mother in watching whatever award-winning film was playing on national television – but it was more than two months since that had happened.

My grandfather was more tense about my upcoming unit tests than I was. He had been chary of the teaching philosophy at Sacred Valley and he could never work out why any school would actively encourage students to shun competition. 'It's never about finishing first but finishing well,' our principal at Sacred Valley loved to say. 'In the words of the great Jiddu, real learning comes about when the competitive spirit has ceased.'

My grandfather's response when my father told him this: 'Hmm. Humbug.'

My mother, on the other hand, couldn't get enough of the green rolling acres of Sacred Valley. Her eyes lit up when I spoke of bird-watching trips and aeromodelling classes, of lessons in pottery, carpentry and artwork. Mrs Chacko was not buying any of it, but she tried her hardest to hide her scepticism. 'Well done, Karthik. I must bake you a cake now.'

My father saw upsides to this style of education, especially at an impressionable age, and wasn't perturbed by the hefty fees – 'If we can't pay to educate Karthik, what is the use of earning?' I overheard him tell my mother – but he was patently uneasy about the complete absence of tests. 'How will they prepare students for their class ten board exams?'

My mother plonked a water jug on the dining table and reminded him that there was a 'looooong time' before we needed to worry about my boards.

My father opened his mouth wide but, gauging her mood, kept the words within himself. My grandfather too stopped himself after a stern 'umm'.

Their concerns occasionally resurfaced over the years – my grandfather held mock exams and threw a fit when I bungled – but my mother was confident that I was going to cope just fine.

Preparing for these unit tests at St George's required me to commit definitions, tables, diagrams, and passages to memory.

Take, for example, History & Civics. It wasn't enough to summarize Emperor Akbar's reign and list out his contributions in our own words. 'You have to mug up the whole chapter, Karthik,' Snoop said when he learned I had never sat for a test or exam before. 'Just by-heart everything that's there, man – Akbar's government departments, his taxation laws, his military strategies, the monuments he built, the religion he founded, his courtiers' achievements – mug it all up. And, oh, don't forget the important dates. Okay? The year he was born, the years of his reign, the years of his major conquests, the year he died ... Mug, mug, mug. That's all it's about, really.' Those who reproduced textbook passages verbatim would score high, Snoop said; the rest would have to make do with middling grades.

Geography wasn't too different in this regard, bristling with passages we had to learn by heart. At least our textbook was peppered with arresting photos that transported me to far-flung corners of the globe. When bored with a lecture on 'Mediterranean farming' I chalked up an itinerary for a world tour, to visit the spots where these photos were shot. One day I would ride a horse through a terraced farm in southern Peru; a week on, I would laze on a hammock in a western Australian vineyard.

'Any questions?' Father Xavier droned, disturbing my reverie.

Bugs raised a hand.

'Yes?'

'Father. I didn't understand what a green harvest is.'

'Have you gone deaf?'

Bugs bowed.

'I just said green harvesting is not important for the unit test.'

'Yes, Father.'

'Don't waste time worrying about useless things, silly fellow.'

'Yes, Father.'

Fax read out the definition of green harvesting from the textbook.

'Understood?'

'Yes, Father.'

'Sit down now. Any more questions?'

No one volunteered.

And Fax jabbered on.

The sciences had no lengthy passages to memorize. I assumed I could get through the portions well ahead of my unit tests, until I realized how pathetic I was at biology diagrams and how long it took to have each one down. My grandfather had budgeted four two-hour blocks for me to practise these diagrams; I wasn't sure if four months were going to be enough, especially after an assignment came back with the plant cell riddled with blood-red x's and our teacher's peppery comments along the margins:

Golgi bodies – wrong shape.

Centrosome – wrong position.

Ribosomes – too few.

Amyloplast – Not marked. Have they gone on holiday?

Mathematics, everyone said, was as straightforward as it got. A problem, a formula, a solution: how complicated could that be? Knowing which formula to apply where was half the battle, and our teacher, Father James, was most supportive, urging us to see the 'beauty in complexity' and to always choose an 'elegant method over the obvious one'. Eager to crack every problem in every exercise set, desperate to be hailed as the Mathematics whiz of 7C, anxious to impress everyone at home, I rushed through the steps, heedless. And the quicker I moved towards the final answer, the more readily I screwed up. Confronted with an unfamiliar problem, or confused by a question's phrasing, I worried I was underprepared. Which brought on waves of panic.

Most of my practice tests were overrun with elementary blunders: multiplication gaffes, substitution flubs, unit mix-ups. A train hurtled at 800 kilometres an hour (when the answer was eighty), a tap magically filled a water tank in twenty seconds, when, really, it took twenty minutes.

My grandfather was in a tizzy over these goof-ups. My father, a bachelor of Mathematics (gold medal), master of Statistics (distinction) and now a financial analyst for a multinational firm, was adamant that anything less than a perfect score in 'the queen of the sciences' was a sign of dimness. The only way to eliminate these mistakes, they were convinced, was to challenge me with puzzles at every opportunity. In the grocery store, could I add up the price of the items as I picked them? My father clutched his hair when my sum was off by eight paise. At the petrol pump, he told me to compute the car's mileage and slapped his forehead when I screwed up the division. During the final stages of an India-Sri Lanka cricket match, I was asked to work out the run rate required after each ball. Caught up in the pulsating finish, I tripped up over and over, which pissed off my grandfather more than India's sloppy bowling. I waited for him to administer a tongue-lashing; what I got was ominous silence.

'Seventeen into nineteen,' a voice demanded, jerking me awake in the dead of night. I turned over, agitated. 'Karthik!' My grandfather shrieked, pinching my arm, 'What is seventeen times nineteen? You have to be able to do these calculations in your sleep!' There was no point even trying, that's how disoriented I was. So I promised to write out the seventeen times table as an imposition. 'And the nineteen times table too,' he said, tugging my sleeve. 'Make sure to write both tables twenty times tomorrow.'

My favourite subjects were the languages English and Kannada. There was nothing to memorize here, no elaborate diagrams and no page-length tables. My mother took great delight in following my progress in English, and often borrowed my texts for her bed-time reading. She never tired of telling people of the time she had taught me the alphabet, going 'a for? b for?' and so on, only to reach 'k for?' and hear me say: 'Karthik'. She had held my hand when I first wrote my name and read the *Panchatantra* tales as she put me to sleep. Nowadays she set aside Saturday afternoons to go over all my essays and assignments.

The English portions comprised the first two acts of *The Merchant of Venice*; five poems, including 'Ozymandias'; and four short stories, starting with 'Tom Whitewashes the Fence'. I often ditched History & Civics and Biology to lap up Shakespeare, Shelley and Twain, and noted down the difficult words to later check in the dictionary.

'What do you have left in English, Karthik?' my grandfather asked on a Saturday, a week before my unit tests.

'I've covered everything, Thatha.'

'You've written out answers to all the sample questions twice?'

'Yes, Thatha.'

'You've gone through all the questions from your assignments?'

'Done, Thatha.'

'Has Amma checked everything?'

'Yes, Thatha.'

'Hmm,' he sighed, shutting his eyes, as if disappointed with how up-to-date I was with my preparation.

'Thatha, Chiku was saying we could play ...'

'Ah Chiku, good you reminded me,' he said and picked out a worn-out textbook from the bottom shelf in his book rack. 'I borrowed this collection of short stories from Chiku. It's meant for class nine but you must read the first story here. Just super.'

My grandfather couldn't stop introducing books meant for higher classes. He had done the same for Physics and Mathematics and, worse, when he asked if I had understood, I was too scared to admit it had gone over my head. 'Yes, Thatha,' I nodded each time, anxious not to let him down.

This time, though, I was curious. The story he wanted me to read was 'The Tiger in the Tunnel' by Ruskin Bond, 'a masterful stylist,' the prologue said, 'who sets his stories in the jungles and remote villages of north India'. No surprise that my grandfather was taken in. He too had grown up in a remote Indian village, so remote that there was neither a bus stop nor a railway station within twenty miles of it, and the fastest way to reach the nearest town was to hop onto a train as it curled around a bend. This had turned into a daily spectacle in my grandfather's village: every evening hundreds of villagers gathered at the bend to watch hyper men sneak into running trains. Many aspirants injured themselves. One died – and later a street was named for him. The successful ones, my grandfather said, were those who had 'mastered Newton's Law of Inertia', men who ran alongside the train until they matched its speed, then latched on to a handrail and floated in. My grandfather pointed out that it was only men who tried such crackpot stunts; the womenfolk in his village steered clear of such idiocy.

'Why are you reading silently, Karthik? Stand up. Read aloud.'

'Yes, Thatha. I was going to.'

The story began with Baldeo, a signalman at a railway station, whose job was to ensure that a certain tunnel was clear for a train to pass. Draped in a shawl on a new moon night, he walked from his hut to the station, unfazed by the jungle's stillness and the sounds puncturing the silence. He knew the ways of the jungle and carried an axe passed down from his forefathers – a weapon so lethal that it could fell a tree in a few rapid strokes.

At the station, Baldeo lit a lamp and made sure the tunnel was clear. He huddled up and was about to doze off when a low, menacing grunt startled him awake. At once, he knew that only one animal was capable of such a sound: the feared tiger that lurked in these parts.

Now his mind was on overdrive. Had the tiger entered the tunnel? Or had it taken off towards the hut where his twelve-year-old son, Tembu, lay unprotected? Clutching his axe, Baldeo searched for clues, until a clatter of stones confirmed that the tiger was approaching, its green eyes blazing against the signal lamp. Baldeo knew retreat was no more an option. So he stood still, his back to a lamppost, and stared firmly at the brute.

The tiger swept its right paw, looking to topple him with a swift blow. Baldeo dodged with a 'marvellously agile leap' – a phrase I uttered with hope soaring – and swished his axe, undaunted. The tiger lunged with a roar. Baldeo let rip another vicious swing and slashed the beast with a blow so fierce, the axe attached itself to the tiger's shoulder.

Now he was weaponless.

The tiger recoiled with a vengeance. Leaping high, it pinned him down and ripped his body as 'night closed on him forever'.

My voice trailed off. But on seeing my grandfather's fervent hand gestures, I cleared my throat and picked up the pace.

Maimed in battle, the tiger lurched into the tunnel, licking its wounds and emitting fitful roars. So acute was its anguish it was deaf to the soft trembles that shook the jungle. By the time the tiger registered the engine's whistle, there was nowhere to hide. The train blasted through the tunnel, and at the next station, the driver saw a large part of the tiger chopped in half by the engine.

Two brutal deaths. Suspense, fury, tragedy and revenge: all packed into four pages. Baldeo's death was a cruel blow for his family but everyone agreed that the village was a safer place.

The signalman's responsibilities now fell on Baldeo's son, Tembu. Seeing the story nearing its end, I thought it respectful to lower my voice.

> Three nights later, he was at the cutting, lighting the signal-lamp for the overland mail.
>
> He sat down in the darkness to wait for the train, and sang softly to himself. There was nothing to be afraid of – his father

had killed the tiger, the forest gods were pleased; and besides, he had the axe with him, his father's axe, and he now knew to use it.

My grandfather was in thrall.

He snatched the book and read the last part aloud: '... he had the axe with him, his father's axe, and he now knew to use it.'

'Aha. What a fine end. Aha. Wonderful.'

In the white space below the story, Chiku had scribbled some notes.

→ Jungle sounds – hammering woodpecker, grunting boar ... Setting the scene.

→ Important relationship between father and son. Daughter and mother not named. Patriarchal society?

→ Significance of axe. Weapon cutting across bloodline. Passed down from forefathers to father to son.

It was only a matter of time before my grandfather would ask for these notes to be expanded into essays. So, looking for ways to distract him, I asked about Baldeo's axe, which spanned generations. Was there anything similar that we, as a family, held so dear? To what could we turn to when faced with danger?

The question roused him into a frenzy. He got off his chair, onto the floor, and, with his chest puffed out and hands working as sculls, bent and unbent his lone leg. Before I could be of any help he had raced to the almirah at the other end of the room, squeaked it open and lunged for his typewriter case in the bottommost shelf. I wanted to tell him that my question was far from serious. But he had already hoisted the typewriter off its case and was now setting it on a short stool.

'Never forget this Remington Monarch, Karthik. It is the axe that saved my life.'

Index finger wound around a rag, he swiped the frame, the knobs and the keypad. He pulled out the type hammers and banished every last speck of dust. Only when the entire machine was sparkly clean did he fit in a sheet of copier paper. He then nicked the jet-black ribbon into position, centred the carriage, crunched his knuckles with a kat-a-kat-kat and typed: The Tiger in the Tunnel.

'Now read,' he commanded, slapping the carriage to the right.

His left pinkie kissed the a, his right pinkie kissed the semicolon. One ring finger hovered over the s, another over the l. His middle fingers bent over the d and k, like sprinters on a start line, awaiting a gunshot. His bushy forefingers danced above the f, g, h and j, and his thumbs dangled above the spacebar, like hammers over an anvil. His ears perked up, his lips parted. Here he was, a soldier on a mission, his eyes fixed on the paper, his ears waiting for my dictation, his fingers ready to fly.

I read slowly.

'Tembu, the boy, opened his eyes in the dark and wondered ...'

My grandfather's fingers galloped over the keys, filling the room with a burst of energy. The typewriter shook to a military beat – clicks, clacks, rattles, clatters, drings, trings – and the type hammers squealed in celebration when they struck the paper, like footballers heading in goals. So hard did he pound the keys, so resolute was his purpose, that my grandfather might as well have been working a foundry: drilling holes, extracting ore, forging each letter, spraying them with paint and fastening them to the page.

More than fifty years ago, he had lost his leg 'for the Brits' in the Second World War. In one stroke he went from being a promising subedar in the British Indian army to an amputee on crutches, in dire need of a job. Employers had rejected him for his disability. The Army had turned its back. As had friends and relatives. When India awakened to the possibilities of freedom, my grandfather was distraught, his world caving in.

Running out of options, he scrounged together his savings, borrowed a chunk from a cousin, and bought the Remington Monarch typewriter. He set up a chair and a table on the verandah outside his humble lodgings, said a prayer to Lord Ganesha, broke a coconut, and started work as a job typist.

For the next twenty-seven years, he provided for his wife and three children by thumping the keys, all day and, sometimes, all night. He typed pamphlets, newsletters, guides and marksheets; resumes, application forms, horoscopes and legal notices. He punched out fliers, manuscripts, affidavits and wills; wedding invites, property deeds, poems and, sometimes, even novels. He typed birth announcements. He typed obituaries. Chika-chik-cha-chika-chik-cha, the Remington rattled along.

Rain or shine he was ready to type. Clients stood by and dictated text, sometimes at high speed, often with indistinct accents. Many scowled when he requested them to repeat words or sentences, and some customers gave him an earful. One tiny slip-up and he could lose his fee; worse, it could ruin his reputation.

He once typed four hundred pages without a single mistake. 'Four hundred pages in one shot! Imagine,' my father would recall. 'He just typed and typed and typed. You know the neighbours would always say: if thieves came to our road at night, the typewriter would scare them off!'

Everyone who knew my grandfather had a story about his typing: how he fractured a hand but refused to take a day off; how he heard a prime minister's speech on the radio and started to air-type the address in real time; how he set up a young couple by typing letters on each of their behalf – their only interaction for six months; how his typing got faster and faster each year, leaving everyone in awe of his swiftness and accuracy. 'Eyes closed, it was like hearing someone burst crackers,' my uncle would reminisce. 'Taka-taka-taka-taka: we had Diwali at home every day!'

I waited for more.

'What more to say, Karthik? One man kept typing for twenty-seven years to support his wife and three children. End of story. Hmm, yes, a success story. Definitely a success story. But no fame, no big house, no scooter, no car, no gold, no expensive clothes. Nothing. No bank account even. Not even a one-line mention in a newspaper. No lifetime-achievement award. No trophy. Just hard work, Karthik. Sheer hard work.'

Even at seventy-seven, with his reflexes slowing and eyesight fading, my grandfather was scaring me with his typing speed. The quicker he typed, the harder he smashed the keys, as if challenging me to up the tempo. So I read as fast as I could.

> Their small rice fields provided them with more than a bare living, and Baldeo considered himself lucky to have got the job of a Khalasi at this small wayside signal-stop.

He kept up word for word, until he reached the end of the sentence and raised his hands with a loud 'oh god'.

'Thatha?'

'Wrong, Karthik,' he yelled. 'Wrong, wrong, wrong.'

I scanned the line he had just typed.

'Just read that sentence again.'

'The same sentence?'

'Yes. Read it from the book!'

'Their small rice fields did not provide them with ...'

'Stop. Read it again.'

'Their small rice fields did not ...'

'Stop. You know what you read the first time? You said, "Their small rice fields provided them with" instead of "did *not* provide them with". That changes the whole meaning, Karthik.'

'Oh no.'

'Always in a hurry. Hurry burry. Always rushing. Rushing with Mathematics, rushing with everything.'

'Sorry, Thatha.'

'How can you ever learn anything if you are so careless?'

'Sorry, Thatha.'

'Few years ago I would have noticed that mistake immediately. Now it is openly laughing at my typing.'

'Very sorry, Thatha.'

He plucked the paper from the Remington and ripped it in four.

'You are the best typist in the world, Thatha.'

'I was,' he said, looking out of the window. 'I was.'

7

Haramkhor

MY UNIT TESTS WENT by without alarm. The question papers were straightforward and left me with enough time to double-check my answers. At the end of the Physics test, I joined Snoop and Ammonia at the bicycle stand to review the question paper, only to discover what all I had botched. From then on, I made sure to avoid those two, afraid to come face to face with my mistakes.

The Kannada test, the last of the set, was on Friday morning. Answer sheet submitted, I clenched and unclenched my fist as if over a squeeze ball. My fingers were sore from the lengthy essays I had composed across twelve pages, in a script that nobody at home understood in the slightest.

Snoop had filled in fourteen foolscap sheets. 'Such a loooong paper,' he said, shaking his head, staring at his inky fingers.

'Screw it man, it's over, that's all that matters,' said Ammonia.

Downstairs, the corridors were shaking with rowdy enthusiasm; boys screaming, cursing and making for the football field. None of our teachers cared to restrain this chaos; they would cut us some slack for a few hours.

Stephen was already on the field, his crumpled shirt untucked, his bag slung over his shoulders. He toe-punched a tomato-sized pebble into an empty goal and turned to examine the tip of his shoe. Soon he picked out another pebble and, dribbling past imaginary defenders, fooled an invisible goalie and scored again, this time jumping to slap the crossbar.

This was the only kind of football I had seen Stephen play. Ditto cricket, where I had only watched him bowl pebbles at trees and swish the air with bat-length branches. I hadn't seen him play a match – either serious or friendly – though Ammonia claimed Stephen was 'born for the sole purpose of playing cricket' and Pocket Rocket raved about his performances in last year's Georgian Shield. Our teachers reminded Stephen that it was not too late to try out for the school cricket and football teams. The director of Physical Education, Mr Suryaprakash, had been on Stephen's case since June, accusing him of wasting his talent and 'letting the whole school down'. He even offered to gift Stephen a cricket kit and a pair of shoes.

Stephen, however, had no choice in the matter. His father had banned him from all sports after he failed the seventh standard finals.

'Belt whips, man. Ten, fifteen bloody belt whips,' Leo had said about the day Stephen went home with a blood-red 'Fail, repeat year' at the bottom of his report card. 'Buckle marks on Stephen's hands and legs, man. Deep cuts in his neck. His pop is a psycho, dude. Seriously. I thought he was going to kill him.'

'Whoa. That's insane. How did Stephen take it?'

'What could he do, Karthik? He just shut his trap and took it like a man. His pop is a monster, man. Seriously. Imagine someone six-foot-two, with a medicine ball for a paunch and bulging muscles. Like one of those Olympic wrestlers. Scary shit. You know ... two days after that first belting Stephen was mad enough to come and play cricket with us. His pop came running with a bat. 'Go home, loafer,' he said, 'or I'll crack your skull.'

It hadn't occurred to me until then that there was someone strong enough, and daring enough, to beat Stephen to a pulp. Still, I could safely assume that the savage belt-whips had not hurt Stephen as much as the ban, that's how obsessed he was with sports. Anyone who hung around with him could see what a natural athlete he was, whether he was sprinting from the canteen to the classroom with those long, fluid strides; or gliding down staircases without needing to look down; or dodging paper pellets with an elegance and agility that could pass for an acrobat's. He could balance a football on his head for a full minute and crack a joke while spinning a basketball on a finger. For Stephen to stand around and watch others playing, to see catches dropped and goals fluffed, was a form of torture.

'Daydreaming as usual, Karthik?' Stephen waved a hand like he was scrubbing a windowpane.

'Hey Stephen. How was the Kannada test?'

'Screw that shit, man. Let's go get your treat in the canteen.'

I had forgotten Stephen had promised me a 'royal treat' for lending him a list of important equations on the morning of the Chemistry test. He later made it known that the last-minute mugging had saved him big time and that it was thanks to me that he could hope to pass.

I blushed, saying it was no big deal.

'Of course it is a big deal, Karthik,' he had hit back. 'Who lent me the list of equations before the test? Was it Leo? Was it Paunchy? When I was in deep shit, it was *you* who was there to give me a hand. That's bloody important, bugger.'

I was happy I had played a part but, with Stephen permanently broke, didn't think he could afford any treat, let alone a royal one. Now here I was, following him to the canteen, debating whether to ask for a burger and a lolly, or a samosa and a packet of Yummies chips. Eyeing the wallet bulging out of his bum, I wondered how much money he had to spare – and whom he had cajoled.

Hands in his pockets, Stephen whistled a tune from a latest superhit movie. I looked around to make sure no teacher was nearby. The song he was whistling started with the lines 'What's behind a blouse? What's under a shawl?' – which had riled up my grandfather enough for him to switch off the television whenever the video came on. Stephen knew the suggestive lyrics by heart – and surely had the answers to the questions the song posed – but now he was intent on mastering the tune. And what a master he was turning out to be! Had someone scheduled an exam to rank our whistling skills, Stephen would have topped our class, no question. He had three different whistles to call upon: a chirp to grab attention, with lips stretched into a boomerang; a hoot for wild applause, sucking on his thumb and index finger; and a soft whistle to pipe melodies. Stephen was the only one in 7C who could whistle the entire national anthem in tune. Now that was serious talent. Leo and Metric could pull off ninety percent but they invariably butchered the last part, when the 'janaganamangala' soared. Stephen aced it each and every time.

Not everyone was impressed though. Early in August, Father Xavier had stopped Stephen in the quadrangle and slapped him for whistling the anthem. There was no warning or scolding, just a swift, decisive slap. Ammonia thought Fax's actions 'hideous'. I disagreed. After all, I would never whistle the national anthem in front of my parents and especially not in front of my grandfather, a former army man who stiffened up whenever he heard the opening notes. And I would never whistle in school. It was just too much of a risk.

Ammonia rolled his eyes.

'What is so hard to understand, man?'

'Let's take these two crimes, Karthik,' he said as if in the middle of an important inter-school debate. 'One: Fax hammering the shit out of poor old Pigeon Lady with a hockey stick. And two: Stephen whistling the national anthem during the lunch break. I think you know who really needs a tight slap.'

The St George's canteen was a shack with two square windows. A swarm of younger boys screeched through the metallic grilles: 'Atiq, pink tuck', 'Atiq, lolly', 'Atiq, burger'... Nudging his way through and tip-toeing over the throng, Stephen asked for two samosas and two Pepsis and continued whistling. So casually did he place the order – with no regard for what I wished to eat – that I was confused who was treating whom. Old Atiq was also confused, for he knew that Stephen couldn't afford even one Pepsi, leave alone two. The moment Atiq recognized the song being whistled, though, his face broke into a grin.

'What man, Steve,' Atiq said, impish. 'Won some lottery, ah?'

Stephen stopped whistling and grabbed the samosas that Atiq held out, each partly concealed in a warped paper plate.

Atiq pulled out two Pepsi bottles from the fridge. He scanned the granite counter while stroking his expertly-manicured grey beard and chanted, 'bottle opener, bottle opener'. No luck. He peeped out of the side door and asked his grandson where the heck he had hidden the opener. The plump kid, relaxing on a ledge, one hand holding a comic book and the other digging his nose, paid him no notice. Atiq threatened to thulp him with his chappals – partly for digging his nose, I imagine, though mostly for paying him no regard. The kid refused to be distracted from his mission. 'See this donkey, man,' Atiq said, turning to Stephen. 'Just eight years old and so much ass-fat.'

Tired of waiting, Stephen unlocked a bottle with his teeth. Atiq beamed, his anger vanishing in an instant. Stephen chewed out the other bottle cap. Atiq gushed, 'Hero, Steve.'

By now the boys around us had moved over to the adjacent window, and were yelling their orders at Atiq's assistant. Stephen stayed where he was. He rested his elbows on the windowsill and, massaging his cheeks with the cold bottle, asked Atiq if he had fully recovered from his heart operation. Atiq withdrew the hand that was waiting for Stephen to hand over fourteen rupees.

'So far so good, Steve,' he said, looking to the roof. 'All thanks to Him. Let's hope and pray for the best.'

'Great to hear that, Atiq. And business? Doing well?'

Atiq looked up again, to thank the one above.

'Great,' said Stephen and turned to consider Atiq's grandkid, who had by now opened the fridge and helped himself to a red ice lolly. 'Fully spoilt, man,' Atiq said, raising his voice so that the kid could hear him. 'Always saying, "Buy me this, buy me that." Never listening to what elders say. Proper headache only.'

Stephen nodded, full of sympathy. Atiq turned to attend to a boy who screamed 'pink tuck, Atiq, one pink tuck'. Stephen took the chance to mumble, 'Credit Atiq, I'll pay next time, promise,' and dragged me away from the canteen.

Thrown off, I was about to lose my grip on the Pepsi and samosa. Stephen made sure I regained my balance and goaded me to 'run faster, fucker'. Soon we were so far out that Atiq knew there was no point chasing after us. 'Abeyooo,' he screeched leaning out of the door, and went on to tell everyone that Stephen was not only a 'one-number loser', a 'loafer' and a 'good-for-nothing' but above all an 'nth-grade scoundrel' and a 'haramkhor' who was out to bankrupt him and ruin his family.

Atiq's curses may have been directed at Stephen, yet he reserved the fiercest glare for me. And who could blame him? Anyone who was friends with Stephen knew he rarely paid for anything in the canteen, that the only times he had any cash was after an arm-wrestling bet match or when Paunchy lent him some of his pocket money. Just last week, Stephen had told us what a miser his dad had turned into. 'This year, he hasn't given me one paisa also,' he had said and asked Paunchy for five bucks to buy a snack. Still, I had fooled myself into believing that Stephen had procured some money for treating me. And had gone along in sheer hope. Now I was marked. Atiq would likely not serve me anything henceforth.

Stephen and I crossed the football field where four games were taking place at the same time. A goal in one game – marked by two black backpacks – served as the halfway line in another game; a goalkeeper in one game stood an arm's length from a midfielder in another; a defender in a third game accidentally blocked a striker in the fourth. The hyper-excited footballers, their white shirts fluttering and their American khaki trousers zigging and zagging, had little trouble navigating this chaos. One boy took his solo skills to the extreme. He stepped on a football, wiggled it one way, swivelled around, tapped it from foot to foot and wiggled it again – all the while staying within a few feet of where he had started. 'Stop showing off, asshole,' cried a teammate, his arms on his hips, like a teapot.

Stephen bawled out instructions, as if he was the coach for all the teams. 'Back pass! Back pass!' 'Oh you got to score there, man!' 'Foul, foul, clear foul.' When one of the footballs flew towards us, Stephen allowed it to bounce off his chest – with one hand holding the Pepsi and another a half-eaten samosa – tapped it from his left foot to his right and blasted it high towards a goal. He then got back to screaming orders: 'All clear, all clear.' 'Worst pass ever!'

I had no idea which players Stephen was addressing, or if he was making any sense even; all I cared about was getting to the other end of the field without suffering serious injury. As far as I was concerned, the field was a massive danger zone. A goalkeeper was cursing me for blocking his view, a striker was calling my mother names for getting in his way. Afraid that boys would crash into me on the run, I looked this way and that, seeking a spot of safety.

Moreover, the threats weren't limited to the field of play. Circling the sky was a soar of Indian kites, who could in only a few seconds swoop down and snatch samosas, burgers, rolls and chips. Unlike the footballers, there was nothing clumsy about how the kites moved. Having eyed their treat of choice, they could hone in at a great speed, pluck the snack from our grasp and rise triumphantly towards a tree branch or rooftop – their entire motion so fluid, their mastery of space and time so complete, as if our Physics teacher, Brother Joseph, had taught them the equation to determine the path for the perfect snatch.

Leaving the field behind, Stephen and I sauntered across the corridors. 'Always take a peek into the ladies' staffroom,' he said. 'Never know what you'll see.' A smirk and a Pepsi sip. 'Looks like they served fish fry for lunch. Yummmm.' A crunchy samosa bite. 'Even pigs won't have such stinky toilets, man, I swear.' We passed four boys playing hand-tennis outside the Chemistry lab. Stephen told one of them to "smash it harder, fool", then proceeded along the lab's sidewall towards the volleyball court that nestled behind.

This was a volleyball court in name only. There was no net and boys usually came here to play trump cards, check out sleazy magazines, goof around, and settle scores. 'Come to the volleyball court if you have the guts and then we'll see,' Leo had threatened Paunchy during a recent argument, for which Paunchy had hit back with, 'I'm going to come there this evening itself and kick your fat ass.' Since nobody played volleyball here, nobody cared to maintain the court and two mangy dogs took their chance to snooze near a baseline. One lazily scratched its neck before returning to its dead state.

Behind the dogs, under a peepal tree, where leafy shadows sliced through a splash of sun, Paunchy and Leo were folding their hands and taking in a lecture from a tall boy. I hadn't seen this boy before but I assumed he was in the ninth or tenth standard; that's how much respect he was being accorded.

Tall Boy was slightly taller than Stephen, though skinnier, and was a prime candidate for a walloping from Mr Suryaprakash. Four reasons presented themselves: i) His shirt was tucked in on the right side and untucked on the left; ii) his hair was too long, so long that he needed to throw his head back to chase away the bangs in front of his eyes; iii) his nails were uncut and grimy; and iv) strands of hair peeked from his nostrils – an observation I wished I hadn't made, for each time I turned to him, I found it hard to ignore the strands in need of a trim.

Stephen addressed him as PK, or maybe it was Peekay. Leo claimed PK was his brother, which could have meant brother or cousin or a friend who Leo looked up to. If Leo thought you his brother, as he did Stephen, you had arrived in his eyes. PK greeted Stephen with a hand-grab–fist-bump–finger-lock–palm-twist. I thought I heard him say 'whatrabro' during this exchange but wasn't sure. Having risen at four in the morning to revise for our Kannada test, I was set for a nap.

Stephen told them about Atiq going nuts in the canteen, then turned to Paunchy and said, 'Dude, pay Atiq fourteen bucks when you go there next.'

'No way, man, no way,' Paunchy recoiled. 'I'm saving up each and every paisa of my pocket money to buy an all-terrain bike.'

Stephen asked Paunchy why he needed a third bike.

'An all-terrain bike is an all-terrain bike, man.'

'And fourteen bucks is fourteen fucking bucks,' Stephen said, teeth crunched, seemingly settling the argument.

PK spoke up. 'Stop taking so much tension, dickheads. No one needs to pay that bullshit fellow Atiq. He makes the wursht samosas and simp-simply shouts at everyone.'

Stephen told them about Atiq's grandkid picking his nose, which led PK to declare, 'That fatty bumbalatty should be royally jacked up with a stump up his buttocks.'

Paunchy was so tickled by this, he turned around and sprayed spittle. Stephen too had some choice words for Atiq's grandson but what stood out was the way he said 'bullshit fellow' and 'wursht' – just as PK had – and threw his head back extravagantly even though there were no bangs to drive away. Certain he was taking PK's trip, I burst out laughing. The four of them turned to me, appalled. And it struck me: Stephen wasn't making fun of PK, he was sucking up to him. Here was Stephen Mohanraj – the strongest of the strong, coolest of the cool, ballsiest of the ballsy – actually buttering someone up!

PK dug out a cigarette from his shirt pocket.

'Doooode,' said Leo.

'Oh, Navy Cut,' cried Paunchy.

'Best,' said Stephen. 'Navy Cut is the best.'

I looked around to check if anyone was watching us. The dogs continued to sun themselves, not in the least concerned if we were alive or dead. To our left, the Chemistry lab's windows were closed, a curtain of cobwebs suggesting they hadn't been opened in years. The lab assistant was not to be seen – though even if Suresh was around, he would have merely asked PK for a cigarette, thanked him with a toothy grin and walked off. If, on the other hand, our Chemistry teacher, Dr Banerjee, saw us, he would shove test tubes full of hydrogen sulphide up our noses. Banner was not to be seen either; he was perhaps racing through his own pack of cigarettes in the Chemistry lab, tapping the ash into a tumbler of coffee before downing that mixture in one shot.

PK dug into his pant pocket for a matchbox, a Cheetah Fight brand on whose box-face a muscular man brandished a sickle at a leaping cheetah. Leo wondered if the man had killed the cheetah or if the cheetah had killed the man – but Stephen shut him up at once with: 'Oh what a crucial question that is.'

PK shook his head, irritated. He sizzled a match and shielded the flickering flame with his cupped palms – a move so stylish, so effortless, he may well have practised it for hours. I had watched many people light matches before – priests in temples, chief guests inaugurating functions, my father during power cuts, my mother in the kitchen, my grandfather during prayer time – but almost all bumbled on the first try. PK had technique: a neat slash from top to down, and a swivel of the wrists and his palms wrapped around the flame as he raised the match to his mouth. Even on a windy balcony he would have required only a single strike.

The moment the cigarette was lit, PK was at ease. The fire and smoke provided all the comfort he sought. Perhaps it was his nonchalant flick of the matchstick towards the compound wall; he brought to mind my older cousin Anish, who usually visited us from Madras during Diwali holidays. Now that chap – a fourteen-year old who looked like a sixteen-year-old and acted like a six-year old – was, in the words of my grandfather, 'a danger-party'. He lit firecrackers straight off candles and flung them in the air just as they burst. He didn't flinch when the crackers seared his fingers and, two years earlier, he had shattered an empty flowerpot by inverting it over a hydrogen bomb. Worse, he had chased after a terrified stray dog to fasten a bomb to its tail – a ploy that made his mother erupt in a rage before storming off in a flood of tears.

None of this, however, gave Anish as much pleasure as taking me down. Like on Diwali morning last year, around the time when night was gently giving way to dawn, with the air shaking with dhooms and dhadams, when he handed me a square, green hydrogen bomb and dared me to 'light it and throw it in the air'.

'How many times should I tell you, Anish?' I said backing away. 'I am not bursting any crackers.'

'Oh god, K the great. Stop being so scared now. It's Diwali today and you *have* to burst at least one cracker in the morning.'

'Who says so?'

'Dei, you need to burst at least one cracker before sunrise on Diwali. Don't you know even this? Ask Thatha if you want.'

'Lies.'

'Okay, no need to throw it in the air. Just burst it on the ground.'

'No chance, Anish.'

'It's just one silly bomb, Karthik. You're not going to die now.'

Hassled by all the firecrackers laying waste to our neighbourhood and fed up with Anish's persistence, I decided to get it over with. That was the only way I could shut him up, especially when he was in a mood to dispense expert nonsense. Stripping an inch off the wick, I set the hydrogen bomb on the edge of our washing stone and pointed a lit incense stick towards the black tail. A puff of sulphur tickled my nostrils. My body tensed up. My hands trembled. Murmuring a prayer, I lit the tip of the wick.

Sparks flew.

I froze.

The explosion was far louder than I had expected. Quicker too. And it startled me enough to toss away the incense stick and rush back into the house, frantic. My eardrums tingled, my head throbbed. A thunderous firecracker went off on the next street. Anish stood exactly where he had been. Chortling, he lit another hydrogen bomb and threw it up. Back inside, he gobbled up two Dharwad pedas and a plateful of ribbon pakodas. In lieu of greeting relatives with a 'happy Diwali', he recounted my reaction with great exaggeration. 'Karthik ran and hid under the bed for an hour, that too because of one silly hydrogen bomb.'

To teach Anish a lesson during dinnertime, I asked my grandfather if it was compulsory to set off at least one firecracker before sunrise on Diwali morning. 'What rubbish, Karthik,' he scowled, gulping down a tumbler of cumin water. 'Diwali is purely a festival of lights. And these bombs and thousandwallas are pure humbug.'

Anish nodded, obedient, like he knew this all along. 'That's exactly what I was telling K this morning, Thatha. All these fireworks are only good for creating noise pollution.'

The cigarette went from PK to Leo to Paunchy to Stephen – who took such a deep drag the smoke must have whizzed through his throat, swirled through his stomach and kissed his intestines before retracing its path. Exhaling through his nostrils, Stephen turned to me.

'Ever smoked before, Karthik?'

My timid nod translated to 'no, and hopefully never'.

'Obviously not, man,' Leo piped up. 'Didn't you guys know: Karthik has a strict 'no shagging, no smoking' policy.'

Paunchy chuckled. Leo smirked. 'Just take a drag, dude,' a dead-serious PK said, pronouncing drag as 'drug' and dude as 'dyood'. I turned this way and that, hoping someone would haul me out of this mess, only for Stephen to hold the burning cigarette in front of my mouth, as if about to take my temperature.

'One drag won't kill you, Karthik. Be a man.'

Before I knew it I was clutching the back of my neck. My breathing was out of whack. My eyes watered. I coughed globs of spit. The piercing guilt was laced with acute shame, for having made such a fool of myself.

Leo and Paunchy emitted hyena-like noises. Stephen crouched to ask if I was okay. This was the Stephen I looked up to, the considerate Stephen, who, back in July, had gathered my belongings from the classroom's rear and helped me turn my life around. Now here he was, ridiculing me one minute and acting all pally the next. Why this Chinese drip torture in the guise of a friendship?

'That was a fucking insane drag, bugger,' he said, patting my back. 'Easy now. Take some deep breaths. Just relax, okay?'

The cigarette was back to where it belonged, with PK, who took another powerful drag and exhaled wistfully, sad that the smoke was leaving his body so soon. Irritated with the way Leo and Paunchy were cackling, PK ordered them to shutthefuckup and then said something so fast that the words may well have coughed, choked, collapsed, passed out and died. I assumed that he was asking them to stop embarrassing themselves.

PK sized me up, raising his eyebrows and tilting his head, making it clear that he had seen hundreds of boys choking on their first cigarettes. His playful eyes suggested he was itching to mock me but there was also a sense of pity in his expression, which marked me out as an incorrigible weakling. I had seen this look before: on Anish, as he watched me light the firecracker; on Paunchy, after he swung his bingo on my first day at St George's; on Aakash, the moment he had trumped me in Last-Letter Geography; on Leo, when he saw I was too ruffled to talk about masturbation; and on my father and grandfather when I fluffed a Mathematics problem. Now it was PK's turn to trample upon me.

PK continued to size me up while taking another deep drag. He didn't ask whether I was recovering. Nor did he care if my breathing had stabilized. The longer I waited for his verdict, the worse it felt. PK didn't say a word. Foremost on his priorities was to tap the dangling ash from the cigarette. That was a far weightier matter. It deserved his full attention. It was what he had to do to be a man.

8

ICU

MY GRANDFATHER HAD MANY unusual theories. In his world, three quick hiccups suggested that a loved one was missing you, your ears itched when someone remotely cursed you, and a string of sneezes foretold five unlucky moments. He ticked me off when I stepped on pillows – 'Don't you dare wake the evil spirits!' – and flew into a rage when I lay down at sunset, a time we needed to be on guard, he said, since Lord Narasimha had ambushed and disembowelled the asura Hiranyakashipu at twilight. Why he equated me to a demon he didn't explain.

By now the divine forces must have informed him of my first puff. A sudden cough or an itchy throat, enough to suspect his grandson had gone astray. The moment I reached home he would ask me about my Kannada test and, on closer scrutiny, sniff out traces of tobacco in my breath. He would drag me to the puja room to draw out a confession and tell my father to report the matter to the principal. That would result in a prompt suspension for PK, severe canings for Stephen, Leo and Paunchy, and major trouble for me – not from the principal but from my classmates, for telling on my friends. The only way out of this muddle was to avoid my grandfather when I got home.

Sneaking in through the back door, I tiptoed across the utility area and slunk into the bathroom. I took a big swig of mouthwash and, counting down from fifty, gargled like never before. Just to be totally safe, I silently brushed my teeth. Only then did I muster the strength to step into the corridor.

My grandfather wasn't in our room. Nor was he in the hall or at the dining table. I took it that he was reading the newspaper in the verandah or picking neem leaves near the gate but the main door was locked, eliminating both possibilities. My mother – her face hastily powdered and forehead dabbed with holy ash – was acting like she had to catch a train. Wiping the dining table at full speed, she toppled a plastic bottle and banged her knee against a chair. She berated the bottle for being a shameless creature but also apologized to it by touching her chest.

'Listen Karthik ...' she said in an officious tone.

Something was seriously wrong:

- Starting a sentence with 'listen' suggested she was worried.
- Her use of 'Karthik' instead of 'K' told me she was upset.
- Her awkward pause indicated she was preparing to roast me.

'Thatha has had a minor setback. Appa has taken him to the hospital. Don't worry. It's all going to be okay.'

'Setback?'

'Yes. He felt a pain in his chest. The doctor says it's a minor heart attack. Don't worry. We're all going to pray and he will be home soon. Everything is under control.'

'When did it happen?'

'Just some time ago. Elevenish. Or a little later. He said the cuckoo clock was slow. So maybe ... around eleven-thirty.'

Elevenish: that was when I had finished my Kannada test. My grandfather would have looked up at the cuckoo clock when Stephen and I had walked to the canteen. Or maybe it was a little later, when we had rushed off from the canteen.

Maybe around eleven-thirty: that was when PK would have popped out his cigarette. Or a few minutes later, when Stephen held the cigarette in front of my mouth, commanding that I be a man. Or was it even after that, when I breathed in the smoke and went to pieces? God no! What if my grandfather had felt the pain in his chest just as I took in the cigarette puff? My violent coughing fit could well have coincided with his heart attack. Worse, what if the first had set off the second!

'I'm going to St John's Hospital now,' my mother said. 'In the kitchen, I've kept rice, beans curry, onion sambar, appalam, everything. Eat soon.'

'Okay, Ma.'

'Don't worry, K. Thatha will get the best treatment. The doctors will do everything they can. Sometimes we don't know the exact reasons for these things. It could be something he ate. Or it could be his age. Don't worry. It's all going to be fine.'

'Yes, Ma.'

'I spoke to Appa just now. The doctors are taking care.'

'Okay, Ma.'

'I will come in the evening. Okay? Maybe around five or five-thirty. Don't worry. Eat your food and sleep for a bit. Watch some TV if you want. Don't go out to play until I come back.'

I waited for more instructions.

'We are all going to pray, K. Everything is going to be okay.'

Two minutes after she had shut the door, my mother was back to pick up a statuette of Lord Ganesha. 'I'm sure Thatha will want to keep this next to his hospital bed … K – why are you not eating?'

'I was going to, Ma.'

Surely she sensed my unease. 'The food will go cold soon.'

'I'll eat, Ma.'

She slammed the door.

A heavy silence descended.

I wanted to run to the puja room and apologize to Lord Ganesha for jolting my grandfather's heart. But I stopped myself, in case my mother came back to check on me.

Clothes changed out, I reeled off a long prayer in the puja room before filling my plate with rice, onion sambar, beans curry and an appalam. The silence around me meant I heard sounds I would have normally ignored. The humming fridge. The ticking cuckoo clock. A window grille's rattle when a lorry passed by. Metal monotonously hammering metal. Construction workers screaming over a whirring cement-mixer. Dogs baying, birds chirping. And a buzzing aircraft deaf to the sounds below.

It was unnerving to have to eat alone, to not have my grandfather sitting alongside, chewing each bite thirty-two times – 'one for each tooth' – and chattering about this and that. I may have just finished with my unit tests but my grandfather, the former army man, would have already drawn up a timetable for the afternoon to make sure 'every minute was a minute well spent'. He would have allocated half an hour for me to read the day's *Hindu*; an hour for an afternoon nap; ten minutes to put away a tumbler of Bournvita; an hour to organize my bookshelf and wardrobe; half an hour to help my mother in the garden; an hour for cricket with Chiku and friends; twenty minutes for my evening prayers; an hour for Tamil lessons; half an hour for dinner; an hour for reading a storybook; and half an hour for the nine o'clock news on television, when I had to jot down the main news items to improve my general knowledge. He would have made sure I was in bed no later than nine forty-five after setting the alarm for six in the morning.

Now my grandfather was likely wearing a patient gown and cursing his stars for having to lie in a hospital bed. I could picture him surveying the unshaven faces and jaundiced eyes around him, and frowning upon all the coughing and groaning. So much about the hospital would have raised his blood pressure. The overpowering whiff of phenyl in the wards, the deathly look on the faces of visitors, the air of uncertainty rife in the corridors. He would have cringed when the doctors tried to buoy him up and he wouldn't have spared any nurse who got too chirpy. If it were up to him, my grandfather would have stayed away from hospitals – or 'drab dungeons' as he called them – where people did little but frown, cough, cry, wail, ack, tsk, sigh ... and die.

Guilty for sitting around idle, I switched on the television. There was no programming on air, just the usual spectrum of grey, yellow, blue, green, pink, red and black bars. My grandfather was certain that Indians spent more time staring at this static image than watching anything worthwhile. 'Millions of people,' he once said, 'they work hard, save money, buy a costly TV. And what do they get? This silly rainbow of sorrow.'

The filler image didn't annoy me as much. To make this spectrum disappear and get a programme to air, it was vital that I too did my bit. 'If you want something really badly, K,' my mother liked to say, 'then don't depend on anyone else, just go and do what you can to get it.' So holding back blinks, my gaze fixed on the monitor, I inched closer and closer to the screen and urged the multicoloured bands to 'go away, go away, go away'. I walked backwards, with my eyes still fixed on the spectrum, assured that the more intensely I focused the higher the chances of my positive energies transferring to the TV screen. If, as my mother had claimed, there were people who bent metallic spoons and toppled bottles with nothing but intense concentration, then surely I too could find a way to get rid of these colour bands?

Halfway into the third lap, the screen dissolved into a sea of black. The 'rainbow of sorrow' gave way to the channel's signature montage – concentric fire rings spinning through space – and signalled the start of a new programme.

Breakthrough!

I punched the air with my fists, thrilled that my determined stares had helped bring a program on air. My unwavering focus had paid off. Millions of Indians who had worked hard and saved up to buy costly TVs would have got a boost. Who knows, my grandfather too may have felt a shot of relief in the hospital.

A science programme began but I was not interested anymore. Victory achieved, I was done with my game. I turned the TV off.

The cuckoo clock chirped twice before the bird disappeared into the pen, unbothered by the boredom closing in on me. My mother had been gone for just over an hour, and was unlikely to be back before five o'clock. Which left me a sea of time to wade through with no plan in sight.

Hands behind my back, I walked around the hall, studying the confusion in the wake of my grandfather's heart attack. The divan's cushions were out of place and a bolster was on the brink. My grandfather would have lain on the divan from around ten o'clock this morning – his back against a wall, his leg stretched out – and scanned the day's *Hindu*. Every half an hour, he would have hopped to the verandah and back to help the blood circulation. Eleven o'clock was when he usually yielded to a catnap, the newspaper over his face rising and falling with each raspy breath. Around eleven-thirty, he had felt a shooting pain in his chest. Cue: my mother's frantic phone calls and prayers.

The teapoy held the day's *Hindu* and the latest *Sportstar*, which I flipped to a random page.

> To survive in Grand Prix racing, you need to be afraid. Fear is an important feeling. It helps you to race longer and live longer. Fear is part of people's life. Some of them don't know how to face it, others – where I include myself – learn coexisting with it.
> – Ayrton Senna, three-time world champion

I re-read the passage, confused, rewinding to a scene from cricket camp. An oversize helmet had wobbled over my head, a pair of pads shielded my legs, an arm guard enclosed my left forearm and a hip guard jutted forthrightly, and yet, when up against 'Big Dog' Suri in the nets, I quailed. Iqbal Sir, behind the net, instructed: 'Watch the ball and move towards it.' I nodded with a firm 'yes, sir'. The moment the bowler let fly, I backed away, terrified, and flailed the bat. The ball caught the inside edge of the bat and thudded into my stomach. Sprawled on the ground and struggling for breath I looked up to see Big Dog imitate my clumsy swish. Iqbal Sir stood over me, a bat in his right hand, ready to split my skull. 'Stop being a chicken, Karthik. If you're so scared, go play marbles.'

Now a world champion racer was saying fear was a good thing, that the answer was not to flee but to make peace with it. How ingenious. If only Senna had been my cricket coach. He could have helped me channel my anxieties and grow into a batsman who gutsed it out. My plucky twenties and thirties could have backed up the big scores from the star players. That might have got me a trial for the school team, or maybe a shot at the under-fourteen state side, who knows...

Setting the magazine aside, I resumed my walk. A radio sat on a three-legged stand. On the wall above it, a painting of baby Krishna gorging on a pot full of butter and, next to Him, a portrait of my late grandmother – which was essentially a portrait of my father at sixty with a sari draped around him. Below her sat a telephone and, under the handset, a chit with two numbers for St John's Hospital.

I dialled the first number.

'Hello, St John's,' said a lady.

I stayed quiet.

'Yes. Hello?'

More silence.

'Is this an emergency? Who is speaking?'

...

'I hear some breathing. Anyone there?'

I hung up.

To my right, a shelf struggled under the weight of books, all neatly slanted at sixty degrees. In the middle rack *Sophie's World, The Story of Philosophy, Zen and the Art of Motorcycle Maintenance, Beyond Good and Evil, The Republic, Meditations*, and at the extreme: an *Oxford Dictionary*.

I pulled out the brick and grasped the spine, the sheer bulk suggesting that I was in possession of something important. The pages crackled, each laid out similar to the next, the same four columns, the same font, yet, every word different, every definition distinctive. There was 'samba': a Brazilian dance of African origin. A few inches below was 'sambar': a large deer native to southern Asia. My grandfather, of course, would have been furious there was no second meaning listed for the word 'sambar', on the lines of 'a lentil broth eaten in southern India'. Once apprised of the omission he would have vowed to write a letter to the editors that would begin, 'It's more with sorrow than with anger that I wish to bring to your attention this all-important matter ...' But my grandfather was forever threatening to write such letters. He never really followed through with these plans.

Rifling through the dictionary, my eyes glazed over complex words – ersatz, fugacious, gendarme, until I reached 'h'. I slowed down, nervously moving to h-e and h-e-a ... and stopped.

heart, n.

Pronunciation: /ha:t/

I. The simple word. * The bodily organ, its function, region, etc.

1. a. The hollow muscular or otherwise contractile organ, which, by its dilatation and contraction, keeps up the circulation of the blood in the vascular system of an animal.

1. Considered as the centre of vital functions: the seat of life; the vital part or principle; hence in some phrases = life.

...

3. a. = mind, in the widest sense, including the functions of feeling, volition, and intellect.

5. a. The seat of one's inmost thoughts and secret feelings; one's inmost being; the depths of the soul; the soul, the spirit.

That was as blunt as it could get. My grandfather was facing an all-out uprising from within. His vascular system was damaged, his feelings under assault. A thousand rebels had laid siege to his intellectual core. The enemies fired gunshots at his inmost thoughts to weaken his resolve. And they aimed to burrow through the depths of his soul, his spirit. This was no 'minor setback'. This was a matter of life and death!

I thudded the dictionary shut and shoved it back in the rack. Something had to be done. Taking my mother's advice, I chanted prayer after prayer to Lord Ganesha. Four shlokas in, I was sobbing myself to sleep.

Back from the hospital, my mother assured me, 'Everything is under control, K, and Thatha will be back in a week or so.' I didn't believe her, especially not after she forgot salt in the fried lady's finger – definitive proof that my grandfather was in big trouble.

My parents spoke in whispers the next day. When I lurked outside the kitchen and strained my ears, only stray words and phrases reached me: 'the big problem ... second opinion ... ICU ... sugar level ... whatever the doctor says ... ICU ... just stop talking and listen to me'. My father walked out in a huff and, on seeing me eavesdropping, recoiled as if he had spotted a gigantic rat. My mother stepped in. 'Forget about all this and focus on your studies, K. That is what Thatha would want. Believe me. He is going to be fine.'

That was obviously bogus. My father wouldn't have called his sister in Madras and asked her to make a 'quick trip to Bangalore' if my grandfather was indeed going to be fine. My mother wouldn't have told the head priest at the Ganesha temple about the heart attack if she wasn't preparing for the worst. Little surprise that Ganesh Chaturthi passed by without fanfare. There was no puja, no yummy kozhakattais, no milk payasam, no crisp vadais. We made a trip to the Ganesha temple in the morning. The rest of the Saturday could have been any other day over the last week: quiet, uneventful and suffused with anxiety.

My parents didn't dissect my unit test results. I had comfortably outscored Stephen, Leo and Paunchy – and done better than half of 7C – but was nowhere near the Maniacs who finished at the top. My Mathematics test had come back with two silly mistakes: the first a basic arithmetic error but the second more infuriating, where I had misread 76 for 67 in a profit-and-loss question and doggedly gone through all the steps. Such 'out-and-out sloppiness' would have burned up my grandfather and he might have changed his mind about buying me a ticket for the cricket match in Bangalore but luckily the news hadn't reached him yet, what with all the problems currently at his doorstep.

My father gave my report card a cursory review, scribbled his signature at the bottom and said: 'Can do much better.' He came along for the year's first parent-teachers' meeting the next day but didn't talk to the proud, angry and worried parents around him, parents whose mood was directly proportional to their boy's performance in the unit test. Like Aakash's mother, her white sari starched and perfumed, collecting praise from every corner; and Stephen's father twirling his handlebar moustache, ready to field a volley of complaints. My father would have normally been on the talkative end of the scale – I mean, let's face it, even if I had scored hundred per cent in every subject, he would still have discussed areas of improvement – but now, fidgeting with his watch, eager to get to the hospital, he kept his chats brief.

Our Physics teacher, Brother Joseph, was happy I was having a positive effect on the 'lazybones' in the last bench. Father Xavier said he had marked me out as someone who could assist him at the Geography Symposium in January. Luckily Fax was oblivious to the Stephanian Geography I was mastering each day – like USA: Under Skirt Activities.

Our Chemistry teacher, Dr Banerjee, skimmed my answer sheet, looked up at my father and said, 'In all honesty, these marks don't reveal anything.' My father nodded in agreement, which in turn sparked off a fire inside Banner. 'I am sure you remember the time when question papers challenged students, dear sir,' Banner said, exuberant, 'a time when we could pose questions that called for serious thinking. And now? 'Keep it simple,' they say – as if such gibberish got anyone anywhere. My dons would have lost their heads if they heard such claptrap. Keep it simple, my foot.' My father kept nodding. He didn't object even when Banner claimed that the eighty-four per cent I had scored in the Chemistry unit test would have been closer to fifty-five per cent back in the day for 'that's how simple these tests are today'. Banner was in no mood to stop talking but, seeing that my father was lost in thought, offered a handshake.

My father and I moved on to Father James, who duly pointed out the two mistakes I had made in the Mathematics test. Seeing my glum reaction, Father James hurriedly added, 'Of course, end of the day, these are really minor things, you know. Tiny mistakes like these can be easily corrected with practice.'

'You mean tiny big mistakes,' my father said with a wry smile.

'No, no,' blushed Father James. 'I wouldn't worry if I were you, Mr Subramanian. Your son is a smart cookie. I am sure he will iron out these wrinkles in a matter of weeks.'

My father acted like he was running an iron box over the table.

'Ha,' beamed Father James. 'He just needs to go on ironing!'

Our English teacher, Father Rosario, pointed out how impressed he was with my gentleman-like behavior.

'His handwriting on the other hand ...'

My father responded with a helpless smile.

'You see ... Mr Subramanian ... there are times when those who correct board exam papers have so little time they assign marks based on neatness. They think a good handwriting is a sign of a good student. It's a terrible state of affairs but what can we do?'

'What can I say,' my father deadpanned. 'With regard to his behaviour – credit goes to his mother. When it comes to handwriting, he takes after me.'

This drew out such a hearty guffaw from Father Rosario that most of the parents and students turned to us, confused.

Overall, I was pleased with how things turned out. I had fallen short of my expectations in the tests but, all said and done, my scores had improved my standing among many in 7C. Paunchy said my marks called for a 'Pepsi treat'; Leo patted me on the back with a 'well done, brother' – the first time he had referred to me thus; and Stephen – who was getting ready for an ass-whipping when he got home – said I had it in me to go places. Even Aakash's hoity-toity mother was impressed; she asked my father if I had used a special guidebook to study for English, a subject where I had come within a mark of equalling her son. 'No no, just the usual,' my father said and proceeded towards the parking lot.

The next morning, after praying for my grandfather's well-being I thanked Lord Ganesha for admitting me to St George's. I walked into school with a spring in my step, belted out the school song at the assembly and asked two questions in Physics class. During the lunch break, I joined Metric and gang in a game of tennis-ball cricket and laughed off swear words that flew around the field. After school, I watched an arm-wrestling bout and found myself giggling at some of Stephen's jokes.

To return home was to plunge into a joyless cave. The TV was not switched on and the radio had gone silent. My mother wouldn't stop mumbling prayers. My father left for work before I rose and returned from the hospital after my bedtime. There was nobody to scrutinize my uniform, nobody to mark a strip of holy ash on my forehead, nobody to remind me to pray on my way to school. When I asked my mother if I could visit the hospital, she snapped 'patience, Karthik' – her tone so charged, I knew I would never see my grandfather again.

Back in June, I hated leaving home in the mornings. Now I didn't want to leave school after the final bell. I had not told my parents about the bullying then. I wasn't going to tell my classmates about my grandfather's illness now. I had cried at bus stops then. I was tempted to cry at bus stops now. Much had changed in the last four months. Much had stayed the same.

PART TWO

9

Centum

OCTOBER WAS DEAD SET on boosting our spirits. The southwest monsoon had taken leave. The cyclonic rains from the northeast were yet to arrive. The routine mugginess eased off, and the winter chill hadn't yet set in. Our world was wrapped in a glorious blue sky, the trees popped in splendid greens and the sun held a warm glow of gold. Had we been puppies we would have frolicked on lush lawns.

We were not puppies. We were droopy big Boxers drained of sparkle, raising our eyebrows as if prepared for doom. It was obvious my father would be up in arms if I turned on the TV, and that he didn't want the radio crackle disturbing the quiet. My parents were in no mood to head out to a park or restaurant, and neither was okay with me playing with Chiku and friends for too long, especially not those tennis-ball cricket sessions that went from four in the evening till the last gasp of twilight, that climactic phase when we flailed our bats in sheer desperation, aiming for a big hit but careful not to connect too well and lose the ball in the enveloping darkness. To play cricket for that long was a 'criminal waste of time', to use my father's words. So I kept to my books for the most part, and let my parents worry about other matters.

On the morning of the second Saturday in October, my eyes on our Civics textbook, scanning the 'Directive Principles of State Policy', and my ears on Chiku and friends playing cricket outdoors, my father interrupted with: 'Get ready, Karthik.'

'Pa?'

'Have you gone deaf?'

'Where are we going, Pa?'

'You want to see Thatha or not?'

'Oh. Surely, Pa. I'll get ready now itself.'

'And set your hair right. It's all over the place.'

'Yes, Pa.'

Every hesitation and distraction melted away. In the ten minutes that my father took to get ready, I washed my face, changed into the blue-and-white checked button-down that my grandfather had gifted me last Diwali, stepped into my black corduroys, oiled my hair, combed either side of the left parting, chanted prayers to Lord Ganesha and scanned the day's *Hindu*, in case my grandfather wished to be caught up on current events. I was reading the local news headlines when my mother offered my father a tumbler of coffee.

'What I am saying is … best not to take the two-wheeler today, no? It's a Saturday morning. Not even ten o'clock yet …'

My father set the tumbler on the dining table.

'So how should we go to the hospital now?' he snarled. 'You know the brake is not working in the car, do you not? Are you saying we should take a bullock cart? Or are you arranging for some special helicopter service? Don't do this, don't do that. Not a good time. Not a good day. I'm fed up with all this.'

My mother tucked her pallu into her petticoat at the waist.

'Oh! Wake up, ask for coffee, read the newspaper, say "what's for breakfast" like some VVIP and then claim *you* are fed up! Who slaves away like a donkey day and night? Who cleans this house after you all mess it up? Who cooks three meals a day? Fed up, it seems.'

Normally, this is when my grandfather would have butted in with 'that's enough'. My parents would have reluctantly obeyed and the matter would have been put to rest … until it was reborn in a different context during another shouting match. Now, on and on they went, raising the volume, hurling accusations at each other and arguing about many things – though, in effect, given how they jumped from topic to topic, arguing about very little. My hopes were raised when my father yelled, 'I am done with this nonsense,' but his emphasis on nonsense only riled up my mother even more and sparked off a fresh round of gunfire.

The cuckoo clock tweeted the time. My mother waited for the bird to finish its ten chirps and clattered a steel tumbler on the kitchen's granite countertop. My father abandoned his coffee. He locked his helmet strap and went on to kick-start the Kinetic Honda – even though the auto-start was working fine. I mounted the backseat and wrapped my arms around his paunch, sensing his violent breaths, gauging his fury. Anything I said would set off trouble, so I pursed my lips and prayed in silence. He too said nothing until we reached the main road, when he channelled his rage to attack the state government for their latest rule that made it compulsory for all two-wheeler riders to wear helmets. 'This is nothing but a bloody money-making scheme,' he said on seeing a policeman grill two young helmet-less riders. 'They will confuse all of us by changing the rule every few months and then make money by taking heavy bribes.'

Like most issues that provoked my father, this too didn't rouse in me any emotion, especially not when I was pondering what to say to my grandfather in the short time we would get in the hospital. There was the major earthquake and Michael Jordan's shock retirement – which had occupied Ammonia and Snoop during the lunch breaks – but I wanted to tell him about the progress I was making with Tamil lessons and the collection of R. K. Narayan short stories that my mother had got for me from the library.

My excitement was dampened by the hospital's mournful air. The staff at the lobby were lifeless. A cleaning woman frowned at us. The peon manning the elevator reeked of body odour. Upstairs, the general ward was abuzz with nervous chitchat. 'When you have no interest in this job, why are you wasting everyone's time, Sister Theresa? Tell me, Sister? Why?'

An irate nurse in a white overcoat drew everyone's stares. At the ward's other end, a younger nurse mopped the floor on her knees, head lowered in shame.

'I'm fed up, I tell you, Sister,' the older nurse thundered. 'All you young sisters are the same. Instructions going into one ear and out of the other ear. I'm telling you, Theresa. I'm fed up!'

Sister Theresa got to her feet, folded her arms across her ample chest and surveyed the hospital floor. Some patients turned from one nurse to the other, as if absorbed in a terrific tennis rally.

'Stop acting like some goody two shoes now, Theresa!'

'Quiet, sisters,' demanded a grey-haired doctor, peeking from an adjacent room.

The cranky nurse stomped out of the ward. A relieved Sister Theresa checked on the nearest patient. And the buzz among patients and visitors returned to its burbling rhythm.

My grandfather was unmoved by this hot-tempered nurse versus pliant nurse contest. Leg folded and brows creased, his tongue searching for stray morsels, he pored over the day's *Hindu* as if studying for an exam. His left palm crushed Boris Yeltsin's nose. His right hand was about to turn the page.

'They are handing out newspapers here now?' my father asked.

'Elei Karthik,' my grandfather cheered, folding the newspaper and reaching for his dentures that bobbed in a glass of water. 'What a special surprise on a Saturday morning!'

'What I was asking is …' my father persisted in a low, firm tone, 'where did this newspaper come from?'

My grandfather pointed to a man napping on the next bed.

'Just borrowed it for two minutes.'

'No, no, no, no. You're not supposed to read anything, Pa. No newspapers, no magazines, no books, nothing. Doctor Baliga has clearly said: no straining your eyes for two full weeks.'

'Not straining, da, just scanning. Don't worry. I've closed it.'

My father clenched his fists and turned to a side window, no doubt hushing up all the angry words flying around in his head.

'Forget all this, Karthik,' my grandfather waved. 'Now tell me: how have you been? What all has been happening in school?'

I ran my hand over his shiny, bald pate.

'Hope you are feeling better, Thatha?'

'I'm okay, da. Don't worry about me. I will be back home soon. But you tell me. Did your test results come? How much in …'

'Did Dr Baliga come on his rounds today?'

This was my father sticking to a plan. 'Don't bring up anything that will lead Thatha to stress,' he had instructed on our short ride up the elevator. 'No politics, no test marks, no Indian cricket. Nothing that will make him take tension. Okay?'

'Yes, Pa,' I had nodded as the elevator door slid open. My father had then led me across a corridor to the general ward.

My grandfather frowned.

'Yes, Dr Baliga was here. He came about an hour ago. Umm. I didn't expect him to come so early on a Saturday morning but anyway, he said everything was looking normal.'

'That's good. I will speak to him before I leave.'

'Yes, you must. And please ask him to discharge me soon.'

'Let's not rush into anything, Pa. We will go by what he says. And that includes not reading the newspaper for two weeks!'

My grandfather took the command through one ear and let it out through the other.

'It is unbearable here, Karthik,' he said, turning to me. 'So much noise, so much irritation. Even my worst enemy shouldn't have to spend this much time in a hospital, I'm telling you. It's just a punishment.'

Sister Theresa cut in and handed my father a prescription.

'Afternoon medicines,' she sing-songed and scurried along.

My grandfather shut his eyes and shook his head.

'This is the worst part, Karthik,' he said, leaning forward. 'They stuff you with hundreds of medicines day and night and then leave it to you to deal with all the side effects. When you can't take the pain anymore, they pump you up with more medicines. Such a big scam this is, I am telling you.'

My father ummed.

'What umm gumm?'

'I'll get these medicines and be back in a minute, Pa.'

'Go. Go get them. I'll swallow them all in one shot and then put up with a stomach upset for the rest of the day.'

'Okaaaaay,' my father said and turned to me.

I knew from his raised eyebrows that he meant: 'You won't bring up anything that will lead Thatha to stress, right?'

'Yes, Pa?'

'Stay right here. I'll be back in two minutes.'

'Okay, Pa.'

Just as my father took leave, my grandfather was re-energized.

'So Karthik ... how did you do in your tests? The results must be out by now, no?'

I adjusted my spectacles.

'Karthik?'

'Are you feeling better, Thatha?'

'Oh god. Leave all that now.'

'Does it pain a lot in the chest?'

'Karthik. I am totally fine. Okay? At my age, these things will happen once in a while. Chest pain, low sugar, loss of breath … it's all no big deal. Now tell me: how did you do in your tests?'

'I did okay, Thatha. But what I was about to tell you is: you know what book Amma got me from the library?'

'What do you mean, "I did okay"? Okay vokay, it seems. What sort of a reply is that. How much did you score in each subject? Tell me properly, Karthik. How much in Mathematics?'

This was bound to happen. You could damage my grandfather's heart and banish him to an Intensive Care Unit in a state so critical that he needed to be force-fed through a maze of twisty tubes but the question that kept him awake at his station halfway to heaven was his grandson's Mathematics marks.

'Don't be shy, Karthik. Tell me.'

I had scored forty on fifty in my unit test. And that would surely stress him out, especially when he learned that the ten marks were lost to silly mistakes. He would demand an explanation for these slip-ups, and crunch his dentures when told that two of my classmates had maxed the test while ten others had crossed forty-five. He would be let down when he gathered that neither my father nor my mother was half as hassled as he. Everything about this would have worn him down.

'Oh, I wanted to tell you, Thatha. I scored fifty on fifty.'

A spontaneous, shameless lie that tumbled out even as I was considering what to say. My voice didn't quiver, there were no ums, no aahs. My eyes confidently met his. My ears didn't twitch. Not only had I blurted out a terrible lie on the spur of the moment, I had somehow pulled it off without an ounce of discomfort.

My grandfather waited, just to be sure he had heard me right, then rejoiced with a clap that stunned the ward into silence. 'Eleeei, this should have been the first thing you told me today, Karthik. Well done. Did you thank Lord Ganesha for this?'

'Yes, Thatha. I went to the temple.'

'Good,' he said, eyes closed, folding his palms at the Ganesha statuette on the side table. 'But remember: this is just the beginning. You must keep working hard and aim to get hundred on hundred in the midterm exams in December. You know the prize, right? A big trip to a cricket match in the stadium.'

'Thatha …'

'I am already feeling better, Karthik,' he said, accepting a glass of water from a panicky Sister Theresa who had assumed his thunderous handclap was a call for help. 'Sister, look here. This is my grandson, and he has got full marks in his Mathematics test in school. Fifty on fifty. What do you say to that?'

Sister Theresa blushed, then checked her watch and made off.

My grandfather ruffled my hair.

'This is just a unit test, Thatha. Nothing major.'

'What do you mean, "this is just a unit test"? This is your first centum in Mathematics, Karthik. Believe me: you will never forget it. How many others have scored full marks in the test?'

'Two boys, Thatha.'

'Hmm. What did your teacher say? Father James? Is it not?'

'He said, "Keep working hard."'

'Good. See, that is a sign of a good teacher. He knows this is just the beginning. As Robert Frost said, you still have miles to go before you sleep and miles to go …'

'Yes, Thatha.'

'What did Appa and Amma say? And how much in the other subjects? Physics?

Chemistry?'

My father, clutching a brown paper bag, strode towards us.

My grandfather beamed. 'How come you never told me about Karthik's test results? The boy has scored a centum in Mathematics and you have not said even one word about it.'

'Aah,' my father groaned, his eyeballs tracing a rapid one-twenty-degree arc from my grandfather to me and back. 'I thought it would be best if he told you himself.'

I could have thrown up then and there, laid low by my father's subtle glance. I wasn't sure what had riled him up more: that I had failed to sidestep the unit test topic, or that I had been brazen enough to lie through my teeth. As calm as he appeared on the outside, he was no doubt boiling within.

My grandfather sensed something was amiss. He turned to me, then to my father, eager to crack open the nervy silence. My first impulse was to blurt out the truth and beg for forgiveness but I could neither summon the guts to own up nor the words to piece together an apology.

My father looked up and took a deep breath.

'Just met Dr Baliga,' he said. 'If you strictly follow what he says, you could be discharged in two weeks.'

'Oh I see.'

'Yes, he was happy that things are going as per plan.'

'Ah. That's good to know.'

'Now we have to get going, Pa. I have some work at the bank. And then a few other things. So I'll come back in the evening.'

'What? Why this hurry?'

'Lots of little tasks, Pa. Plumber said he will come at twelve.'

'What is this, da? I'm seeing Karthik after so long.'

'I'll see if I can bring him next week.'

'Tcha. Okay. Karthik – take care of yourself. Keep working hard.'

'You please take care, Thatha.'

'Don't worry about me, da. I'll be back home in two weeks.'

'Okay, Thatha.'

'And don't forget to pray every day. That is most important.'

'Yes, Thatha.'

'Right. God bless.'

And with that, we made our way out.

My father didn't say anything on the way back home, nor did he bring up my lie over lunch. All afternoon, he busied himself sorting through files and paperwork. Assuming he was waiting for the right time to fire a rocket, I loitered in the bathroom when he searched through the almirah near my desk, and later sought refuge in Chiku's place. I made sure to dodge my father's eyes during our evening prayers and, when spoken to, kept my replies short and my manner respectful. Chiku saw no need for my elaborate charade. 'This is no big crime, dude,' he said when asked for advice. 'It's just a silly little lie. Stop acting like you've got ants in your pants.'

I got back after a session of table tennis, emboldened. My father was watching the news, a glass of orange juice in hand. 'Nelson Mandela and F. W. de Klerk have won the Nobel Peace Prize, Karthik. It's a big day. Note it down in your GK notebook. De Klerk is two words. D, E and then KLERK starting with a K.' For the first time in a month, he appeared free of all tension. Chiku was probably right; my father understood the reason I had lied about my marks. Now he had moved on.

On Sunday morning, just as my mother and I returned from the Ganesha temple, my father called out to me. 'There is a big sale at Paragon Books, Karthik. Let's get there as early as possible.'

I was reminded of the Paragon book sale last year, when I was laid low by viral fever. Chiku had made the trip and got hold of eight Tintins and six Asterixes at a bargain rate, including a brand new Obelix and Co that many of us dearly wanted.

'Karthik?'

Chiku would surely raid the store again and crow about his latest treasures. The only way to shut him up was to go myself.

'Have you gone deaf, Karthik?'

'Two minutes, Pa. I'll be ready.'

'Uyyo! What drama. I thought I was talking to a stone.'

'Coming, Pa,' I blushed, and bolted down the corridor.

The Kinetic Honda swerved past the gaping craters on 15th Cross Road. 'Same old story for the last ten years,' Mr Chacko had moaned last week. 'They will first dig up the road and then they will re-route traffic to re-lay the road. I heard one minister saying that we are soon going to be a superpower. Such high hopes!'

My father didn't curse the state of the tarring. Nor did he bother about the motorists overtaking on the left. Over the last month he had limited himself to crunching his teeth and sucking air when faced with reckless drivers. Sometimes, like today, he launched into shlokas invoking Lord Ganesha and Lord Vishnu and his booming chants drew stares at a traffic signal. I was embarrassed by all the attention but my father – his forehead banded with a thick strip of holy ash – wasn't ruffled. In fact, when he saw he was being judged, he raised his volume with a sunny smile.

At the bookstore, parts of which were as congested as a public bus at rush hour, my father headed to the Philosophy section. I made my way to the comics corner where I saw a tubby boy blindly stuffing comic books into a cloth bag. It was as if his father had won the state lottery and commanded that he exhaust the winnings in the next ten minutes. A special issue of *Amar Chitra Katha* jutted from a middle rack. Yes, it was likely to be too expensive; yes, it would soon be available in the local library; and yes, my father didn't like me wasting time reading 'useless comic books'. Still, I made sure to get my hands on it before Tubby could. Someone had to stop this madcap and quickly.

Two more glorious wins followed, in a game Tubby didn't even know he was part of, before I headed off to show my father the loot – three special issues for which Chiku would happily exchange three Asterix comics. My father crumpled his forehead. He scanned the jackets to add up the prices and with a gentle 'okay' put them on a pile by his side. I waited for a blunt put-down to follow – something on the lines of 'terrible idea' or 'utter waste of money'. But he said nothing more.

'Thanks a lot, Pa.'

'Hmm. Now look here, Karthik,' he said, pointing to the three white bricks that sat by his side:

Tell Me Why
More Tell Me Why
Still More Tell Me Why

'These are very good books, you know. Great for improving your general knowledge. I am thinking of buying them for you.'

'All three?'

'Of course. They cover a wide range of topics. And there's lots of interesting trivia also. I'm sure you'll like them.'

'That's great, Pa.'

'Umm. Read and see. You'll understand what I'm saying.'

There was something so enchanting about his manner – not to mention the tenderness in his voice – that I felt a wave of happiness rising within. I eagerly flipped through the *Tell Me Why* and took in the wispy fragrance from the pages. If only I could have slowed down time then and there, clinging on to these precious seconds with my father, sipping in his affection and seeking out his guidance. This was how most weekends had been before my grandfather's heart attack, when my father would take me to some bookstore or the other and introduce me to a treasure trove from across

Mathematics, Science, Literature and History. Not only had we stopped visiting bookstores in the interim, he had stopped reading out trivia and nuggets from the newspaper, stopped quizzing me on difficult words and stopped challenging me to games of chess. Finally, we were turning a corner.

Overcome with gratitude, I skimmed the *Tell Me Why* subheads: 'Why is a foot twelve inches?' 'Why do dogs bury bones?' 'Why does the moon shine?' – and read the explanations. My father was immersed in a stack of books, reading blurbs, scrutinizing prices and weighing what he wished to read against what he was willing to pay. There were almost no words exchanged between us but sitting there and riffling through the pages, in the midst of these wondrous books, was enough to bring us closer. The murmur in the aisles, the chaos at the billing counter, the squeaky ceiling fan: none of it mattered. When I asked if he was aware that zebras couldn't see the colour orange, he raised his eyebrows, impressed. And a bubble of joy popped in my head.

I got through an entire section. My father shoved a set of books into a cloth bag. 'Now come,' he said, setting out towards the billing counter but slowing down as he reached the Science and Maths aisles. I secretly hoped he was going to pick out *Science Can Be Fun*, a book that Chiku often referred to for fun experiments.

Squatting at a Mathematics rack, he drew out a stout textbook.

'Pa?'

My father held the white brick an inch from my face.

'This is a terrific Russian textbook for high-school Mathematics, Karthik,' he said in a low, frightening tone. 'You must borrow a copy from the library when you go there next.'

'Okay, Pa.'

'Take it from me: if you can solve all the problems in this book you may actually get full marks in Mathematics some day.'

'Pa …'

Shoving the brick in my hands, he made for the checkout line.

I didn't know where to look. Lurking in the aisle and glancing through the textbook, I felt minuscule. In the next aisle three middle-aged men discussed 'network theory', while I stood among the book racks, coming to terms with my uselessness. If only I could slink out through the backdoor and dissolve into the bustle of Church Street. There, nobody would know my test scores. And nobody would care.

Ringing in my head were the words *you may actually* and *some day*. Not only was my father furious about what I had done, he wasn't sure if I was going to improve. Now that was nothing short of a stinging slap.

None of this should have been a surprise, really. My father had a knack for showing me my place when I least expected. Yet, I couldn't help but feel cheated by this withering attack. It was too planned, too underhand. He had bided his time most of Saturday, lured me to the bookstore this morning and softened me with these *Tell Me Whys*, only to knock me down as we were about to leave. He knew I was thrilled with the comic books I had found. Still he chose this moment to deliver his message.

And for what? Because, under pressure, with no time to think, I had made my grandfather happy with a lie and not stressed him out with the truth. Was that such a horrible thing? Did it merit this sort of punishment?

My father didn't say anything on the ride back home, didn't chant any prayers, and it took all of a long nap and a strong coffee for his mood to look up. At dinnertime, he gushed about the "extraordinary variety" at the book sale and suggested that we should plan a visit to the annual bookfair in December. There was talk of chess, and how we had not played in a long time. Having surgically carved me up in the morning, he now got to staunching the bleed.

10

Robo

OUR MORAL SCIENCE TEACHER Father Mendoza was nicknamed Robo Pop for his stony face, his staccato voice, and the way he walked without moving his arms. He had black globules for eyes, which, some boys said, were sockets that held cameras and his bald head supposedly doubled up as a solar panel. He spoke as if programmed, pausing in the middle of his sentences. 'Have you … Finished … your homework?'

One Tuesday, in the middle of October, as all fifty-two of us flocked to the chapel for our Moral Science lecture, Mangu asked Ammonia if he had ever noticed Robo breathe. 'What are the chances that he is really not human, man!'

Ammonia slapped his forehead.

'Ever thought of thinking before talking, Mangu? Try it.'

The class began with Robo reading out 'The Mischievous Dog', an Aesop's fable about a dog that bit people's heels. The dog's master fastened a bell around his neck but, assuming this was a reward, the dog shook the bell back and forth and proudly tinkled it in the marketplace. This carried on for a few days until an older, wiser dog had had enough. 'Why are you making a fool of yourself?' he asked the mischievous dog. That bell is actually a mark of disgrace, a public notice that you must be avoided.

'Not a prize … but … a punishment,' Robo swivelled his head, panning across the breadth of the chapel. 'Not a prize …'

It was odd to see the word 'mischievous' in the title. Was that the best description for a dog that bit people's heels? Wouldn't 'ferocious' have worked better? Or 'vicious'? If only I had slipped my pocket thesaurus into my bag.

'Any questions … so far?' Robo rumbled.

I wanted to shoot my hand out and suggest an alternative title. But one had to be careful with Robo. Sometimes he was forthcoming but occasionally he could lose it, like when he told Baab to 'take your … preposterous questions and fling them … into the dustbin'. Additionally, many in 7C had come to see me as a showoff. Metric had asked me to take a break from 'kissing ass' and stop throwing out big words at the first opportunity. Musu had gone on to label me a 'walking-talking dic' – and though he meant dictionary most assumed otherwise. So any question connected to a word or a phrase was bound to bring on taunts.

The time for the question passed.

Robo listed out the lessons we could take from the fable. I picked up my fountain pen to jot down his points, when I noticed Paunchy, sitting to my right, snickering.

To Paunchy's right sat Leo, and on Leo's lap was a glossy magazine open to a nude lady stretched across a double-page. I tilted my head for a clearer view, hoping that this image was a figment of my imagination, but there she was, this sultry model, lying on her side, biting her lower lip, squinting her eyes and grasping her knees. Her legs were a pair of tangled vines, her hair the head of a coastal palm. The chapel's bleak lighting obscured her torso but her face radiated an impish glow. How pretty she would have turned out with clothes on!

Leo was sketching her in his notebook. He traced her breasts with his pencil and applied soft touches to her cleavage. Paunchy did well to suppress a torrential laugh. Leo outlined her puffy nipples. Paunchy's belly wiggled, unchecked.

'A prize and a punishment … are two sides … of the same coin,' said Robo at the head of the chapel. 'Is that … understood?'

Leo was not listening. Proud of his artwork, he pinched the nude's nipples, pawed her breasts, imitated her lip bite, narrowed his eyes and thrust his hips back and forth with soft groans. Paunchy stuffed a handkerchief in his mouth, and crouched low to hide behind the boy in front. Leo moved his hips faster, and his moans got raunchier, as if nearing a climax.

I turned away, repulsed. Not only had I let my attention drift, I now couldn't erase the nude's curvy tits from my mind. An angry image of Lord Ganesha flashed in my head. The Jesus figurine at the head of the chapel glared at me with contempt. Tendering a silent apology to both, I turned back to Robo.

'The mischievous dog … is nothing but a personification …'

I took a peek into Mangu's notebook, anxious to note down what I had missed, when a terrible explosion shattered the quiet. It was halfway between a violent cough and a loud sneeze but I knew it was more dangerous than either of those. This was Paunchy, going to pieces, his rampant cackle ripping through the chapel's still air and prompting fifty heads to turn towards us. Many of them had their mouths wide open.

Robo thudded the book shut. His dazzling robe quivered with rage as he stormed the pew like a phosphorescent ghost. So fast did he advance, so jerky his movements, it was a surprise he didn't trip and shatter his ovoid head. Leo shoved his notebook into his bag. He tried the same with the magazine but the nude, in the heat of the moment, flew from Leo's fingers and launched herself onto the aisle. The magazine landed and flopped open along the centre of the spine. The double spread lay wide open. Paunchy flinched. Leo froze. Surely for the first time in St George's history a priest beheld a naked woman at his feet in the chapel.

'Is this … your magazine?' Robo thundered. 'Tell me … Leo … is it yours? Or … whose is it?'

Leo stuttered.

Robo thumped his face.

Leo bowed.

Robo swung at his sorry head.

'Sorry, Father.'

Robo slapped him on the neck and smacked his right ear, confirming what everyone in the chapel already knew: this almighty thwacking would go on until Leo came clean.

'It's … it's Stephen's magazine, Father,' Leo mumbled.

A collective gasp sliced through the chapel. Leo – who was loyal enough to back Stephen in arm-wrestling bouts against tenth-standard boys and mental enough to call them cheats when they won – had given Stephen away.

Robo kicked the magazine aside and moved to the row behind us. There, Stephen rose from his bench and folded his arms in earnest. Robo had no words to waste on him. He swatted an invisible fly on his cheek, twisted his ears until they were pink as piglets and backhanded a blistering slap across his face.

Stephen, as ever, was unmoved: a rock numb to crashing waves.

'Get lost now,' Robo roared. 'You have polluted … the sanctum sanctorum. The Lord will make you pay … for this grave sin.'

Stephen wore his bag and made for the exit, carrying not a molecule that was defeated, nothing to suggest he was about to face severe punishment. So upright and confident was his gait.

A shell-shocked Leo followed him.

Robo grabbed Paunchy by the collar, yanked him out of his seat and dealt a searing slap. Paunchy lugged his bag and dashed out.

Robo came around to my side. I had done nothing wrong but he held on to his rage anyway, as if to pass on a message to the rest of the class. He twisted my right ear and pricked the lobe with his nails. 'You are … a donkey … your face should be covered … with manure.' Everyone laughed at this insult. None was pulled up.

'Sorry, Father.'

'Get lost, Karthik,' he barked, pointing a finger to the exit. 'This is what happens … if you mix with the wrong crowd.'

I packed up my backpack and trudged out.

I was welcomed by a sharp blue sky, fluttering jacaranda leaves, chirpy sparrows and a gentle breeze. So tender was the scene that I briefly forgot I had been humiliated.

Stephen, Leo, Paunchy and I had to stand outside the chapel until the period ended. Here was a chance for all our teachers to see that we had misbehaved. The vice-principal might come by and demand an explanation. The principal could spot us on one of his supervisory walks, and deepen our shame.

Stephen peered down the stairwell to check if anyone was coming up. Confident we were alone, he grabbed Leo by the collar, shoved him against a wall and cursed his mother. Or maybe it was his sister, I couldn't make out. He definitely cursed Paunchy's grandmother and stunned him with a bingo.

'Why the fucking fuck have *you* been thrown out, Karthik?'

I glared straight back.

Looking away, he leaned against a pillar to steady his breathing.

Leo sat on a stair and put his hands over his ears. Paunchy massaged his groin. I turned to the football field and spotted a stray, perhaps a 'mischievous dog', near the canteen. How differently things may have turned out had I asked my question about the story's title. Robo might have walked towards our bench as he responded. Leo would have closed the magazine. Paunchy wouldn't have turned into a madcap. And none of us would have been outside. Yes, I may have been tagged a 'word-whore' but that was trivial compared to what had happened.

'Why is Robo always thulping us, man?' Leo asked, breaking the lull. 'Every time he has to hammer someone.'

'He's a priest, dude,' Stephen said, turning his head away.

Leo turned to Paunchy, curious.

Paunchy turned to me.

Identifying this as a version of Passing the Parcel, I turned to Stephen.

'This is Clifford's theory, man,' Stephen went on, referring to his elder brother who had recently started pre-university. 'These priests spend so much time by themselves ... no girlfriends, no wives, no flirting ... so they are pissed off all the time. And they are just waiting for a chance to show off their strength.'

'Oh. What a theory, dude.'

'And then some genius goes and opens a porn magazine in the chapel.'

'I never thought of it this way, Stephen.'

'That's because your world starts and ends with your dick, Leo.'

Paunchy shook his head, unconvinced.

'Your pop beats you often no, Stephen? But he's not a priest ...'

'Exactly,' Leo butted in. 'My pop has always been beating someone. First it was me, then it was my brothers. I don't think your theory works in our case.'

'Fool. I never said it has to work in every case.'

'Ya, like Father James. He never hits us.'

'You're such a blind bat, Leo.'

'What do you mean, man?'

'You haven't seen Father James loitering near the ladies' staff room or what? He is there so often, ready to make small talk with any lady teacher who smiles at him.'

'I thought they have some meetings there.'

'Ya, right. Father James and about ten lady teachers, most of whom teach in the junior school. That sounds like an important meeting.'

'No way, man!'

'You're such a dickhead, Leo. Seriously. First stop sketching nude chicks. Then maybe you'll notice some of this.'

Leo shook his head, shamefaced.

'Anyway, one thing is for sure – a horny bastard like me can never become a priest.'

'You never know, Leo.'

'What?'

'Did you know that four Popes have popped while doing it?'

Leo looked to me, astonished, as if to check if this was part of the Moral Science syllabus, which I may have covered in advance.

Stephen pinched his Adam's apple: 'I swear on my mom, dude.'

Leo crossed himself.

Paunchy stuffed his mouth with the handkerchief to contain a giggle.

The bell went off.

Robo led us to the principal.

Father Menezes took in the metronomical narration without a flicker of shock. Now that I think about it, he gazed upon us like we were the latest in a long line of boys caught ogling nudes. Robo only had to mention the magazine. Quickly, the principal dished out our punishments.

Stephen and Leo were suspended for two weeks. Paunchy was dealt ten cold ruler strokes. I was given a warning, though it was my presence that irked the principal the most. 'It's time you stop playing with fire, Karthik,' he commanded, glaring at me over his rimless spectacles. 'I am not going to inform your parents in this instance but, remember, this is going to be a final warning. Stay away from such rubbish for your own good.'

By next morning, everyone had a view on the Case of the Pornstar in the Chapel.

- Kulla called Leo a horny toad who had no better work in life.
- Snoop couldn't believe Paunchy was not suspended.
- Aakash simply said 'yuck'.
- Ammonia's assessment: 'This crap was waiting to happen.'
- Baab had no idea why Robo had thrown me out.
- Bugs asked why I 'of all people' sat next to those morons.
- Pocket Rocket accused Paunchy and 'nobody else'.
- And Paunchy had the gall to fault me. 'You should have just put up your hand and asked Robo some question, man,' he snapped. 'Then none of this would have happened.'

St George's had no students' union to review our punishments. There was no committee set up to hear our appeals. But let us consider the bare facts for a moment. Stephen was suspended not for scanning the magazine but for owning it. Stephen was, in the principal's words, 'the root cause of the deadly virus'. This, we all agreed, were flimsy grounds to suspend someone. For, had Robo opened every boy's bag, he would have found posters, James Hadley Chase paperbacks and at least one X-rated video tape. Had Robo opened Musu's bag, he would have spotted a floppy disk (aka 'floppy dick') with raunchy photos. And in TP's bag he would have found an Archie comic with Betty and Veronica in low-cut bikinis on the cover, with handmade captions splashed all over them.

Neither could anyone make sense of why Leo had caved in so willingly. 'He could have just said it was his magazine, man,' said Musu. 'Why drag Stephen into this?'

'Stop over-analyzing this silly thing, dudes,' said Ammonia in his typical dismissive style. 'Don't you realize that Robo, Leo and Stephen were simply following the rules of the chapel?'

For once, the boys waited for Ammonia to continue talking.

'See ... The priest's job is to find the origin of the sin. And once caught, the sinner has to confess the truth. Leo knew that. And Robo knew Leo knew that. Anyone who aids the sinner has to accept punishment. Stephen knew that. There is nothing more to this, guys. In the chapel, people don't go by any other logic.'

'But what if ...'

'It's just how it is, Karthik. You know, when you guys were thrown out, Robo said Stephen and Leo were similar to the mischievous dog in that Aesop's fable. Like the dog, they had been proud of their beatings before but this time they were ashamed. Robo had made it clear that what was being handed out was not a prize, but a proper punishment.'

11

Athai

MY GRANDFATHER RETURNED HOME to a hero's welcome.

His bed was neatly made, the almirah dusted clean and the full-size mirror all shiny. I made a 'Welcome Back' placard and cellotaped it to a wall in our room. The head priest from the Ganesha Temple stopped by to hand over a packet of holy ash blessed at the legendary Vaitheeswaran Temple, where Lord Shiva was incarnated as the God of Healing.

Mrs Chacko baked a large, brown sugar-free cake – which she had wanted to shape in the form of a heart until her husband dissuaded her. 'This is what Peter does whenever I have an interesting idea,' she said, frustrated. 'He acts like I am a full-on mental case and tells me I have no sense of occasion – whatever that means!'

If only Mrs Chacko knew that my grandfather wasn't going to be offered any cake, with or without sugar, heart-shaped or regular, and that it would be many weeks before he was permitted to indulge. My mother joined her palms and said, 'Very sweet of you.' My father smirked. 'Not that sweet,' he would pronounce later, helping himself to a generous chunk. 'Not that sweet at all.'

Mr and Mrs Naik, who lived next to the Chackos, walked in with a bouquet of roses. A single sneeze from my grandfather was all it took; my father seized the blooms and consigned them to the utility area behind the house. 'One can never be sure what he could be sensitive to in the next few days,' the doctor had warned at the time of discharge. 'If you notice anything that causes him even a slight irritation, please act. And please call us if things don't improve.'

A surge of visitors meant that my mother had to set up camp in the kitchen, hastily preparing cups of coffee in between glassfuls of lime juice. My father turned away some guests at the main door, mostly neighbourhood uncles and aunties whom we barely recognized. Soon he tired of manufacturing excuses, and we welcomed everyone who came calling, including a bearded man in a kurta – 'an intellectual type,' according to my mother – who didn't reveal his name, only said, 'We stay opposite the Ganesha temple.' He seemed to know my grandfather well, so well that he didn't ask him about the heart attack. Rather, he chatted about the special pujas scheduled at the Ganesha temple, the holy sites he hoped to visit during his monthlong trip to Tamil Nadu and the Indian cricket team's chances in the Hero Cup.

My grandfather was enjoying his time with this bearded man – the kind of company he had craved in the hospital – until they were interrupted by a distant cousin who grilled him about his health and the time he had spent in the Intensive Care Unit. 'Enough about me now, tell me, how have you been?' my grandfather ventured, fed up of listing the stockpile of medicines he had been prescribed. 'My life as usual,' the cousin deadpanned. 'But … the ICU must have been terrible, right?'

Four days after my grandfather returned home, his only daughter arrived from Madras, her hair windblown and her waist-deep plait slackened from an eight-hour train journey. Savitri athai was appalled at hearing the doorbell tring so often. She informed visitors that my grandfather – her father – had been advised plenty of rest and that it would genuinely help if they kept their visits brief. 'We know you have the best intentions but please understand his situation also,' she said to Mr and Mrs Nagaraj – who, accustomed as they were to my excessively polite mother, hadn't accounted for so much bluntness. Savitri athai wasn't going to leave it at that. She flitted in and out of the room when the Nagarajes were in, and was at the ready to barge in and cut short their conversation if they overstayed.

Savitri athai, 'all of five-foot-nothing,' in my grandfather's description, carried enough energy to fix all of Bangalore's electricity worries in one shot. My grandfather only had to request a glass of water and she would rush to his bedside as if attending to an emergency. 'Never ever forget to take your tablets, Appa,' she said over dinner, the same evening she arrived. 'I know you get angry when I say this, and I know you think that we unnecessarily worry about your health. Of course I know you hate taking medicines. But please, for the sake of your ageing body, for the sake of all of us who are praying for you day and night, for the sake of your dear grandchildren, please don't forget your tablets.' It didn't matter in which part of the house Savitri athai was talking, everyone heard her loud and clear.

On the first Saturday in November, Savitri athai woke up sniffling. I assumed that, like most mornings, she was tearing up out of concern for my grandfather, calling to mind all the medical troubles he had put up with in the last month and a half, not to mention the countless hardships he had overcome in his seventy-seven years on earth. But no. She had caught a cold.

'This city simply hates me,' she cried, blowing into a white hand towel. 'What a terrible, terrible cold it has given me now!'

My uncle Raju athimber offered her a curt 'umm' – an 'umm' that had a perfect measure of his wife's state of mind – and drifted out of the room.

Savitri athai glanced around. My grandfather was engrossed in his astrological almanac. Worried that she was about to turn to me for comfort, I whirled around to face the window and zoomed in on two aunties on their morning walk – their ears stuffed with cotton and jazzy sneakers peeking from under their saris.

'What is the use of the sun coming out if it's going to be so cold,' Savitri athai continued, volume raised, irritated that nobody was listening. 'I can't even keep my eyes open in this weather. Tcha. Just feel like sleeping all the time.'

The city of Bangalore was in for a lashing when Savitri athai visited in the cold and damp months. She couldn't bear to dry her clothes indoors, what with all the musty smells getting her blood to boil. She asked Lord Rama what grave sins she had committed in her previous births to deserve such chilly feet every morning, and made it known that only mad people – presumably my mother and I – wore socks and sweaters indoors.

A few years ago I was unsettled by Savitri athai's complaints, and felt partly responsible for her plight. I considered apologizing on Bangalore's behalf, and asked my mother, on one of our temple trips, if the time had come to relocate to Madras. 'Don't be silly, K,' my mother had shot back, her response so sharp it instantly lifted my spirits. 'People will say all sorts of things. You can't keep worrying about any of that.'

Gradually it dawned on me that Savitri athai's protests were no cause for alarm, that residents of Madras and Bangalore took delight in tearing each other's eyes out. Madras, as my mother loved to say, was the fiery mother-in-law in this relationship. Bangalore was the new-age daughter-in-law, happy to laze about in the chill. Where

Savitri athai railed against Bangalore's drizzles and biting chill, Mrs Chacko, a loyal Bangalorean, brought up Madras's godawful heat and humidity. Savitri athai looked down on barefaced laziness – 'In which self-respecting city do grocery stores open at 11 a.m.?' she once screeched. Mrs Chacko saw no need for rabid enthusiasm – 'Only nutcases will open their restaurants at 5 o'clock in the morning.'

Now Savitri athai rubbed her nose with Vicks Vaporub. 'I don't know why I ever leave Madras,' she said, massaging her temples. 'It's time to book our return tickets now itself.'

'No tickets vickets, Saavi,' my grandfather said, shaking his head, still peering into his astrological almanac. 'November is a good month, and I see … the third Sunday is an auspicious day.'

'Oh god,' said Savitri athai and turned away, irritated. 'This is exactly what we need at the moment: a family function!'

My grandfather crinkled his eyebrows and puckered his lips. Gauging his displeasure, Savitri athai made sure to stay quiet.

'Good day for what, Thatha?' I asked, softening the edge.

'The time has come, Karthik,' he said, clearing his throat. 'It's time to take your first big step towards adulthood.'

'Thatha?'

'I am planning your sacred thread ceremony.'

'Oh.'

'The gods have already sent me their first call, Karthik. Somehow I survived that.

It won't be too long before They call me again. So we must get this done as soon as possible.'

'But Thatha ...'

'No ifs and buts. Okay? I know what I'm doing. Just leave it.'

Savitri athai was ready to inhale steam from a pot. My grandfather got back to his almanac. Unsettled by the news, I slinked out of the room only to run into Raju athimber in the hall.

'Karthik?'

'Yes, athimber?'

'Athai will get better soon. Don't take tension. It's just a cold.'

'Yes, athimber.'

'No need to be so worried, da. Believe me. It's all normal.'

'Not worried, athimber.'

'Then why do you look so upset? Something is wrong for sure.'

'Thatha was saying …'

'Uh?'

'… he is planning my thread ceremony.'

'Ah. Yes. I heard there was a plan. Isn't that exciting?'

'Umm.'

'It's a simple function, Karthik. Remember, you attended Anish's thread ceremony two years ago? Same thing only.'

'Yes, athimber.'

'So you know why we wear the sacred thread, right?'

'I know little-little.'

Raju athimber shut the Tamil magazine in front of him, removed his spectacles and pinched the skin between his brows. 'You see,' he said, puffing out his chest and surveying the ceiling as if pondering a national crisis, 'a sacred thread ceremony celebrates a Brahmin boy's coming of age … right … one of the ways to mark a boy's passage from childhood to adulthood … okay? But who knows … some say that in the olden times it was the moment when a boy was independent of his mother … you know … the time when he was no more hand-fed by her … right … so basically what is a sacred thread ceremony … it is to signify a time when a boy is capable of leading his life entirely on his own … what you call adolescence, puberty, etcetera …

'But you see … these days the whole thing is a bit of a humbug … you know … most boys don't understand the meaning of the prayers being chanted during the ceremony. Sometimes even the boy's parents don't understand the significance of the shlokas. Actually leave the parents, even some priests don't know the exact meaning of these chants. They blindly recite what they have memorized, collect their fee and go home …

'So in the end, what is a thread ceremony … it is another occasion where you will eat good food and get many gifts … okay? … a chance for, what you call, a family reunion … right … and once you wear the thread – one secret: the thread is great for scratching your back but don't tell Thatha I told you that – so anyway … where was I … yes, once you wear the thread you will have to say a set of daily prayers and chant the gayatri mantra a hundred and eight times each morning … nothing complex … just basic things … understood?'

Raju athimber rarely spoke when his wife was around. But when it was just me and him, the words could tumble forth in a great haste, as if relieved to be set free. Bolting from one thought to the next, he chattered till he ran out of breath. Then a swift inhale … before the onrush continued.

With the date for the thread ceremony finalized, it was time the planning got going. What style of invitation card should be designed? My grandfather said 'traditional'. My mother preferred 'semi-formal'. My father went with, 'whatever you people decide'. The bigger issue was the venue. 'Home,' said my mother. 'Maybe temple?' my father suggested. 'No, no. No temple,' my grandfather said. 'Kamala is right in this case. Let's have it at home only. Maybe we can set up a shamiana in the vacant plot next door.'

Savitri athai shook her head. 'I always dreamed that Karthik's thread ceremony will be a grand celebration in a big hall,' she said.

'No need,' went my mother, unmerciful, crushing Savitri athai's hopes like they were ants clambering up a sugar bowl.

An hour later, with the matter still unresolved, my mother stood up from her chair. 'We can't even decide on where to hold this function … so let's just cancel it,' she said, ready to walk off.

My grandfather tsked to rein her back. Raising his hands, he announced that the function would be at home, perhaps with a shamiana installed in the next plot – with only close family and friends in attendance. 'Sixty guests max,' he declared, clapping his hands to settle the issue, 'and let's print a formal invite for relatives and a semi-formal one for the rest. Kamala, go ahead and get that organized.' My mother returned to her seat, revitalized. 'Alright,' my father said, upbeat.

The wheels were set in motion. My parents called on friends and relatives to inform them about the thread ceremony and handed out invitation cards. The head priest from the Ganesha Temple came home to chat with my grandfather about specific plans for the ceremony. Raju athimber left for Madras to get back to work but not before he booked his return ticket for two weeks later. And Savitri athai, having recovered from her cold in three days, was back to her talkative, hyperactive best.

Just as I assumed everything was going as per plan, my grandfather informed me that:

- I had to shave my head for the big day
- I had to wear earrings for one part of the ceremony, and
- I had to invite some of my classmates for the function

'Earrings!'

My grandfather let out a hearty chuckle.

'Thatha? Honestly?'

'I knew that would shock you, Karthik,' he said, full of mischief. 'Such a frightened boy you are, I tell you. It's so funny to see how easily you panic. Anyway, don't worry. I have told the priest that there is no need for any earrings gearrings and all that. You see, that was an old custom. We can't keep holding on to all that in 1993. We need to keep up with the times.'

'You also no, Thatha. So no need to shave my head, right?'

'What's the problem with shaving your head, Karthik? It is very much part of our culture.'

'Please, Thatha. My classmates will make fun of me.'

'Who are these foolish classmates of yours? You can't keep worrying about what people will say. Your hair will grow back in a month, I'm telling you. Don't make a big fuss about this.'

'Thatha ...'

'Stop acting silly now, Karthik. Look at my head. See how bald I am. Look at your father's head. He will be bald in five years. And you will mostly go the same way. There is already a tiny strip on top of your forehead. As if some cows have had a good time grazing there.'

'Cows?'

'That's a joke, da. A joke! What has happened to you today?'

'Thatha ...'

'What Thatha vatha? Tell me?'

'Do I *have* to call my classmates for the function?'

'Oh yes, no question about it. Don't call the whole class, please. That would be madness. We don't plan to spend so much money on food also. Just call a few boys you are close to.'

'I am close to no one, Thatha.'

'Uh ho. Just call two or three boys who you sit next to in class.'

'But Thatha, if I invite only a few, the rest will feel bad.'

'Silly fellow. Quietly hand out the invitation cards to two or three boys who sit next to you and tell them to be here at eleven o'clock on Sunday morning. What is the big problem in that?'

'They can't keep secrets, Thatha. Everyone will find out.'

'Aiyyo Rama, stop it, Karthik! It's going to be really odd if none of your classmates come for the function. These are happy occasions and it's important to celebrate them with people of your age. Please don't argue with me now. Just do as I say.'

'They are Christians, Thatha. They won't know anything about the ceremony.'

'Uh ho. What is there in that? I too had Christian friends in the army and some came for my wedding. Robert, Jesunathan, Manikkam, Francis … Such great fellows. You know, Robert could run hundred metres in eleven seconds – a proper cheetah. And Manik, oh Manik was so funny. Always up to some comedy or the other. Anyway, forget all that. What I am saying is …'

'But Thatha …'

'Who are these Christian friends of yours?'

'Uh …'

'You forgot their names?'

'Thatha … the problem is that …'

'Names, Karthik. I want your friends' names!'

'Stephen and Leo.'

'Ah. Stephen what? Leo what?'

'Stephen Mohanraj.'

'And?'

'Leo Pinto.'

'Great. We will be honoured to have Mr Mohanraj and Mr Pinto at the ceremony. Please invite them tomorrow.'

That is when it hit me: in a span of a few minutes I had climbed a ladder, fastened a noose around my neck and kicked the ladder down. I had painted myself into a spot where I had to invite Stephen and Leo home. And what could be more embarrassing than that? My classmates would see me topless and bald – and tell everyone in school about it. My grandfather would meet the loafers I hung around with in school – and likely have another heart attack. Head spinning with panic, I burst out.

'Uh ho,' my grandfather said, alarmed that the issue had taken such a serious turn.

'You can't keep crying for these little-little things, Karthik. Trust me, you are going to look really smart with a shaven head. And everything is going to turn out fine.'

A dismal sky hung over St George's the next morning. The classroom was murky – the lone tube light having blown its choke weeks ago. It was hard to read the date at the top right-hand corner of the blackboard. An overreaching drowsiness took hold of us. Minutes before the first period Stephen let out a giant yawn and, head resting on the desk, caved in. Seeing how content he was with eyes closed, I found myself yawning.

Our English teacher, Father Rosario, walked in.

'Good morning, Father,' we chorused, standing up as one.

'I see you are all here for a funeral,' he barked. 'Who died?

'Morning, boys,' said Father Rosario, emphasizing the boys.

'Good morning, Father,' we hit back, this time at top volume.

'That's more like it. Now open your textbooks to chapter seven. We have plenty to cover today. The story we are going to read now: "God Sees the Truth but Waits". By Leo Tolstoy.'

Stephen, who had only recently returned from suspension, searched his bag for his textbook.

'I am hundred per cent sure I put it in here, man.'

'Then where could it have suddenly disappeared?'

'How do I know, Karthik? Someone has obviously stolen it.'

'Oh please ...'

'Shut up. As if you've never forgotten anything ...'

I nudged my open textbook towards him.

'Now which of you wants to read the first part of the story?'

Pocket Rocket raised a hand, and set off a murmur. Everyone knew he was about to murder the prose with his singsong style.

'Quiet, everybody. Yes, you, please go ahead and read.'

'In the town
of Vladimir
lived a young merchant
named Ivan Dmitrich Aksionov.
He had two shops
and a house of his own.'

'Useless fellow. This is a short story, not a nursery rhyme.'

The class erupted in laughter.

'So-orry, Fa-ather.'

'And please read faster, boy. We don't have all day for this.'

Pocket Rocket continued, trying his best to be arrhythmic.

Stephen was distracted after a few paragraphs. Tearing a blank page from his notebook he went about rolling paper pellets, which would catapult off rubber bands during the breaks. Stephen didn't see I had dragged my textbook away from him. Neither did he check on Father Rosario. He had escaped into another universe where nobody else was allowed entry.

Pocket Rocket picked up his reading speed.

Father Rosario's gaze was riveted to the textbook.

I waited for Stephen to finish rolling up his next paper pellet and snuck an invitation card under his notebook.

'What the …'

'I'll explain later.'

'You're getting married?'

'Oh please, man!'

'Upan …?'

'Upanayanam. Sacred thread ceremony.'

'Whoa.'

'Read it later,' I hissed. 'And don't tell anyone. It's a secret.'

'Secret?'

'Ya. Just for you, Leo and Paunchy.'

'Why?'

'Because I can't invite the whole class, man.'

'So don't invite the whole class. Why is it a secret?'

'Oh god. Just don't tell anyone.'

'Dude, stop acting like you're inviting us to watch a porn film.'

'Shhhh.'

'Why the fuck is this a secret, Karthik?'

'I'll explain later.'

'So weird you are.'

'It's totally fine if you can't come also …'

'Is it this Sunday?'

'Ya, at eleven o'clock.'

'Will there be hot chicks?'

'Just stop it, man.'

'Relax Karthik. That was a silly joke. Stop looking at me as if I killed someone.'

'Shhhh.'

'This Sunday huh? Is there a dress code for this function?'

'No. But please, no shorts.'

'What?'

'Just don't wear shorts for the function, man.'

'Why the fuck would I wear shorts for a function?'

'I don't know. Just telling you.'

He suppressed a cackle.

'Please, Stephen. All my relatives will be there.'

'Okay, dude. I will make sure that Leo, Paunchy and I wear shorts for the function on Sunday. Okay? Happy?'

'Please, man.'

'It's the in thing nowadays, bugger. Everyone wears shorts to religious ceremonies. Haven't you heard?'

'Please, man. Just for one day.'

'That's what I'm also saying. We'll just wear it for one day.'

'Fuck you, Stephen.'

Mouth agape, he surveyed the rows in front and to his left, hoping that he wasn't the only one who had heard me. The rest of the boys were dutifully following Tolstoy. Stephen wobbled his head in a daze, to confirm he was indeed awake.

'Sorry Stephen … I didn't …'

'Unbelievable, dude. Just unbelievable.'

'Please, man. No shorts for the function.'

'What an angry young man you have turned into!'

'Please! I really …'

'Yes, Stephen, Karthik, what are you two jabbering on about? Seems like some really important matter is being discussed.'

Stephen stood up and looked straight ahead at Father Rosario, even as he slid the invitation card under his notebook.

'Sorry, Father.'

'Yes, Stephen. You want to run a few laps around the field?'

'No, Father, sorry, Father.'

'Please enlighten us about the story?'

Stephen scrunched up the paper pellets in his left fist.

'Yes, Stephen? Have you gone deaf? Answer …'

'Aksionov,' I whispered, my lips stationary and slightly apart.

'Father …' went Stephen. 'The story is about … Axeiyano.'

'You mean Aks-iyo-nov,' said Father Rosario, temper rising. 'And what happens to Aksionov in the story? Go on …'

'Jail,' I rustled, again without betraying facial movement.

'Father …' Stephen drawled, buying some time. 'Father … in the story … Aksionov goes to jail … yes, Father, jail.'

Father Rosario checked his watch. There was still half the story to read, a discussion to be overseen and homework to be assigned. 'Now sit down and pay attention,' he said, saving his anger for a time when Stephen misbehaved in the future. 'And that goes for you too, Karthik. Don't think you're off the hook.'

I stood up.

'Sorry, Father.'

'Sit down now. You two have wasted enough of my time.'

I returned to my seat.

Father Rosario asked Ammonia to read the next part of the story.

Stephen unrolled a paper pellet. He scribbled on it with his Reynolds ballpoint and tossed the crumpled ball towards me.

'Thanks. And fck u too.'

His handwriting, as always, was delightful.

My head was tonsured the day before my thread ceremony, and Raju athimber captured a photograph of my grandfather and me – both baldheads, our foreheads striped with holy ash, our noses chiselled from a template – gawking at the camera. Raju athimber didn't warn us before he clicked; his idea of a good photograph was a candid photograph.

The day whizzed by in a gust of gossip.

'Remember the tension at Mala's wedding?'

'Ooh, who can forget. What a big fuss the boy's side kicked up about the filter coffee. I thought they might even call it off.'

'I told Balu: don't put up with their snide comments. If it means we have to find another boy for Mala so be it. She was hot cake those days. No shortage of suitors.'

I gathered that no event was complete without drama, confusion and an outpouring of emotion. Someone had to have yelled at someone else. Someone had to have sulked. A few years ago, at Savitri athai's housewarming ceremony in Madras, most of the talk had been about KRS, the oldest grump on that side of the family.

Savitri athai had been in her element the day before the function. Her sweaty green blouse clung to her skin and she took every chance to bark at Anish.

'Just as lazy as your father,' she snapped at one point while sweeping the kitchen in their new three-bedroom apartment – so new that I stopped myself from touching the pristine white walls assuming that the paint hadn't dried.

'Now switch off that stupid cricket match and go clean your room, Anish! Otherwise I'll tell KRS what all drama you are up to. You want me to do that?'

Unnerved by the threat, Anish began organizing his room at once.

The next morning, KRS lounged on an easy chair in one corner of the spacious hall and flipped through Tamil magazines for close to an hour, when Savitri athai realized that he was livid.

'Was the breakfast okay?' she asked, apologetic.

'The point is not whether the food was okay or not, Savitri,' KRS bellowed. 'The point is: nobody had the decency to ask me about it. Here I am, eighty-five years old, sitting quietly in a corner. Do any of you even care if I am alive or dead?'

After the puja, KRS refused lunch – which many deemed as the ultimate insult. He later told Raju athimber that he had 'suffered enough for one day' and that nobody should bother inviting him for family functions henceforth. At the time it was seen as a fit of rage, and a classic stunt. That turned out to be KRS' last function after all. Two months later he suffered a terrible stroke, collapsed on the granite floor in his bathroom and died.

Since then Savitri athai had taken it upon herself to monitor the elders in order to avoid 'another KRS-type situation'. One quick scan of the hall and she would pick out a granduncle or grandaunt who was left unattended. Soon she was by their side, holding a tray of coffee tumblers and another with a scattering of milk biscuits and other eats. 'Maybe some mixture to crunch? Oh please, at least a banana?'

With no assigned responsibility at the thread ceremony, I stood around with my face plastered in a smile. Occasionally, a relative put forth an obligatory question: 'What's your favourite subject, Karthik?' 'What do you want to become when you grow up?' Many stroked my shaven head as if petting a kitten. Others took it upon themselves to grant me advice. 'Study hard now and the rest of your life will be a cakewalk, Karthik,' said a grandaunt, pinching my cheeks with more passion than was necessary. 'And remember: the next four years are the most important years of your life. They will decide everything.' I asked Savitri athai if that was indeed true. 'Nonsense,' she said with a wave of her hand and continued on, serving coffee and water and persuading elders towards milk biscuits.

The ceremony began at nine o'clock on Sunday. Four priests on a freelance outing from the Ganesha temple sat around a holy fire and belted out prayer after prayer at high volume. The smoke plumed into the multi-coloured shamiana. My grandfather sat behind me, and whenever he got the chance, slipped in the significance of a shloka. Presently he left my side, seeing that the head priest was rousing the flames with mango leaves, coconut shavings and ladles of ghee.

Stephen, Leo and Paunchy walked in as the ceremony was winding down. Attired in collared shirts and ironed pants, the three of them stood at the gate, hesitant. Savitri athai welcomed them in and requested that they sit on the cloth mat. The three did as told but remained uncertain, as if hoping for Savitri athai to return with more instructions.

'Hey,' I said walking up after my work was done. 'Nice to see you guys made it.'

Stephen didn't recognize me in my bald, topless, veshti-clad avatar. Leo and Paunchy, meanwhile, hadn't even noticed my arrival, nervously looking this way and that.

'Whoa,' said Stephen, when the light bulb finally came on. 'You're looking like a really tough dude, Karthik.'

'What?'

'Seriously, man. A bald head suits you well. Now all you need is to build up some muscles. And everyone will be scared of you.'

I blushed, expecting a massive put-down to follow.

'It's all about how you look, Karthik. Seriously. There's one guy near my house, Pablo. He's a scaredy cat of the highest order but he works out in the gym and walks around with this serious look. Nobody messes with Pablo.'

'Really?'

'Ya, everyone is a little careful with him.'

'But they will soon find out he's a chicken, right?'

'Still. They will still think twice before acting smart with him.'

'You sure?'

'Ya, dude. You have to look tough and act tough. Then everyone automatically thinks, 'Umm, maybe this guy is really tough.'

'I don't know, man.'

'You should try it, Karthik.'

'No, no. I won't be able to fool people like that.'

'Seriously, dude. Lift some weights, eat eggs. Build up muscle. Puff your chest out. Don't smile. Then see how everyone acts.'

This was weird. Stephen didn't curse every few sentences, didn't interrupt me mid-sentence and wasn't searching for ways to put me down. Since we didn't have to talk in whispers, like we did during class, I could challenge his wild theories and ask him to elaborate on each one. Stranger still, Leo and Paunchy seemed genuinely interested in our conversation. They didn't make fun of my new look and, hands folded, listened in silence. Were it left to me, this steady and back and forth with Stephen would have gone on and on and on.

'Kaaaaarthik,' my grandfather screamed from a distance. I turned. A couple of young men were prostrated in front of him.

Stephen stopped talking, looking to me for direction.

'Such tall, strong friends you have, Karthik,' my grandfather cheered as I guided them to the verandah across the crowded hall.

'So who is Mr Mohanraj among the three? Ah, the tallest. Super. And you must be… Mr Pinto. Wonderful. And you? Paunchy? A nickname. Ah, I see why. Very funny. Or should I say, "very tummy"? Haha.'

My grandfather was thrilled to get away from men and women his age, exhausted with all the chatter around heart attacks, diabetes, hypertension and cholesterol. He usually steered clear of anyone over sixty-five – especially those who had a 'terribly negative attitude' and those who were prone to mishear, and misunderstand, whatever he said. When it came to my friends, though, he didn't have to worry about being mistaken. He could bring forth all his enthusiasm without the fear of judgement.

'Why are you fellows so late? You missed the entire ceremony.'

They had waited for a bus for more than half an hour, Stephen explained, before they took an auto-rickshaw and lost their way.

'These auto fellows are rascals, I tell you. They just take a much longer route to make extra money. There is nothing more to this.'

Stephen clarified that it wasn't the driver's fault.

'No way, no way. You boys are not to be blamed at all. After all, this is the first time you are coming here. These auto-wallahs are not to be trusted, I tell you. They will try every trick to make some extra money. Don't believe anything they say.'

'Yes, uncle,' said Stephen, giving up on the argument – which actually put off my grandfather as he greatly enjoyed ripping into auto drivers. Now he had to find another topic that irked him as much and hope my friends would take interest.

'So anyway, forget all this for now. Tell me: how did you boys do in your unit tests? Let's see … how much did you score in …'

'They did alright, Thatha. Now they're hungry and …'

'What hungry vungry? Of course, we will make sure they eat to their heart's content. But first tell me, how did you do in Mathematics? Karthik has scored fifty on fifty. Isn't that great?'

This was the heights. My lie had turned into a cockroach that just wouldn't die. I had been exposed in front of my father; now I was about to be embarrassed in front of my classmates. One careless lie was causing so much damage. God forbid if my grandfather found out that Stephen, Leo and Paunchy had all failed in the Mathematics test. The mere thought of his grandson hanging out with these numbskulls would shatter his fragile heart. All the happiness that the ceremony had brought on would evaporate. Now I had no other choice but to lie again.

'Thatha,' I began, but was interrupted by Stephen.

'We did better than last time, uncle,' he said, full of cheer. 'We all hope to score as well as Karthik someday.' Leo and Paunchy nodded along.

Sensational! This was essentially the truth. Not the whole truth but a white lie that would pass quietly, like a pedestrian jaywalking across a deserted street. I would have never been allowed to get away with such a vague response but Stephen was a guest, and was not going to be subjected to fierce cross-examination.

'Good, good. I take it that all of you are preparing for the midterm exams that are coming up?'

'Yes, uncle,' said Stephen. 'We are all getting ready for it.'

'Excellent. Now before the food gets cold you must get started. And please eat without shame. Treat this like your own home.'

12

Mid-terms

THE THREAD CEREMONY WAS done but like the food that was left over, my grandfather's excitement too wasn't going to be wasted. He shifted his energies to my mid-term exams, due in a week, drawing up a time table and taping it to the wall.

'I have to wake up at four o'clock every morning?'

'What is the problem with that, Karthik?'

'Why not six, as usual, Thatha?'

'No six vix and all, please. That will be way too late. Believe me, the earlier you rise the sharper your mind will be.'

That may have been the case for my grandfather and father, uncles and aunts – and that whole side of our family tree hell-bent on being awake in the wee hours – but my mind was a drawer of muddled thoughts. At four o'clock, chapters I had revised multiple times began to look unfamiliar. Then came the panic. For if I couldn't recall passages, definitions and tables at will, what chance did I stand in my exams? Snoop had spelled out the recipe: 'The more you can remember, the higher your marks.'

By the time exam week came around, I was certain I would blank out. The English Language and Literature papers provided some relief but the tension snowballed on Monday evening, when I mapped out all the ways I could bungle History and Civics.

Triiiiinnnnnngggggg: the alarm went off at four in the morning.

A knot of toads kicked up a racket outside. I brushed my teeth and washed my face.

Random names and dates flashed in my head.

Four-thirty came along too fast. The tenets of the Bhakti movement slipped from my grasp. My yawns stretched out, my eyes begged for more sleep. Reading the text aloud, my sleepy voice emitting garbled notes. I jotted down the main subheads from the first chapter but a page in, I was ready to doze off.

The clock struck five. Monuments from the Sultanate period became hard to recognize. Sher Shah Suri's achievements? Only vague recollections. Year of the Battle of Haldighati? 1577? 1576? Babur, Humayun, Akbar, Jahangir: blur blur blur.

The paperboy came around. The milkman couldn't be far behind. My grandfather, sleeping on the divan in the hall, would be up soon. There was a good chance he would conduct an impromptu quiz and make me feel inadequate. Now did I understand why he had asked me not to waste so much time over the last month? Now did I regret watching the Hero Cup semi-final and final?

The pinkish-orange sky prepared for sunrise. The birds cheep-cheeped to welcome the new day.

In the hall, M. S. Subbulakshmi poured out prayers from our tape recorder. My father and grandfather bickered over Prime Minister P. V. Narasimha Rao's latest foreign policy initiative.

'PVN knows what he is doing. Leave it.'

'Even Karthik knows more about foreign policy than PVN.'

My mind switched off. My eyes glazed over the text.

This was it, the high point of my studiousness, when all those hours of slogging came to naught. There was no coaxing the memory anymore. Just pack away the textbook and pray.

'Karthik!'

'Yes, Thatha.'

'Revision over? All prepared?'

'Yes, Thatha.'

'Good. See what I told you? Early to bed and early to rise makes a man healthy, wealthy and wise. It always works. Always.'

●

The History & Civics exam didn't end too badly. I put together a comprehensive essay on the architectural legacy of the Slave Dynasty and surprised myself with all I remembered about the Tughlaqs. Passages that I feared had abandoned me were tucked away in deep pockets of my brain, and I was relieved that they emerged when called up.

This boosted my confidence somewhat. Early next morning, when panic threatened, I knew I could count on my memory to bail me out. I refused to close my textbook and leave it to the gods. The passages were all seeping into my head, I assured myself, and they would be by my side when the need arose.

Thankfully nobody at home was too fussed about the Geography and Chemistry exams on Wednesday. My grandfather had just two instructions before I left: 1) 'Don't forget to double-check your papers', and 2) 'Don't forget to pray.'

The instant I returned home, my mother advised that I eat an early dinner and get enough sleep before the Mathematics exam the next day. My father reminded me to stay 'totally calm', as if he was confident that the stress was going to get to me. My grandfather couldn't stop talking over dinner, telling me which chapters I should focus on now and which ones I could set aside for next morning. Given a chance, he could have ridden a bus to St George's the next day, sat at my spot in the 7C classroom, and blown the twenty questions to smithereens.

Each time someone passed on advice, I worried I was underprepared. Yes, I knew all the formulae by heart. I had written out the proofs for the geometric theorems multiple times. I had solved every problem in every exercise set. Yet, at 4:30 in the morning, chewing on the butt-end of a pencil while wrestling with a straightforward problem on Simple Interest, I could only visualize how everything was about to go wrong.

This was madness. Maybe boys who ran the hundred-metre dash on Sports Day understood my dread. Or those who lined up for penalty shootouts in big finals. Or those who sang or played the violin in front of thousands in giant auditoriums. Who knows. I hadn't experienced any of that. On my big day, there was no audience, no cheers, no drumroll. Just me and a problem set, battling quietly. Still, I too was up against mighty expectations. I too had to guard against the tiniest of slips. I too needed to stay calm under pressure. For Mathematics was way too important for everyone at home. With each test, each exam, the aspiration was clear: it was hundred per cent or nothing, perfection or bust.

Naturally, everyone was up by 5:30, voices lined with a marked pep. My grandfather's puja ran ten minutes longer than usual. My father set the newspaper aside and took up the task of polishing my shoes, and my mother went about preparing 'hot-hot dosas with coconut chutney'. This might have been *my* Mathematics mid-term but our family honour seemed to be at stake.

Of course, we had run this to script before, back in April, on the morning of my entrance exam to St George's. Then too the anticipation had simmered at dawn, and with ten minutes left for us to leave, my father decided it was quiz time.

'Just two or three questions, Karthik. Ready?'

'Yes, Pa.'

'Ganeshaaa,' he said, flipping open my textbook.

'Is zero a natural number or a whole number?'

'Whole number, Pa.'

'Umm. Ganeshaaa … is one prime or composite?'

'Neither prime nor composite, Pa.'

'Ganeshaaa … is three by four rational or irrational?'

'Irrational, Pa.'

He eyed me from above the rim of his spectacles.

'Listen carefully, Karthik,' he said, lowering the pitch when he uttered my name. 'Is three by four rational or irrational?'

I knew I had messed up.

'Karthik?'

'Irrational.'

He crinkled his brows and rechecked the textbook. Only when he looked up did he realize that I was being deliberate.

And out came a ferocious forehand, thudding into my left cheek.

'Rational or irrational?'

'Irrational,' I wailed, partly sobbing, partly choking.

Another slap. Same cheek but harder.

'Rational or irrational?'

'Irrational, irrational, irrational,' I screamed and collapsed to the floor, trembling with fright, but also proud for not backing down. I had stuck with the wrong answer, and suffered a hammering, but that was so much better than being a weakling who surrendered. My father recognized my moral victory. Rather than thump me further – and harden my resolve – he threw the textbook down and walked off.

My mother rushed to wipe off my tears with the end of her sari.

'Why are you torturing the poor boy, of all days today?'

My grandfather asked if we had all gone fully mad, which was his way of asking us to shut up.

The clock struck eight. My mother handed me a glass of water. 'Forget everything and just pray on your way to school, K,' she said, setting my hair in place with her fingers. 'The gods will take care of you during the exam. Don't worry, okay?'

My father hadn't quizzed me since. He left it to my grandfather to grill me on exam mornings.

'Karthik, all prepared for the Mathematics mid-term?'

My grandfather applied a thick strip of holy ash on my forehead.

'Yes, Thatha.'

'You remember all the formulae, right?'

'Yes, Thatha.'

'Hmm. Let's see now. What is the area of a trapezium?'

'Half the sum of parallel sides into perpendicular distance.'

'Right. And the volume of a cone?'

'One by three pie r squared h.'

'Right. Surface area of a sphere?'

'Thatha, the spheres chapter is not in the portions.'

'So? I'm asking: what is the surface area of a sphere?'

'Thatha, for the portions ...'

'Portions vortions. Leave all that. The surface area of a sphere is four pie r squared. How difficult is it for you to remember that?'

'Thatha ...'

'Just repeat the formula now.'

'Four pie r squared.'

'Good. Keep the formula in mind. No harm at all. The human brain is a marvel, Karthik. It never runs out of space.'

'But Thatha ...'

'What but vut? Yes, I know it is not in the portions. But nothing stops them from asking questions that are outside the portions. Okay? How hard is it to remember one extra formula?'

There was no time for rebuttals. I still had to pray, eat breakfast, sharpen my pencils, and pack my bag.

'Okay, Thatha. I'll remember the formula.'

'Have you prayed?'

'Now I'm going to.'

'Dosas getting cold, K ,' my mother wailed.

'Pack your bag, Karthik. Your pencil box is on the dining table.'

'Coming, Ma. Coming, Pa.'

'And oh,' my grandfather clapped. 'Don't forget to double-check your answer paper, okay? Triple-check if possible.'

'Okay, Thatha. I have to leave soon.'

'Oh god! How many times should I tell you, Karthik! Never say you are leaving. Always say you will go and return.'

'Sorry, Thatha. I will go to school and safely return.'

Stephen stood outside the classroom, hands on a concrete ledge, eyes gazing into the horizon. His hair was a weaver bird's nest, his face grubby and jaded.

'Hey Stephen …'

I might as well have been addressing a corpse.

'Stephen!'

'Hey baldie. Why are you screaming now!'

'You didn't hear me, dude.'

'What crap.'

'I swear.'

'Okay. What do you want now?'

'Nothing, man. I was just asking if you are all prepared.'

'Obviously not.'

'Then?'

'What then?'

'You'll somehow manage?'

'How much you want to bet this is my last Maths exam?'

'What are you saying, man?'

'The princi has already made it clear, Karthik. If I fail the Maths mid-term, I won't be able to write the finals.'

'Don't think of all that now. You won't fail.'

'Let's bet. Any amount.'

'Stephen, this is the time for positive thoughts and ...'

'What's the bet, Karthik?'

'I mean ...'

'Just give me a bloody number, man!'

'Five bucks.'

'Done. You better pay me when I fail this exam.'

'Listen to me, Stephen. Out of twenty questions you need to just get eight right. Learn these formulae now and you'll be fine.'

He grabbed the sheet that I held out and took a peek.

'What is this?'

'Important formulae!'

'Why the fuck can't you write neatly, Karthik?'

'Just fuck off, Stephen. I am the one trying to help you here.'

Stephen looked away, chastised, and scanned the formula set. My 'fuck off' had centred his attention. These were the only times I allowed myself the liberty to throw out a swear word. It was empowering to surprise Stephen now and then. The curses served a purpose; he took me seriously when I spoke his language.

'I don't know any of these formulae, Karthik.'

'Just mug them all up.'

'I won't know when to use them.'

'You'll figure it out, Stephen. Don't worry.'

'No way, man.'

'I'm going in now. See you soon.'

'Okay. Bye.'

The 7C classroom was a milk pot on a stove, bubbling with expectation. The Maniacs stood around and chitchatted. Other boys sat at their desks and skimmed their textbooks.

'Do we have spheres?' Musu howled, using up more effort than it would have taken to memorize the formulae.

'No man,' Baab howled back.

'Only till cones.'

Once in my seat, I sharpened my pencils, filled my fountain pen with blue ink, spilled a few drops on the desk and wiped the blobs with a rag. In my geometry box, the metal compass gleamed. The protractor, set squares and ruler were all shipshape. The brand-new eraser hoped for a light workout but the divider, ignored for many months, yearned for action. Until recently I hadn't seen the need for a divider – after all, a compass with a pointy pencil did the same job – but Snoop had told me about a boy nicknamed Sphinx who, after failing in the tenth standard, secluded himself near the back gate, slashed his wrist and neck and took off heavenwards. His mugshot had made the newspapers the next day, along with an obituary that mentioned the weapon of destruction: a brand-new steel divider.

Father James walked in with a sheaf of question papers in one hand and a rolled-up newspaper in another. Spurred on by the whiff of cyclostyle in the air, the boys shut their books and brought out their stationery. Father James wasn't about to wait for everyone to settle down. He asked us to 'say the Lord's prayer, quick', then got Pocket Rocket and Kulla to help him hand out the question papers and foolscap answer sheets. 'No hanky-panky, boys,' he said sternly. 'If caught cheating, you are in deep trouble.'

Leo turned around and, in a low volume, inquired if it was 'hanky-panky or hanty-panty'. Eight of us heard him. Nobody, not even Paunchy, cared to offer a response.

One glance through the question paper loosened the knots in my stomach. Of the ten questions in the first section, four looked familiar. There was a distance-speed-time problem for which I already knew the answer. The other six questions seemed fairly straightforward. It was time to doodle a Ganesha curl at the top of the first answer sheet and set off on my merry way.

To my left sat a frosty Stephen, in no hurry to get going. He took his time to fill in his name, class and section at the top of each sheet before turning to his unsharpened pencils. I moved to the second question (Ratio and Proportion). Stephen opened out his palm and measured the angle between each pair of fingers with his protractor. I attacked the third question (Simple Interest). Stephen plunged a set square into a groove in our desk and watched it hold a pose like a yogi on one leg. I dealt with the fourth question (Profit and Loss). Stephen engraved his name with a compass on his white eraser.

In just under forty-five minutes I was done with the first section, and thanked Lord Ganesha for whispering solutions into my ear. If only I could have snapped a photograph of my answer sheets right then. There was not a single line crossed out. My handwriting shone through. And the right margin, reserved for rough work, was entirely blank. Here was an answer paper that would have made my mother so proud she would have hovered her palms over the pages – as if it were a holy flame – and devoutly raised her fingertips to her eyes. 'A-one, Karthik,' my grandfather would have said with calm, reassuring nods.

Stephen looked up, as if hoping for the roof to cave in.

Father James sat on the chair at the head of the room. His face was hidden behind a spread newspaper and his feet tapped the floor in step. Assured that he was engrossed, I turned to my left.

'Why are not you writing anything, man?'

Stephen flinched, as if in the middle of a psychic exercise.

'Start solving!'

'This is a nuclear bomb of a paper, Karthik.'

'It's not so hard. Start with question three.'

'Question three? I have no idea about Simple Interest.'

'Uffo. Question four then.'

'Uh. I don't know the formula for that.'

'It was in the formula set I gave you!'

'I couldn't read any shit in there, man.'

'Get lost, Stephen.'

'I told you, Karthik, I'm going to fail.'

'If you fail here, you can't write the finals.'

'Oh. Like I don't know that.'

'So what are you going to do?'

'Do you have any bright ideas for me, Karthik? No. So shut up.'

'Stop shouting, man.'

'Mind your own business.'

Father James turned a page of his newspaper. I admired my flawless answer sheet. Stephen rested his chin on his palms and looked up, as if seeking a divine command for his next move.

Question 11: Prove the Base-Angle Theorem (5 marks)

I drew an isosceles triangle and marked the vertices A, B, C. I dropped a line from vertex A to the triangle's base when I saw Stephen packing up his geometry box, getting ready to leave.

'What's wrong with you, Stephen?'

'Why simply waste my time here? I'm anyway going to fail.'

There was something pathetic about those helpless eyes.

And something within me snapped.

Setting my pencil down, I snatched Stephen's answer sheets with one hand and his ballpoint pen with the other.

'What the …'

'Shhhh,' I said, nudging my answer papers towards him.

'What the hell are you doing, Karthik?'

'Quiet.'

'Bloody hell.'

'Shhh! Act as if you are writing something in my answer paper.'

'Karthik! You're going to fill in my answer sheets for me!'

'Keep quiet, man.'

'Holy mother!'

Positive that Father James was immersed in his newspaper, I started to solve the first section in Stephen's foolscap sheets, mimicking his handwriting with a ballpoint, like I had done for so many of his assignments over the last four months.

I knew he crossed his sevens and triangulated his fours; that he curved his z's and tagged his o's with a wick; that his cursive writing slanted at twenty degrees; and that I always finished up his proofs with 'Hence Proved' and mine with a 'QED'.

Rarely had I felt so invincible. Formulae spilled onto the page. Fractions simplified themselves with minimal effort. X's and y's and z's did as told. I didn't need to think before any step, so determined was the flow, And I ignored voices that claimed I had lost my head. All that mattered was to knock off the first section and ensure that Stephen passed. That was the least I could do as a friend. Memories from my early days at St George's flashed by. I was little more than a human dartboard in the first six weeks, until Stephen had gathered my backpack's contents at the classroom's rear. How differently my life would have turned out without his intervention: my optimism shattered, my confidence crushed, my every step fraught with danger. Stephen had thrown me a lifeline when I most needed it. Wasn't it my duty to pay him back?

Before I knew it, I was done with the first section, the ten solutions neatly packed into six foolscap answer sheets.

'Fuckin' rockstar,' Stephen said, recharged with a familiar zest.

'Shhh.'

'Is this a dream, Karthik? What has happened to you, man?'

I exchanged my answer papers for his.

Stephen looked to the ceiling and crossed himself. He shook his head, unsure of how to convey his thanks. As if to confirm all this was really happening, he flipped through his answer papers, then turned to me, shock intact. Clearly I had pulled off a stunt that he didn't think possible. What were the odds of that?

Father James folded the newspaper, stood up and puffed out his chest. 'Last twenty minutes, boys,' he said, peering at his watch. 'Write your name, class and section at the top of each sheet. Your papers won't be corrected otherwise.'

Last twenty minutes!

Shaken, I checked my watch. The hour hand inched towards the eleven. The minute hand marched from the eight to the nine, untroubled by gravity's relentless pull. My heart went thud thud thud, refusing to believe that – despite my confidence at an all-time high – this exam was going to end in a shambles. I now had ten problems to solve in twenty minutes. Unwinnable. Useless. Hopeless. By choosing to rescue Stephen I had blown my own exam, blown all those hours of preparation, blown a chance to make my family proud. My grandfather's hopes? Now up in smoke. My parents' dreams for me? Crashing, burning. In one split second of utter lunacy, I had let them all down.

Three and a half problems – that's all I got through before an electric bell confirmed my defeat. The shock and desperation wrecked my handwriting. Most of the steps were left haywire.

'Hey Karthik. Hope you checked all my answers, man?'

'Get lost, Stephen.'

'What a stud you turned out to be, dude!'

'I messed up my own paper, man. All because I helped you.'

'What are you saying, Karthik? You were killing it.'

'I answered just thirteen questions!'

'Bugger, that's more than enough. Way more than enough.'

'Shut up.'

'Stop being greedy now, Karthik. You know what the Bible says? Greed is the root of all evil.'

'Just shut up, man.'

'Here, take your five bucks. No way am I going to flunk now.'

My head felt heavy, my brain numb. I tossed my geometry box into my bag and walked out of the classroom. Snoop asked if I too had been confused by question eighteen. Leo patted me on the back: 'All-time great move, Karthik.' I relieved myself in the toilets and tried to process what I had just done. What the heck?

On the bus journey back home, with a breeze fanning my face, the fog began to clear. What had Lord Ganesha made of all this? Was he going to forgive me at all? I closed my eyes and laid out a scenario: if nobody got off at the next stop, I would take it that Lord Ganesha was willing to pardon me. If, however, someone did get off, it was confirmation that He was fully pissed off.

The bus honked as it sped past a lorry. Our driver called the other driver a drunkard. He was promptly told to shut his ass. As the stop approached, I tripped over words, my prayers frantic. A lady in a blue salwar kameez walked to the front exit. She seemed to want to get off, until she checked something with the conductor and took a hesitant peek outside. Maybe – under orders from Lord Ganesha – she had changed her mind? Eventually she did step off but once out on the street, she was unsure of which direction to proceed in. What was I to make of her indecision? Perhaps Lord Ganesha too hadn't made up His mind about my situation. I could set the same test at the next stop, of course. But I was too scared to fail once again.

My stop arrived with the bus almost emptied out. An overcast sky painted the outlook a drab grey and a row of flower vendors outside the Ganesha Temple packed up, anticipating rain. A man stood near a corner store and smoked a cigarette, hiding it behind his back after each puff. To his left, a barefooted boy whipped a bicycle tire with a branch as he charged down a slope at high speed. Given a choice I would have tracked this boy, his face flush with joy, lashing the tire and weaving past hawkers, pedestrians and cyclists. But the skies were going to open up and my mother would already be worried. So I made my way home.

I walked up the street that led to our house. A group of middle-aged men hung around on our driveway, some in black jackets, some in sober full-sleeve sweaters. The tallest among them leaned against a wall, arms folded, his expression stiff. I opened the gate and passed him by, denying him any eye contact.

In the middle of the hall, the head priest from the Ganesha temple was readying an altar of bricks for a holy fire. My father was on the phone, talking at an unusually low volume, which was weird by itself but weirder still given the loud chatter that engulfed him. My mother stood at the apex of an isosceles triangle and popped out words like pain, heart and attack even as the neighbourhood's aunties – who formed the triangle's slants – did their best to comfort her. 'One can say he lived a full life,' said Mrs Chacko. 'Good he wasn't bed-ridden,' said Mrs Naik. 'Amazing how happy he was till the end,' said Mrs Nagaraj.

My grandfather lay on the red-oxide floor, unfazed by all the jabbering. His lips were parted and his face free of worry, just like it was during his afternoon naps. His forehead was banded with three thick strips of holy ash and his cheeks and neck were clean shaven. Everything was normal … until nothing was normal. Not the puddle of urine on his white veshti. Not the rice grains strewn around his head. Not the incense stick that swirled vapour up to the heavens, charting his final voyage.

Barely four hours had passed since we had spoken, when he had asked me to learn the formula for the surface area of a sphere. Had he known he was so close to the end? Was there a warning sign? His final words to me? 'Never say you are leaving, always say you will go and return.' And now he had left for good.

Three months ago, when he was fighting for his life in the hospital, I had wondered how we would react if he were to die. My parents: I had expected them to restrain their emotions. Me? I would be crouched over him, I thought, clasping his palms, kissing his hands, petting his cheeks and sobbing on his chest. The sorrow, I assumed, would rush out like jets from a sprinkler.

Now he was gone but I wasn't crying, wasn't shivering and wasn't choking. Standing over his motionless body, I could only think of what a terrible grandson I had turned into: forging assignments, puffing on a cigarette, lying about my marks, getting thrown out of the chapel, being warned by the principal, swearing at Stephen and, worst of all, cheating in an exam – a Mathematics exam no less – and ruining my chances. Surely my grandfather had sensed all that was happening. Each of these transgressions must have worn him down. The cheating, though – the mere recklessness of it – had surely shattered his heart.

Wherever I looked, the guilt intensified. The priest shot me piercing glances as he rattled off shlokas during the final rites. My father repeated these chants, as if accepting that this was absolutely my fault. In front of them raged a holy fire, into which I was probably going to be flung soon. Mr Chacko eyed me suspiciously. Mrs Chacko whispered something in my mother's ear. 'Don't worry about tomorrow's exam, K,' my mother said, clasping my shoulders. 'We'll ask for a retake.'

'Okay, Ma.'

'The Maths exam went off fine, no?'

I bowed, ashamed.

'Leave it, K. Don't break your head.'

'Yes, Ma,' I said, my head still bowed.

A gentle rain accompanied my stretchered grandfather to a large black van. I asked my mother why they weren't taking my grandfather's crutches along. 'Don't worry K,' she said, hugging me tight. 'Where he is going, he won't need them.'

My father and grandfather left for the crematorium in the van. His friends followed them on their two-wheelers. The neighbourhood aunties scattered to their homes, with Mrs Nagaraj shielding her head from the rain with a fold of her sari. My mother, perhaps seeking some quiet, headed to the bathroom. Which left me to deal with the silence in the hall. The cuckoo clock's pendulum had come to a halt, the time stuck at 10:30.

Clueless how to occupy myself, I wandered from the verandah to the hall to the kitchen and back to the hall. I skimmed through the day's newspaper and read jokes in *Reader's Digest*. I took a long walk around the house before moving to our room and stopped, startled. Not because of the unmade bed or unfolded sheets – a mess that would have raised my grandfather's blood pressure. Not because his studded gold ring lay on the side table. No. In front of me was the Remington Monarch typewriter: his loyal aide for over forty years, freed of its case and left to itself on a short stool. I had no idea who had brought it out, and why nobody had packed it into its case, but after all these years, even with my grandfather gone, this squat machine was as eager as ever, ready to be called up for service.

Winding a rag around an index finger, I expelled every last speck of dust from the frame, knobs and the keypad. I fitted an A4-size copier paper and reminded myself to strike each letter slowly, decisively, making sure each finger struck the right key.

The quick brown fox jumps over the lazy dog.

Pack my box with five dozen liquor jugs.

How quickly daft jumping zebras vex.

...

'A pangram is a typist's best friend, Karthik,' my grandfather had said before my first typing lesson. 'They were by my side when I learnt to type. Practise them. They won't let you down.'

Jinxed wizards pluck ivy from the big quilt.
A large fawn jumped quickly over white zinc boxes.
...

By now I was in flow, the fingers in harmony, thumping the keys with gusto. If only my grandfather had been around to see how effortlessly I was acing this exercise: looking straight at the paper 'like an expert' and not glancing at the keys 'like an amateur'. He would have been thrilled that my elbows were at a higher level than my palms – 'that's vital to get the blood circulation going' – and that my pinkie fingers had no trouble pressing down the a and the p. Finally, happy with both my speed and accuracy, he would have, briefly, let slip a contented smile.

Ten pangrams done, I stopped.

The tears gushed out, unrestrained.

13

New Year

THE DEATH THREW ME off in all sorts of ways, starting with the prickly question of how to carry myself in front of relatives and friends. My mother was uplifted when I seemed unfazed – as per Chiku, she had told Mrs Chacko that I was coping 'so well, so well' – still, it was an act I was keeping up. I was afraid to come across as childish and attention-seeking so I wore a thoughtful expression that gave way, only when I was spoken to, into a smile. This created a fine impression on many who visited, including one of my father's friends who called me 'the most mature twelve-year-old' he had seen.

Inside me, the guilt gnawed away, reminding me of what a terrible grandson I had become. I often slept through alarms and jolted myself out of bed, just as my grandfather would not have wanted. I wolfed down meals – in so much 'hurry burry,' as he often said – instead of chewing each bite to pulp. One morning, flipping through the *Hindu*, I accidentally ripped a corner of the sports page. My father turned around. I waited for him to grit his teeth and flay me for being a clumsy oaf, to demand that I cellotaped the page this instant. At least someone would be monitoring my screw-ups now that my grandfather was gone. All I got was a muted 'umm' before he returned to tallying accounts. Perhaps he didn't want to growl at me at such a delicate time. Still, such a tepid response made me feel much worse.

My father, mother, uncles and aunts – and other relatives who came calling – were nowhere as unsettled as I was. They had all witnessed multiple deaths and had worked out how to keep their emotions in check. Or so I assumed until, on the tenth day after my grandfather's passing, I was jolted awake by Savitri athai's manic howls. Having bottled up her grief for days she was now pouring it all out in one monster blast, weeping into her palms, into a hand towel, between sips of coffee and weeping as she shaved a coconut. Even when she was about to lose her voice she couldn't bring herself under control.

My uncle, Raju athimber, ignored his wife's blubbering. He sat at the dining table and scanned the newspaper, and didn't look up even when his wife shut herself up in my room. Only when he looked around for a pen to solve the crossword did he note the awkwardness on our faces. Raju athimber set the newspaper aside. He spoke of the soul's journey once it departed the human body, and assured me that my grandfather was going to be reunited with our ancestors 'very soon'.

One of my father's cousins – Bamu they called him – interrupted with a vehement 'no, no, no, no'. Bamu said my grandfather's soul first had to reap the benefits of his good deeds and then atone for his sins – 'I know, it is unlikely there are any sins in this case but why assume anything, right?' Then he could be reborn.

Raju athimber's response – mouth open, eyes narrowed, brows furrowed, translated to: 'Who the hell do you think you are?'

My father took a lengthy sip of coffee. The antennae that tracked his brother-in-law's temper was now extended, alert. My father may have agreed with Bamu but there was no way he was going to refute Raju athimber. So he pulled up Bamu for his 'baseless theories' and asked him to 'do proper research'.

Raju athimber shot Bamu a lethal stare, while, a corridor away, Savitri athai continued to bawl her guts out.

Eventually, when the house was emptied of relatives, I came to realize that my father hadn't moved on from his loss. He had retained his poise through the final rites, lightened the mood with his typical puns and highlighted how lucky we were that my grandfather hadn't been bedridden for a lengthy stretch – but I now saw that these were merely a series of deep, meditative breaths before he eventually plunged into a pool of sadness. He sat on the rocking chair and stared at the ceiling, disregarding the folded newspaper in his hands. He did hundreds of laps across the verandah, with his head down and hands locked behind his back. Often, he sat quietly in the puja room late into the night. Some evenings he skipped dinner. When he ate, he hiccupped and coughed while gobbling down his food. My mother turned to him, as if trying to recall how many teaspoons of chilli powder she had sprinkled over the fried potato curry. 'No, no, nothing,' he said, coughing dangerously close to his plate. 'Don't worry. It's all fine. All fine.'

My parents were never going to head out of the house in this mood. Not even for the Residents' Association get-together on New Year's Eve, where a dinner buffet was usually followed by musical chairs, dumb charades, housie and antakshari. Nor were they likely to watch the three-hour 'mega entertainment' broadcast leading up to midnight. True to form, we went through the evening imprisoned in our respective zones and maintained a studied silence over dinner. Having watched a few minutes of the nine o'clock news, we retired for the night. When 1994 came along, no doubt ushered in by the Association president – a bald, retired bank manager – calling on the youngest kid to slice a cake, the three of us were fast asleep.

School was to resume two days later, offering a welcome escape from the ghostly quiet. My mother wasn't fussed about my new term until Monday morning, when she asked if I had covered my notebooks in brown paper. My father reminded me to polish my shoes, his tone so lukewarm that he was obviously not going to inspect my brushwork. I too was blank and sluggish. Though neatly washed and ironed, my uniform had faded with use. There was no stirring whiff from the fabric, no twinkling sleeves. My belt buckle had lost its sparkle, and there was no one to supervise as I polished it.

Getting back to school provided a respite from the overarching glumness. But it also required me to confront my mid-term exam results. How differently things would have turned out had I aced the papers. My grandfather would have been so proud of me, smiling from above, clapping with delight, raving to everyone about how hard I had worked and how earnestly I had prayed. Despite everything that had happened in the last few months, he would have known that academics remained my top priority.

The reality stared me in the face by Monday evening: seventy-two in Biology, seventy-six in History & Civics, eighty in Chemistry and sixty-two in Mathematics – depths I hadn't plumbed in my worst practice tests. As predicted, the first part of my Mathematics paper was peppered with ticks and praise that went 'excellent' and 'neat'. The last two pages, though, were overrun with Father James' scribbles in red:

'Incomplete proof'
'Too hasty'
'??'
'Forgot to answer the rest?'

In the evening my mother asked if my results were out. Without a moment's hesitation, I claimed they were not. Only when I returned home on Wednesday and found the radio on and my parents chatty, did I steel myself to reveal my marks, subject by subject, alternating between the reasonably good scores and the forgettable ones. Mathematics, of course, I reserved for last.

My father switched the radio off.

'Sixty-two?'

'Yes, Pa.'

'As in sixty plus two?'

'Yes, Pa.'

'This is out of hundred, right?'

'Yes, Pa.'

'Oh …'

My father turned to my mother.

My mother turned away.

'Really tough paper or what, Karthik?'

'Pa …'

'Forget about it, K,' my mother cut in, signalling to my father to stop with these searching questions. 'Just treat this like a bad dream and focus on preparing for the final exams. Okay?'

'Okay, Ma.'

'And how well you did in Kannada, K! We were wondering whether to ask for a retake or not. But see, we did just what Thatha would have wanted. And that worked out perfectly.'

'Yes, Ma.'

My father downed a tumbler of water, taking his time to absorb the shock and disappointment. My mother sat down next to a mountain of clothes that needed folding. Seeing that my father was setting himself up to blurt out something mean – perhaps one of his cutting put-downs that would ring in my head for years to come – she nudged a ball of bedsheets and towels in his direction. As far as she was concerned, this discussion was over.

Even in his 'wildest dreams' Stephen hadn't seen himself failing in only one subject in the mid-terms. Better still, his path to the finals was clear after a 'fifty freaking per cent' in Mathematics, which was five marks more than he had scored in any Mathematics test ever. 'I go tell my pop my marks and the first thing he says is: "What bloody cheating you did, man, loafer?"'

Paunchy vomited a laugh.

Leo poked me in the ribs.

'I'm going to sit next to you for the final exams, Karthik. I'll have nothing to worry about then.'

We were outside the canteen, sucking on Chocobars. Stephen had borrowed money from Paunchy to treat me to lunch. I hadn't wanted to be a part of this 'celebration'. But Stephen wasn't about to accept my nos.

'Just shut your trap and come, dude,' he said, tugging my arm. 'I would have been kicked out of school by now if not for your help. Stop acting all pricey now, Karthik.'

'Leave it, man.'

'What do you mean leave it? I need to pay you back big time. Seriously.'

'Come on, Karthik,' Leo said. 'What are friends for?'

'Karthik, Karthik,' Paunchy chanted. 'Come on, Karthik.'

Stephen wouldn't stop gushing even after buying me a burger and the Chocobar. 'Whenever you want something in the canteen, just tell me. I'll buy it for you.'

'No way, man,' Paunchy cut in, flustered by Stephen's offer.

'Nobody is talking to you, Paunchy.'

'Oh really? I have nothing to do with this then?'

'Maybe I'll ask for a little cash now and then. Okay? Is that such a big deal? Stop acting like a drama queen, Paunchy. Everyone knows you have enough cash to treat the whole school.'

'No chance, Stephen. I'm saving up to buy a video-game set.'

'Oh really? Then why the fuck did you buy an apple cake just now? And that Pepsi yesterday? Saving up so well, Paunchy?'

'Whatever, man. I just can't keep treating everyone all the time.'

'Okay fine. So let's say …' said Stephen, softening his tone. 'Let's say Karthik is willing to help you with your extra assignments. You'll spare some cash to treat him then at least?'

Here was Stephen acting like he was solving a problem when he was muddling it up. We all knew the principal had summoned Paunchy to his office, laid into him for failing in four subjects in the mid-terms and informed him that he would have to do one extra assignment per subject each week. Only if Paunchy showed 'significant improvement' would he be eligible to sit for the finals. Now Stephen was telling him to pass on those extra assignments to me – with no regard for my take on the matter.

'Nothing doing, man,' I said, shaking my head.

'Listen, Karthik,' went Paunchy in a pleading tone I knew well. 'Just two assignments a week. And I promise, I'll buy you anything from the canteen.'

Stephen clapped his hands and threw Paunchy a high five. He tried the same with me, as if to put a seal on the agreement.

'Two assignments a week? Gone mad or what?'

'Oh come on, Karthik,' said Stephen. 'You can finish two assignments before Paunchy runs one round around the field.'

'No chance, man. It's going to be …'

'Fucking hell.'

Stephen gobbled a chunk of the Chocobar and flung the stick.

'You buggers sort it out. I need to piss badly.'

Now that he had sensed an opening, Paunchy began to act like a salesman for water purifiers. Each time I refused, he was more fired up, and he went so far as to accuse me of ruining our 'great friendship' over 'a few silly assignments'. When that didn't work, he tried flattery. Then fake sulking. And finally outright begging.

Exhausted, I agreed to doing two assignments a week for him. I would answer five out of ten questions in each, I said. But, as the finals approached, I would stop helping altogether.

'Perfect, Karthik,' he went, offering me a bite of his apple cake. 'You should have said this first itself. I am totally cool with it.'

This, I thought, was a good win:

- I wouldn't have to waste much time on these assignments. To answer five questions would take me twenty minutes at most.
- With the deal done, Paunchy would stop persuading me. As per our agreement, I would hand him two half-assignments on Friday evening and he would pay me ten rupees. The rest of the time, we could go our own way.
- The extra workload would help take my mind off my grandfather. Instead of analyzing the reasons for his heart attack and considering the what-ifs, I could lose myself in coursework and make him happy. That would also keep my parents off my back. The moment they saw I was keeping busy with books and assignments, they would let me be.

The same evening, I stayed back in 7C after the final bell and mimicked Paunchy's handwriting for a Mathematics assignment. Four questions in, I stopped for a sip of water – only to rewind to that fateful Thursday in December, when I had sat at the same spot during my Mathematics mid-term. Just like on that day, my eraser and sharpener were nestled in a worm-shaped groove in our desk. Our rickety wooden bench wobbled from side to side. The teacher's chair sat at the same location where Father James had read his newspaper that morning. And, just as it had on that day, a cool breeze roused my shirtsleeves to a flutter.

My grandfather had yelled out in pain at 9:15 that morning, as my mother recalled. His moans had got weaker and weaker, soon to be replaced by an ominous silence. The doctor arrived at 9:30. He took my grandfather's pulse and pumped his chest only to confirm what my mother had already suspected.

Oblivious to the events at home, I had gone about solving the first section of the Mathematics paper. There were no hiccups to warn me of my grandfather's condition, no scratchy ears, no serial sneezes. It was only at 9:45 – with my grandfather gone from this world – that I had turned to Stephen. And a further minute before I had lost my mind altogether and snatched his paper.

When I heard the sequence of events, I was relieved that it wasn't my atrocious lapse that had provoked my grandfather's downfall. My mother's theory – that his time had come, that no force on earth can stop the god of death on his mission – was a persuasive one. As the days wore on, though, I remembered something my grandfather had mentioned after his discharge from the hospital, that back in September, when he suffered a shooting pain in the chest during his first heart attack, he had been able to glimpse the future. Even when in agony, struggling for breath, he had known that an ambulance was about to carry him to the hospital, where a doctor would assure him that everything was in control. He had foreseen the bypass surgery, and knew he would recover soon. He had even had a vision of me draped in a silk veshti with a sacred thread across my torso.

Surely, when the pain had returned in December, he must have again perceived what was to come. His mind's eye would have grasped that I was going to abandon my answer sheet and start work on Stephen's paper. He would have known that I would lose forty-five valuable minutes as a result and have no time for the last seven questions. And there was nothing he could do to prevent this. So acute was the letdown, he had obviously lost the will to live. What use of battling each breath and willing himself on when his own grandson was hell-bent on wrecking his future?

'Wake up, silly fellow!'

One of the school peons, Eric, stood at the head of the classroom, waving his broom and dustpan as if casting a spell.

'Finished cleaning, Eric?'

'Just swept the whole classroom, man. Gone blind?'

'Oh.'

'Time is 4:30. SP sir will go mad if I delay.'

'SP sir?'

The very sound of those letters uttered one after the other – raising visions of our hot-tempered director of Physical Education, Mr Suryaprakash – hastened my heartbeat.

'I have to lock up and then go and give SP sir the classroom keys, man.'

'Oh, really?'

'Ya. Some days sir only comes and locks up.'

'What! How come I've never seen him?'

'He comes sometimes after hockey practice.'

'Oh.'

'That's why I am always telling you useless fellows: get out of the classrooms before 4:30, get out before 4:30.'

'Okay, Eric. I'll leave now.'

'Go. Hurry. Fast!'

Downstairs, on the cricket field, a bowler thup-thupped through his run-up. A batsman tapped the ball and yelled 'two, two, two'. Someone gave chase. 'Keep it to one. My end, my end,' the bowler screeched but the batsmen scampered through for two runs. 'Keep it tight, boys,' went a cry. 'Come on, fight!'

St George's were batting in one of the early games of the Georgian Shield cricket tournament. A third of the field was under shadows. The rust-brown pitch and a wide sweep of the leg side were being nourished by the evening sun. On strike was a stout St George's batsman wearing a chest guard and grilled helmet, looking like a Lego Man. A wiry bowler in a white jumper sprinted in, leaped high and let fly. The ball grazed the bat edge, and as the bowler spun around with 'Howsthaaat!', the umpire raised a finger. All the fielders ran in to celebrate.

Lego Man swished his bat and chided himself on his walk back to the pavilion. The new batsman didn't say anything when their paths crossed. He adjusted his cap, twirled his bat, strolled to the centre and marked his guard with 'leg stump, umpire'. He crouched into his stance a foot outside the crease, a kind of risk only an elite batsman would dare to take. The bowler charged in and let go. Bat met ball with a sweet tookh. Out came the bowler's left arm, but the ball raced past it, past the umpire, past a fielder, all the way to the boundary, a stroke so assertive that nobody bothered to give chase. 'Shot, man, Anto,' went a cheer from the pavilion, where his teammates were clustered.

Mr Suryaprakash, who sat on a chair with his arms folded, didn't move a muscle. As the next ball arrived, Anto eased down the track and lofted a straight six with such abandon, his teammates stampeded down the pavilion steps. SP stood up and glared at the batsman, willing him to take his time before venturing into such daring stroke play. Anto left the next one alone. He defended a straight ball with utmost care and let another one pass by, unharmed. Somewhat assured, SP sat down. I checked my watch. It was time to head home.

The early matches in the Georgian Shield kindled little interest. Hardly anyone stayed back to watch and even Musu and TP, who were part of the team's reserves, didn't bring up the games in the classroom. The Georgian Shield may have been an annual tradition for forty-five years, and now the most coveted prize for the city's schoolboys – where a standout performance was rewarded with a newspaper mention, and sometimes a mugshot – but none of this was apparent. Spectators were often outnumbered by the flock of pigeons near the scoreboard. Fielders were left to egg each other on. Gorgeous stroke play received only ripples of applause. When a ball shaved the edge of the bat, 'catch 'im', 'howisthat' and excited howls cut through the quiet. Most of the time silence reigned, especially during stretches when batsmen didn't attempt to score. They shouldered arms and let the ball go, waiting for the best time to make an impact. Like a St George's batsman, who, after a prolonged calm, unleashed a pull shot so striking, his bat could have caught fire. The ball scattered the pigeons on its way to the boundary. The batsman held his pose: left knee in mid-air, right leg upright, like Lord Nataraja at the peak of his divine dance.

I hadn't accounted for these flashes of brilliance when I agreed to do Paunchy's assignments. Twice a week on my way out I paused under the jacarandas – right behind the bowler's arm – and with the breeze on my neck, watched the small triumphs pile up.

The next evening I told Snoop that he should stay back and watch a few overs, given that he had watched 'almost every game of the Georgian Shield' last year.

'Waste of time, Karthik,' he said and headed towards the back gate.

Something had come over Snoop in the new term. Ammonia too couldn't figure out why Snoop was acting like 'a different person each day of the week'. I took it that Snoop was shaken by his mid-term results, especially the fifty-six and fifty-eight he scored in Physics and Chemistry. Having finished fifth in class in the unit tests, he had now fallen outside the top thirty. Snoop's dad was a Chemistry lecturer at St Thomas' College, and Pocket Rocket reckoned that he had dealt Snoop a proper thumping and told him to focus on the finals. The theory got a boost when, last week, Snoop backed out of the inter-house swimming competition, even though he had won a silver in the 100-metre freestyle and a gold as part of the 100-metre relay last year. An irate Mr Suryaprakash asked him if a screw had come loose in his head. Snoop shrugged and coolly announced that he had given up swimming for good.

Even St George's making it to the semi-finals of the tournament wasn't good enough for Snoop. About a hundred others stayed back, though, many of them dotting the perimeter of the field, clustered in tiny islands, chatting, joking and popping peanuts.

I joined Stephen among a group of six.

'This is so damn boring, Leo.'

'It's the semi-final, Stephen! How can you go?'

'Screw it, man. Going to be a shit game.'

'What the fuck is wrong with you!'

'I don't have any hopes for this shit team.'

'Karthik,' went Leo. 'You have watched so many games. Is this a shit team?'

'I have played with most of these players, man,' Stephen said, as if insulted that I, and not he, was being asked for an opinion.

'But what if it's a really close match? You'll miss it.'

'So? The sky won't fall.'

The game eased along, unexciting. St Ignatius' openers defended the straight balls and let go of anything wide of the stumps. Five overs in, Stephen wore his backpack, ready to make his way out.

'You're just jealous that you're not in the team, Stephen.'

'Shut your trap, Leo, or I'll thulp your ass so hard ...'

Leo continued to needle Stephen, goading him to hit back with threat after threat until our star bowler, nicknamed Bazooka, hurtled in and knocked the middle stump out of the ground. Klatak – the abrupt rattle injected the crowd with frenzy.

That was the end of Stephen and Leo's sparring. Bazooka had given them reason to join forces. Pumping their fists and shrieking woohoo and fuckinghell, 'Jakkalakka, jakkalakka,' they screamed. About ten others responded with: 'ooh aah ooh aah'. Another 'jakkalakka, jakkalakka' from Stephen and Leo. An even louder 'ooh aah ooh aah'.

The new batsman was welcomed in with a mean lifter. He fended at it and ballooned a catch back to the bowler. The crowd was unstoppable. The buzz spread to the canteen and the basketball court. Georgians streamed in from all directions, and many took out textbooks and pencil boxes to create a din. They slapped plastic water bottles against each other: clat-clat-clat. One chap inflated a balloon and jumped on it. Boom. He jogged around the boundary rope and handed out whistles. From the teachers' quarters, a priest craned his neck to ascertain the score. 'Holy crap,' went Stephen. 'What great bowling!'

Bazooka turned the rock-solid St Ignatius line-up into jelly. He targeted their chests and neck first up, softened them with blinding pace and then burst through their defences with low-flying missiles. Even when he didn't get a wicket, Bazooka stirred. We knew the lethal ball was around the corner.

Six wickets in eight overs – Bazooka's torrid spell of fast bowling had knocked over St Ignatius for a miserable fifty-four. And all it took was forty-five minutes for St George's to race to victory.

Minutes after the win, SP motored in our direction.

'Fucking hell,' said Leo in a fit of panic.

Stephen adjusted his hair, unshaken.

'Let's get out of here, man.'

'What the fuck for, Leo? We've done nothing wrong.'

Leo slunk away towards the canteen.

Stephen stood still, tracking SP from the corner of his eye.

'Good evening, sir.'

'Good evening, boys. Good evening.'

'What a win, sir.'

'Fine win, Stephen, fine win. But now we have a problem.'

'Sir?'

'Ashok Selvaraj.'

'Sir? He's batting so well.'

'His grandmother passed away this afternoon.'

'Oh.'

'Ya. She was ailing. Pancreatic cancer.'

'Terrible, sir.'

'Ashok can't play the final now.'

'Sir …'

'He was very close to his grandmom. Poor fellow.'

'That's terrible, sir.'

'Yes. Terrible. So … what do you think?'

'Sir?'

'What, man, Stephen? You'll play or not on Saturday?'

'Sir, my father won't let me …'

'Oh god. Stop it. I've heard this Ramayana about your father hundred times. Enough. But listen. I'm not asking you to play some itty-bitty match in some silly tournament. This is the final of the Georgian Shield. Our tournament. Which we haven't won for three years. And you are saying, my father this, my father that.'

'Sir but …'

'All I'm asking for is six hours, Stephen. Six bloody hours.'

'My father won't let me, sir.'

'Then call him to school tomorrow morning. Eight-thirty sharp. I'll meet him outside the principal's office.'

'He won't come if it's about cricket, sir.'

'Then tell him you're going to be thrown out of school.'

'Sir?'

'Just make up something, man.'

'Okay, sir.'

'Okay what?'

'I'll tell him, sir. I'll tell him to come and meet the principal.'

It was 8:20 by my watch when Rubin Mohanraj arrived outside the principal's office. Stephen had taken a chance by telling the truth. Mr Mohanraj had agreed to come, despite his factory shift starting at 7:30 every morning. Right hand snuck in a pocket and left hand caressing his handlebar moustache, he surveyed a rectangular plaque that listed gold medallists from years past. His checked white shirt stretched around his tummy. His expertly pressed trousers were ready to be inspected by SP. Stephen stood behind him, head bowed. SP treated Mr Mohanraj to a firm handshake and led father and son to the principal's office.

Paunchy and Leo relaxed on the staircase that wound its way up to the chapel. I cannot say exactly what it was that drove me to walk halfway across the field to join them but I was soon in their company, settling a couple of stairs below. A part of me wished to find out if Stephen would play the final. But there was also a part of me that was fascinated by how much seemed to happen around Leo, Paunchy and Stephen. Arguments, insults, whacky theories, simmering tension, back slaps, rumours: it was hard to feel bored in their company.

'What if,' Paunchy went, 'what if Ashok Selvaraj was lying about his grandmom? Maybe he just didn't want to play the final.'

'What's wrong with you, Paunchy?'

'Seriously, Leo. I think there's more to this Selvaraj story.'

'Everyone is not like you, Paunchy. Killing grandmoms every few weeks just because you don't have time for homework.'

'Not just me, man. Lots of guys saying Ashok chickened out.'

'That's just bullshit. Why won't Ashok want to play?'

'Never know, man. Last year also he didn't play some games.'

'So? He must have had a solid reason last year also.'

'Someone was saying Ashok always misses important games.'

'And you will believe anything anyone says?'

'Never know, Leo. Lots of people are talking.'

Paunchy and Leo moved on to other arguments, insulting each other's mothers and grandmothers along the way. That was until Stephen walked out of the principal's office, head still bowed. His father, pinching his moustache, towered over him. Behind them, radiating a generous smile, was SP, a spring in his step.

It was a smile that spoke a thousand words. The principal had somehow convinced Mr Mohanraj to permit Stephen to play in the Georgian Shield final.

14

Torch of Life

SATURDAY BEGAN WITH A tiff over curdled milk. My mother blamed the milkman. My father blamed my mother for not ordering an extra packet of milk every day. My mother said this was a silly idea since it would lead to wastage. My father slapped his forehead. My mother told my father to stay out of these kitchen matters. My father accused my mother of not being able to think straight without her morning coffee. My mother sniggered. 'Everyone knows you are the coffee addict!'

This was the point when my grandfather would have boomed: 'You two have no better work or what?' – not as much a query as a demand for quiet. My parents would have had no choice but to dial down the temperature. My father would have walked out to buy milk, and thereby retired this argument, at least for the time being.

Now, with my grandfather gone, my parents were unstoppable. Worse, I was stuck in the crossfire.

'You've already had a bath, Karthik?'

'Yes, Pa.'

'Oh. Going somewhere?'

'School, Pa.'

'School? On a Saturday? Some special class?'

'Final of the cricket tournament, Pa. Georgian Shield.'

'You are in the cricket team?'

'Not playing, Pa. Just watching.'

'Oh god, Karthik. Don't tell me you are going to waste a whole day watching some silly cricket match?'

'Please, Pa. Just today.'

'What nonsense is this. One day for a cricket match. One day for some birthday party. One day for this, one day for that. When are you going to concentrate on your studies, Karthik?'

'Why are you controlling his life now?' my mother hollered from the kitchen. 'He is old enough to know what to do.'

'He is not old enough for anything, Kamala,' my father announced, slapping the dining table. 'Just look at his mid-term results. I have nothing more to say.'

'Oh please. There was so much going on. So much tension. You know how worried he was when Appa was in the hospital. Plus ... new school, new friends. There were ink marks on his shirt on most days. Despite all that, he did okay in the mid-terms.'

'He did okay? Are you serious? Your son has got sixty-two in Mathematics.'

'Nothing can be done about that now, okay?' my mother said, slamming the refrigerator. 'He is working hard. Up to date with all assignments. And he hardly goes out to play these days.'

'That's all fine. But end of the day, only the marks matter.'

'Shall I tell you something now? School is not just about exams and marks, okay? It's high time you understood that.'

'Ya, ya. That's all easy for you to say. Everyone knows how hard it is to get into a top college these days. Even ninety per cent is not enough, you know? Plus all this reservation nonsense.'

'Karthik is just in the seventh standard. I don't know why you keep worrying all the time.'

'There you go. Same old excuse. His board exams are just three years away! From now, every single test and exam is important. The time to worry is *now*!'

'Stop making this into a life-or-death situation. Please. The world is not going to end if he goes for a cricket match today.'

'I have said whatever I have to say. Rest is up to you.'

My mother locked the jar into the mixie. My father grabbed his money pouch and made off to buy milk.

'So this cricket match, K,' my mother said, once the mixie had pulverized the coconut chunks into a chutney, 'when will it finish?'

I wasn't sure. Four o'clock seemed a reasonable estimate. But given how my mother had stood up for me just now – given how she had perceived my troubles during my early days at St George's and yet hadn't embarrassed me by bringing it up – I decided it would be best if I left the game midway through the second half.

'It will finish at two o'clock, Ma,' I said, shaking my head confidently.

'Ah. That's good. Finish some homework in the next two hours, then. Okay? You can leave at nine-thirty. And make sure to be back by three.'

'Okay, Ma.'

'Good. Eat breakfast now. Idlis are hot-hot. Chutney is here.'

I reached school not long after ten, sprinting from the bus stop to the cricket field only to be met by an unsettling quiet. About thirty boys were scattered around the field's perimeter, and most weren't watching the game. Some peered into trump cards, some chitchatted. A group of boys loafed around near the canteen, oozing the sort of disinterest that would get Mr Suryaprakash's blood to boil. None among them noticed when a ball narrowly whizzed past an outstretched bat. 'Well bowled,' went a lone cry from the pavilion followed by a 'come on, boys, come on', but it was a far from worthy atmosphere for a home team vying for their first title in four years.

The game was in its eighth over, with St Thomas off to a steady start. Bazooka, at the top of his mark, had set an attacking field: three slips, a gully, point, mid-on, mid-off and square leg. The only boundary rider was at third man – a roly-poly boy with hands in his pockets, tracing a circle with the tip of his sneakers. Bazooka charged in. Roly-Poly Boy inscribed a triangle within the circle. The ball was wide of the stumps, to which the batsman duly shouldered arms. Roly-Poly Boy didn't look up from his diagram until SP screamed, 'Stop daydreaming, donkey.' At once he erased the drawing and waved, all serious.

Stephen was fielding at mid-off, his white trousers mud-stained from what must have been a full-length dive. He egged Bazooka on when he got back to his mark and walked in for the next ball, crouched, eyes alert. I considered calling out his name and flashing him a thumbs up but Stephen was so gripped by the game – even in between deliveries – I didn't want to disturb him. This was not the Stephen who lay into 'shit bowling' and 'crap batting' from the sidelines. This was a quieter avatar, watchful, committed. When his teammates bore down on the batsman to rubbish his technique, Stephen didn't join them. He walked back to his fielding spot and got ready for the next ball.

Leo stood near the scoreboard, arms folded across his chest. Behind him, Paunchy sat on a ledge and chomped on chips.

'Hey Leo, when did you come, man?'

Eyes still on the game, Leo held up eight fingers.

'Whoa. Early bird. Did Stephen bowl in practice?'

Leo scrunched up his eyes and shook his head.

'Where do you think he'll bat? Four?'

He held up five fingers.

'What if SP surprises us by sending him at number three or four?'

'Got him!'

I turned around.

The umpire declared the batsman out, and handed St George's their first wicket. The boundary edges crackled with high-pitched howls. Leo pumped his fists: 'fucking yes'. Paunchy, with his hands cupped around his mouth, shrieked 'woohoo'.

'Up, up,' went Leo.

A few of us responded with 'George's!'

'Up, up,' he squawked once more.

'George's!' came the reply, with more voices joining in.

'We want ...'

'... Vic-tory!'

'Come on the blues ...'

'... Never lose.'

'Whiskey, brandy, soda, pop ...'

'... We want George's on the top!'

'Whiskey, brandy, soda, pop ...'

'... We want George's on the top!'

'George's!'

Clap, clap, clap

'George's!'

Clap, clap, clap.

'George's!'

Clap, clap, clap.

St Thomas brushed off the fall of the wicket with a steady partnership. The crowd deployed drumbeats, whistles, rattles and chants. A St George's fielder had to merely field the ball and fling it in; a throng of Georgians raised their arms and erupted with delight. One of the St Thomas batsmen reeled off three successive fours – each shot so expertly executed that it would have brought a happy tear to every cricket coach's eye. The crowd was coerced into silence until Hippo, a hefty tenth-standard boy, unfurled a massive St George's flag: its sky blue and milky white sparkling in the mid-day sun. Hippo jogged along the boundary rope swishing the flag. He pranced and screamed in between heavy panting.

Hippo was soon chanter-in-chief:

'Up, up, George's
We want victory …'

… and he urged his team to kick St Thomas' butts:

'Ek do teen char
Thomas ki gaand maar.'

Bazooka picked up the second wicket with a sharp in-cutter.

Hippo upped the volume.

'Hundred thousand people say
Hundred thousand people know
Un-gayya un-gayya
Thomas chooth le papaya.'

Hippo thrust his pelvis in the course of bawling out the last line. His hands rammed an imaginary papaya into a hapless groin.

With so much going on, I couldn't help but look elsewhere when something important happened on the field. Every time I missed a wicket, I scolded myself for losing sight of play. To get back into the game I started tracking field changes and counting the number of strides in the bowlers' run-ups. Our captain bit his nails after each over. Stephen mouthed 'fucking bullshit' when Roly-Poly Boy let slip a ball through his legs. I was happy to be immersed in the action until a Mexican wave started rippling around.

The crowd had ballooned to roughly four hundred.

Bazooka picked up another wicket and brought everyone to their feet. Once more, I was a split second too late to the action – a lapse in concentration that would have made my grandfather lose his mind, irrespective of whether I was watching a game or practising my typing or solving a problem. More than a month after he had left us, I was still seeking out ways to let him down.

A rampaging finish catapulted St Thomas to 193.

'Too much, man, way too much,' said Paunchy.

'Stop this negative bullshit,' warned Leo.

Most of the boys around us weren't hopeful. From what I had seen of St Thomas' bowling, this was possibly a winning total for them.

Leo and Paunchy headed to the canteen.

'Come, Karthik,' said Leo. 'Paunchy is treating.'

'Fucking hell,' said Paunchy.

I stopped myself.

'That's Stephen's pop, man.'

'Holy crap,' went Leo. 'That's him.'

'Unbelievable.'

'You know what? I had a feeling he might come off.'

'Seriously?'

'Remember he was at the junior final last year? He kept shouting instructions to Stephen until SP told him to chill out.'

'Oh ya. He knows SP from before, right?'

'Ya. They played in the same league.'

'What? Stephen's pop played cricket?'

'Long, long back, man. Club cricket.'

'Whoa. Was he good?'

'Stephen says he was a madcap batsman. Whacked sixes but got out for twenty-thirty each time. Mental Rubin, they called him.'

'Mental Rubin! What a name!'

'Then one day he just gave up cricket.'

'What! Why?'

'God knows, man. Stephen says his pop came home one day and said he had thrown his bat and kit in a lake. That's all. He never played again.'

'Stop fucking woaling, Leo.'

'I swear to god, Paunchy. That's what Stephen told me.'

'Are you serious?'

'I swear on my mom, pop, grandmom, everyone.'

'That's crazy, dude.'

'Ya. It's nuts.'

Leo and Paunchy were yelling to be heard. Many in the crowd were slitting the air with honks, trumpets and whistles. Empty plastic bottles smacked empty plastic bottles. A boy with a drum led a chorus of 'We Will Rock You'. The jam-packed pavilion heaved with each throbbing 'rock you'. At the opposite end of the field about fifty boys from St Thomas egged their team on. It didn't bother them that their screams were drowned out by a tidal wave of boos. The booing, in fact, spurred them on.

The St George's openers began cautiously in their run chase. Five overs passed, then ten, with neither attempting a shot in anger. There was no urgency in their running and twice they missed out on misfields. In the twelfth over, they failed to communicate and were lucky to escape a farcical run out.

'Why can't these fools just get the fuck out, man?'

'Ya. They're having a tough time.'

'Seriously, Leo. Why can't they just throw their wickets?'

'Because SP will whip their asses.'

'Balls. You know what SP will be mad about? This shit batting.'

'They surely have a plan, Paunchy.'

'Oh really? Then I guess the plan is to lose this match.'

'Shut your trap now.'

'I knew it, Leo. These chaps are going to throw this final. I told you that day itself. Selvaraj's grandmom didn't die. The bugger just made that shit up.'

'Will you shut your goddamn mouth right now?'

Paunchy was about to respond when one of the batsmen nicked a catch. The crowd's murmur turned to a hush. Leo was unsure if the wicket was good news or bad news. Paunchy slammed a fist against a palm. 'Good riddance!' Two balls went by when the other batsman spooned a catch to the bowler. The ambient hush gave way to a gasp. Leo covered his face, concerned. Paunchy was unsure if this wicket was good news or bad news.

Anto, with his cap at an angle, ambled to the crease as if woken from an afternoon nap. There was not a shred of urgency in his approach, no hint that he was anxious about the two quick wickets. The first ball he slashed to the fielder at cover, bat meeting ball as crisply as a wet towel would a washing stone. The second ball brought another a cover drive, the ball hurtling to the boundary this time, a shot of such unalloyed brilliance that Leo closed his eyes and turned away with a euphoric 'oooooof'. Paunchy was too stunned to shape his mouth to make words.

Anto's batting partner, the right-handed Dorai, loved his short-arm jabs and punches. He appeared in a tangle when he set up for strokes but found a way to find the gaps. Stephen had once said Dorai was too jittery, too weak against pace, but it was Dorai's contributions that had brought St George's to the final.

Anto slashed, Dorai punched. Anto creamed drive after dazzling drive. Dorai nudged, chipped and angled his bat to add on the singles. Seventy came up in twenty overs, a hundred in twenty-six, one hundred and twenty-four in thirty. Anto's walk transformed into a swagger, and, once, when he uncoiled a rapturous straight six, Hippo flung the school flag high in the air.

> Wherever we go-oo,
> People want to know-oo,
> Who we are,
> So we tell them,
> We are the Georgians,
> The mighty, mighty Georgians …

The chant was approaching a crescendo when Anto missed a fast, straight ball and was bowled – the middle stump uprooted, flying over the turf, the bails launched in opposite directions, the deathly rattle knocking the wind out of the mass of spectators. Even the St Thomas boys couldn't believe what they had seen. 'Holy mother of god,' went Leo, speaking for the crowd.

Stephen slid to the centre, windmilling his bat over a shoulder and squinting at the dipping sun. His top button was off and he wore no helmet or cap, nothing that could disturb his slick mop. Leo expected the first ball to be aimed at Stephen's head – and it was – but he didn't 'blast it for six' as Leo hoped, just swayed out of its way and glared at the pitch. The next ball was also a lifter, which Stephen, on his toes, defended straight back.

I had heard so much about Stephen's batting, I expected him to announce himself with a flurry of fours and sixes. What I got was Stephen handing the strike over to Dorai, and Dorai handing it back to Stephen: a trickle of singles that returned the innings to a steady tempo. There was nothing spectacular or explosive about Stephen's shot-making. Rather he instilled a sense of calm in the crowd, tapping the ball in the gaps and gliding across the turf. Dorai proved an ideal partner, geeing him up and alerting him to field changes. In between overs, the two righthanders tapped bats and punched gloves, and once, after scampering three runs, shared a joyous high five. Gradually, unobtrusively, they trimmed the target to forty-four off thirty balls.

Then thirty-six off twenty-four.

St George's were within striking range, yet everyone in the crowd was wary of Sonic, the standout fast bowler through the tournament. His missile to dismiss Anto had sent a shiver down our spines and another lethal delivery now would spell big trouble. Even the sun didn't want anything to do with Sonic; it hid behind the clouds when he came on to bowl and enveloped the ground in a blanket of grey. 'Sensible, sensible,' said Leo when Dorai was beaten by a brutish outswinger. Paunchy looked to the sky and cursed the sun for being a 'pansy, a chickenshit'.

Twenty-eight needed off eighteen balls.

Then twenty off twelve.

Sonic began the penultimate over with a blast of energy, pelting through his run-up and grunting on delivery. The first ball was too fast, too vicious, so fast that it was reduced to a hazy red blur on its way in and took off at a steep angle to thud into Stephen's chest. 'Fucking shit,' screamed Leo and turned away, terrified. Stephen grimaced but only briefly. He adjusted his gloves and glanced around the field, then re-marked his guard and gave Dorai a thumbs up. Pissed off with this delay, Sonic dashed in and, leaping high, launched a fireball. The fuzzy sphere landed on a length and was about to shoot through low and shatter the stumps when Stephen brought his bat down just in time.

'Oooh,' went the cry from the pavilion steps.

'Oooh' went Dorai, a hand on his chest.

'Oooh,' went SP, his palms pressing his forehead.

Sonic stood at the centre of the pitch and glared. Stephen dusted the toe-end of the bat, making sure to avoid eye-contact.

Twenty needed off ten, with every single spectator on his feet.

Mr Mohanraj towered over a group of nervous boys near the canteen. Eyes enlarged and cheeks strained, he kissed a clenched fist. Leo crossed himself and muttered a prayer. Paunchy bit off a grimy fingernail. Fearing the worst, I screwed up my eyes.

Sonic galloped to the crease, gathering pace through his run-up, and let go with an intimidating urghh. The ball wasn't short, it wasn't full, it wasn't wide. It was straight and on a good length, neither rising awkwardly nor keeping low. It was quick, but not quick enough for Stephen who took a step down the ground and swung with such ferocity that it was a surprise the bat didn't fly off the handle. A sudden ttaaaack tore through the silence.

And how the ball flew! Shrinking as it soared into the distance:

an apple over the field,
a peach above the canteen,
a plum among the jacarandas,
a grape against the grey sky,
and an orange pip that cleared the compound wall and dropped onto the main road

– maybe injuring a motorist or denting a car – leaving behind eight-hundred spectators gasping for breath.

The bowler turned skywards. So did every fielder. The umpires swivelled their necks. And boys near the basketball court rushed across the boundary rope to get a clear view. SP waved his hands and told the ball to, 'Go, go, go, go.' The principal squinted. Mr Mohanraj raised his hands over his head as if to signal six. Stephen tracked the ball even as his bat continued its smooth follow-through. His feet, a dancer's feet, held their poise.

What. A. Shot.

Stephen could have chipped the ball over midwicket. Or shuffled across the stumps and whipped it through the vast gap at square leg. Or driven the ball wide of cover. He could have chosen to turn over the strike to Dorai, who was one of the highest scorers in the tournament. But no. With tension mounting and light fading, with the bowler spitting fire and the pitch playing tricks, with the game on a knife-edge and the crowd wracked with dread, Stephen went for broke. And, unlike those watching, he carried not an ounce of disbelief, as if he had always known that he would be on strike at the climax, ready to launch the ball when the time arrived.

Dorai ran up and hugged Stephen tight. The St Thomas captain covered his face with his palms. Their wicketkeeper was on his haunches, shaking his head. Up in the pavilion steps, Georgians screamed, hugged, danced and slapped high fives. SP returned to his seat and crossed one leg over another. The principal, Father Menezes, in what was surely a first, broke into a smile.

It was all so heady, so feverish, and I knew the match was ours. I didn't yell or clap or pump my fist, didn't prance around like Leo or thump my chest with animal noises, like Paunchy. Watching the ball disappear into the grey sky, I could only think of how my grandfather would have reacted to this thunderbolt, screeching 'sixerrr' as the ball went soaring, clapping his hands, slapping his thighs and recalling his favourite sixes. 'Just like Kapil,' he may have said. Or, if truly impressed, 'Ah, just like Viv.'

Over the last month, desperate to move on from my grandfather's death, I had tried hard to suppress my memories of our times together. Every time his face popped up in my mind, I had distracted myself with other thoughts and thrown myself into assignments and homework. The best way to cope with my sadness, I told myself, was to tune it out. Only then could I somehow eliminate the grief. Stephen's mighty strike, though, and the sight of the ball getting tinier and tinier in the distance, stirred something deep within. Thrilled as I was with the shot and its outcome, I was also on the brink of tearing up. The game was in the bag, yes, but it struck me that my grandfather, like that red ball, was gone forever. One moment I was so happy.

Then, I was overcome with loss.

The field was awash in blue and white. Hippo clambered onto the canteen's roof and waved the flag. Paunchy splashed Stephen with a bottle of Pepsi. Leo shrieked his heart out, arms spread-eagled. Dorai was drenched in lime juice. Anto was about to be drenched, when he led the team on a victory lap.

Our principal stood on a make-shift dais and took in the chaos. When handed the Georgian Shield, he examined it from multiple angles and blew off dust from the crown. 'Hello, mike testing, hello,' a peon announced and asked us to gather around the dais for the presentation ceremony. 'Mike Tyson?' asked Paunchy, gawking at the irate peon.

Father Menezes thanked all the volunteers who had worked tirelessly for three weeks. He made sure we handed the 'gallant Thomians' a big round of applause. 'This historic tournament has produced many unforgettable games,' he said, tapping the Georgian Shield on its cheek like it were his pet puppy, 'but this was the most gripping game I have been fortunate enough to watch.'

A cheer of 'George's, George's' went around. We waited eagerly for the medals to be handed out.

'Sports can be a wonderful thing, boys,' Father Menezes said, arms spread out. 'A civil war in Senegal was halted because the great Pele was passing through. Think about that for a moment. A footballer halted a war!

'This is why I tell my students: academics is important, yes, but it can't teach us what sports can. Sports helps us understand ourselves, it teaches us to work as a team. Each time you get on the field, you test the limits of your excellence.'

'Blablafuckingblah,' said Leo under his breath.

Paunchy ran off to the toilets, confident that he would make it back before the prizes were handed out.

'I know you're all tired and excited,' said Father Menezes, 'but allow me to share with you a small anecdote that will shed light … on the crucial role that sports can play in our lives …'

'Holy Christ,' muttered Leo, 'this is the height of bullshit.'

'Two days ago I met a boy and his father … in my office,' the principal said, scanning the crowd. 'The father, who I am happy to see among us, was worried that cricket and football were distracting his son from his studies. "Sports didn't get me anywhere," the father said, and he felt it wasn't going to get his son anywhere either. "It's just… it's just a massive waste of time," he said.

'This came as no surprise to me. I understood his concerns and told him that his logic was perfectly sound. After all, even the best cricketer in school has to do well in his exams, he has to get into a good college and he has to then get a good job. All that is no doubt true. Still, I tried to impress upon the father the value – often unrecognized – that sports adds to the experience of growing up. One can learn a lot from books, I said, but some lessons are best picked up in the cut and thrust of competition.

'My task was made easier when I recalled a poem I had read as a young man, a poem that had such a profound influence on me … that I have framed it in my office to constantly remind myself of the lessons that sports instills. I am glad the poem had the desired effect on Mr Rubin Mohanraj. And I am thrilled that his son Stephen turned in a performance that none of us will forget. Let me tell you: it was the best cameo I have seen under pressure.

'The poem is called "Vitai Lampada", or "Torch of Life", and it was written by Sir Henry John Newbolt in 1892.

Please bear with me as I read it out.'

There's a breathless hush in the Close to-night
Ten to make and the match to win—
A bumping pitch and a blinding light,
An hour to play and the last man in.
And it's not for the sake of a ribboned coat,
Or the selfish hope of a season's fame,
But his captain's hand on his shoulder smote
'Play up! play up! and play the game!'

The sand of the desert is sodden red,—
Red with the wreck of a square that broke;—
The Gatling's jammed and the Colonel dead,
And the regiment blind with dust and smoke.
The river of death has brimmed his banks,
And England's far, and Honour a name,
But the voice of a schoolboy rallies the ranks:
'Play up! play up! and play the game!'

This is the word that year by year,
While in her place the school is set,
Every one of her sons must hear,
And none that hears it dare forget.
This they all with a joyful mind
Bear through life like a torch in flame,
And falling fling to the host behind—
'Play up! play up! and play the game!'

15
Chhakka

MY MOTHER DIDN'T CARE for the dramatic Georgian Shield final. Nor for the outpouring of emotion that followed the game. Rubin Mohanraj hugging Stephen tight; SP choking up during his speech; Anto holding the Georgian Shield aloft; Bazooka weeping; the crowd bawling out the school song: none of this made a jot of a difference to her. She had put up with a domestic scuffle this morning for my sake – and she had been supportive enough to let me go for the match assuming I would be back by three o'clock. Now here I was, worn out and unrepentant, ringing the doorbell a little after six. 'What Appa said was right only.' She turned away in a huff. 'Whole day wasted.'

I shut the door and stayed quiet. The best way to limit the damage was to a) put on a helpless expression, and b) say nothing at all, making it plain that there was no reasonable excuse for my three-hour delay. This was as submissive a response as I could muster – and it had worked in my favour when I had announced my mid-term exam results few weeks ago – but now, the same mute cluelessness got her blood to boil.

'What is the use, Karthik?'

'Sorry, Ma. It was …'

'No, Karthik. No. Don't say sorry when you don't mean it.'

'Ma, it was …'

'No. Don't. Stop it.'

Subdued, I bowed my head.

'You yourself think and see, Karthik. Ya. Think about what you have achieved all day. And then see if you are really sorry …'

'Ma …'

'And how are we to know that you are not lost or kidnapped? How many times have I told you: call from a phone booth and tell us that you will be delayed. But no. You won't listen.'

'Amma …'

'I have said what I have to say, Karthik. If you have made up your mind not to listen to anything, I can't help you.'

Silence.

'Look at how dirty your shoes are. Tcha. Wash up.'

My father sat still on a rocking chair with his face blocked out by an *India Today* magazine. He could have picked that moment to say any number of things but – now that matters had turned out exactly as he had anticipated – he quietly basked in his victory. It was, after all, my mother who had allowed me to go for the match, so he would leave it to her to clean up this mess. As for me, he could always teach me a lesson some other day. 'Best you stop wasting time on useless cricket matches, Karthik,' he might say after beating me in a game of chess. 'Believe me: there are far more sensible ways to spend your time.'

My father scanned magazine after magazine. My mother retired to the bedroom as early as 7:30, without telling me about the rava upma and tomato chutney that she had set aside in the kitchen. I ate quietly at the dining table – not daring to turn on the TV – and analyzed what I could have done differently.

- I could have been upfront and told my mother in the morning that the match could stretch till five o'clock, but that could have backfired. 'So late, K!' she may have said, reconsidering her decision to let me go. 'Better stay at home then.'
- I could have left halfway through the St George's innings, as planned, and got back home by three o'clock. That would have put my mother at ease, but it would have meant missing Stephen's cameo, the heady climax, those hysterical celebrations, the principal's speech and the prize distribution. Plus, I would have had to suffer Leo and Paunchy going on about how I had been dumb enough to abandon the 'greatest fucking cricket match of all time'.

The only way to resolve my confusion, at least for my own sake, was to ask: what would my grandfather have made of my delay? Over the last month or so, putting matters to the Thatha Test had thrown up valuable lessons. In this case, he would have blasted me for my hopeless time-sense and pointed out that such 'criminal unpunctuality' would have led to an unceremonious dismissal from the army. He would have ordered me to clutch my earlobes, with my arms crossed over my chest, and do twenty squats in the puja room. And he would have banned me from all sports until my final exams. These outcomes would be unavoidable.

At some point, though, perhaps after my prayers, he would have asked about the game and settled down into his cane chair to extract a detailed account. Feeding him a brief summary of the final would not have cut it. When told of a batsman hitting a four or a bowler picking up a wicket, he would have asked for specifics. 'What kind of ball?' 'Outswinger?' 'Full length?' 'Batsman on the front foot?' 'How was his timing?' 'And the follow-through?' Approaching the climax, he would have dissected each ball and each big shot as if this were a World Cup final. The post-match review would have unfolded at dinnertime, which meant my parents too would have been forced to chime in. Through the evening, cricket talk would have taken precedence. And the mood would have automatically lightened.

Now my grandfather was gone. And the house had fallen silent.

On Sunday, my father spoke to me only when he wanted something done. 'Replace the bathroom bulb, Karthik.' 'Keep the garbage out, Karthik.' 'Turn off the heater, Karthik.' My mother resumed normal communication but it was obvious she wouldn't grant me any leeway. So no cricket with Chiku and friends, no TV, no comic books and no tapping the ball against our driveway wall. These could wait until my finals were done.

It was up to me to prove I was repentant. I dusted the furniture, watered the potted plants and scrubbed the windowpanes. I helped my father wash the car and scooter, then organized the bookshelves, the cassette rack and the stack of newspapers. I prayed aloud in the puja room – loud enough for my parents to take note – and made sure to accompany my mother to the Ganesha temple that evening. Next day, I woke up at five o'clock, went over the day's lessons, bathed, prayed, ate my breakfast and left for school at 7:40. I finished a Physics assignment over the lunch break and didn't stay back to watch Stephen, basking in his stardom, take on three ninth-standard boys in a push-up contest. Back home, I washed up, prayed, did my homework, ate dinner, revised the day's lessons and retired at nine. The more predictable my schedule, the lesser the chances of trouble.

The only time I broke from the strict routine was on Friday, when I told my mother I had to stay back for an extra half hour to help Mrs Andrade catalogue books in the library. This, of course, was a barefaced lie. I needed that time to blitz through Paunchy's assignments: an act of forgery that was too risky to carry out at home. The moment the classroom emptied out, with some boys heading home and others wandering to the football field or volleyball court, I got to his assignments, solving not more than five questions in each. Neatness wasn't a factor here. I didn't review answers, didn't label most diagrams. Paunchy didn't care, anyway. He would rather I did a sloppy job and keep it above suspicion.

I was midway through this slapdash routine when Snoop walked into 7C with his shirt mangled and a couple of buttons ripped off. His trousers were wet and his cheeks flaming red. Ignoring my presence, he sat in his spot in the third row and, with his face buried in his palms, broke down. A minute passed. Snoop kept sobbing. He took a break, sobbed more and slowly quietened. I assumed the worst was over. He raised the volume, releasing a bucketful of tears.

Maybe he had been dipped in the fountain. Or sprayed with a hosepipe. Or dunked in a puddle. Having myself suffered so, I knew the possibilities were endless. I also knew that he would rather deal with his agony by himself – as I had preferred back in June, when my first instinct on being strong-armed was to escape all company. And anyway, what could I have said to him? Offered false hope that things were going to get better? Or made him feel worse by prying out details of the bullying? No. The most practical move was to let him be. Only by emptying himself of his sadness could he make space for hope to sneak in.

So pronounced were Snoop's mood swings, and so unpredictable his behaviour over the last few weeks that he became saddled with nicknames like 'Screw-loose', 'Mental' and 'Touchy-feely'. Someone had claimed he only needed to be touched to be tickled. Leo tested this theory by walking by his bench and fondling his ribs. Snoop squeaked and squirmed, which brought on a caress to his neck. A helpless Snoop cowered in his seat. Paunchy was all set to attack him from behind when someone announced that Father Rosario was on his way to the classroom. Leo and Paunchy hurried to their seats and Snoop was left alone for the English period. Come lunch break, though, and the pestering inevitably resumed.

Each new stunt hacked into Snoop's confidence. His butt cheeks quivered when he walked, wary as he was of being bullied. One PT period, during a team relay, he sprinted like no one I had seen before, flailing his arms as if in a blindfold, desperate to escape from a pack of mad dogs. Metric and Musu collapsed in a torrent of laughter. The PT teacher – SP's deputy – didn't pull them up, only chuckled and asked Snoop why he was 'running like a frightened girl'. Snoop complained of a headache. He fled to the basketball court, flopped onto a bench and shyly crossed a leg over another, dangling his limbs like a pair of scissor blades.

'Now I get it, man,' Leo proclaimed. 'Snoop is half boy, half girl: a chhakka.'

That blew up like dynamite. Someone set off a rumour that Snoop had a thing for fair-skinned boys. Someone else glued a poster of a topless male model on Snoop's desk. Paunchy claimed that Snoop had once made a pass at him, and though nobody was mad enough to fall for that – 'even a toad won't make a pass at you, dude,' Leo had clarified – it solidified the narrative. Each time a new fiction emerged, Snoop didn't stamp it out. Rather, he only withdrew further into himself.

Four days ago, a Monday morning, with the magnolias in full bloom and two red-wattled lapwings tweeting didyadoits, Snoop surprised us by talking about his trip to Bannerghatta National Park. For the first time in more than a month he resembled his old self, especially when he recalled minute details – like the pitch of an elephant's rumble and the length of a bear's yawn. 'And so many crocodiles,' he went on, eyes aglow, 'fifteen, twenty of them at least. And they were so close to us, you know! Suddenly two crocodiles climbed the rocks and were watching us with mouths open. Woah. We nearly died of shock!'

'This is such an amazing story,' said Musu. 'So how did it feel when a crocodile bit off your prick and ate it for lunch?'

Overwhelmed by the boisterous laughter, Snoop turned around and rushed off to the library. The crocodile fiction spread like fire around the football field. Later that morning, Metric bingoed Snoop and announced: 'Pretty sure there's nothing down there!' During the break, Paunchy and Leo sneakily followed him to the toilets to investigate 'how exactly he was pissing'. Snoop saw he was being pursued. And he stayed away from school for the next two days.

Assignments completed, I packed my backpack and made for the exit when a sweaty Paunchy, his leather shoes smeared in wet mud, bounded into the classroom.

'Work over, Karthik?' he demanded, ruffling his moist hair. 'Oh. Look who's here! His royal pansiness – Chhakka.'

Snoop didn't look up from his desk.

'Stop being a cry baby, Chhakka. Enough of this drama.'

Not a peep from Snoop.

'This is what I don't understand, Chhakka. You've just got royally screwed in the volleyball court, and instead of going home you're now back to class to get your ass kicked again.'

'Paunchy, just leave him alone, man.'

'You cork up, Karthik.'

'He's been crying for the last fifteen minutes.'

'Thanks for that bit of info. Where are my assignments?'

'Here but …'

He grabbed the sheets and held out a crumpled ten-rupee note. 'Now go. Enough yakking.'

I refused.

He closed in to stuff the note in my shirt pocket.

'I don't want your cash, man.'

'Someone is acting really funny today, I see. Okay. Fuck it then. If you don't want the cash, don't take it. Now get the hell out.'

Folding my arms in front of my chest, I stayed put.

'Chhakka, why don't you tell this nerdy dickhead to get the fuck out of the classroom? That way you can take your clothes off and I can take a great photo with my new camera. Wooohoooo!'

'Everyone knows that's a toy camera, Paunchy.'

'Oh really, Karthik? But what if I have another camera that takes real photos? Huh? What then?'

'Liar.'

'Just wait till you see the photos I'm going to click today. They're going to be such a big hit. Everyone will finally see what Chhakka has down there. Hohohohohooo. The ultimate proof that we have a girl in an all-boys school!'

My first impulse was to fling something at Paunchy. There had to be some way to register my protest. My pencil box and half-full water bottle were within reach. The green duster sat on the teacher's table, not too far away, and my Physics textbook was in my backpack, ready to be called up on a suicide mission.

'Just get lost, Karthik,' Snoop pronounced, kneading an eyeball with the base of a palm.

'Huh?'

'I said: leave. Get out. Go home.'

The anger in his voice was laced with disgust. Clearly Snoop was repulsed by what a terrible friend I had turned into over the last two months, standing by and doing nothing as boys shat all over him. He must have waited for me to come to his aid, to do something – anything – to lessen his torture. Perhaps he had hoped I could persuade Stephen to put an end to the ragging. Or to at least comfort him when we made small talk during the breaks. All he had got from me was a mountain of indifference.

'Get lost, Karthik,' Snoop screeched, shooting me such a stern gaze that Paunchy was taken aback. 'Just leave right now.'

Paralyzed, I looked him in the eye, to confirm if he really meant what he was saying. An enraged Snoop turned to Paunchy, then to me and back to Paunchy, as if ordering him to boot me out.

I stepped out of the classroom onto the corridor, unable to bear the mounting shame. It was one thing for Paunchy to think I was a pushover. For Snoop to feel the same was a punch in the gut. The only way to redeem myself was to rush back into 7C and take Paunchy on, which would give Snoop a chance to run away. There was a good chance I would be overpowered but at least Snoop would know I was willing to fight for him, that I didn't mind risking serious injury to save him this indignity.

Out in the corridor, I unzipped my bag and picked out the metallic divider from my geometry box. That would surely throw Paunchy off. Or would it? Conflicting voices popped in my head. This was a reckless move. This was my only option. I had to think this through. No, I had to act fast. I had to act now.

Clutching the divider, I steeled myself to run towards Paunchy. The idea was not to stab him, only rattle him enough for Snoop to escape. I took a deep breath to drive away all doubt. Something wasn't right. Another deep breath. More uncertainty. Turning left and right, I made sure no one else was around. I strained my ears to latch on to faint sounds ... when it struck me.

Mr Suryaprakash!

Surely he was somewhere in the vicinity. His voice was muffled but its rumble unmistakable. All it took was a moment's focus to realize that he was two classrooms away. I checked my watch. The time: 4:20. No wonder. SP must have been supervising as Eric, the peon, dusted the 7A classroom.

I dropped the divider in my bag, held it low and tiptoed across the corridor, hunching below the windowsills as if playing hide-and-seek. The 7B classroom was vacant. By now, I could clearly hear SP from within 7A, recounting how his scooter had broken down on Queen's Road and how 'not a single idiot' had stopped to help.

Crouching lower, I took a quick peek through the classroom entryway and saw SP and Eric near a far window, their backs turned to me, their eyes unmindful of my presence. I slithered past 7A and hid behind a pillar at the corridor's end.

This was it. One false move could ruin everything. Eric would soon finish dusting 7A. SP would lock up and they would move to 7B. Five minutes later they would reach 7C.

Under the circumstances, only two options remained:

Alerting Paunchy about SP	**Alerting SP about Paunchy**
Best for Paunchy	Worst for Paunchy
Good for Snoop today	Great for Snoop in the long run
What Stephen and Leo would have done	What my parents would have expected me to do

I took two deep breaths to calm myself.

It was too late.

Peeking from behind the pillar, I saw SP and Eric lock the 7A classroom and proceed down the corridor, past 7B, and all the way to the 7C entrance. SP only needed to take a peek to be overcome by a fire so intense he leaped across the threshold. Eric, his broom raised as if about to murder a rat, followed him.

My time was up.

So I ran ...

... down two stairways, across two corridors, past the principal's office, the bicycle stand and the Pegasus fountain, out of the school's main gate, past Canara Bank, a peanut vendor and a bhelpuri cart, and all the way to my bus stop where I collapsed onto a bench. Three middle-aged women turned to me, concerned, but I was in no position to explain my shock. The more urgent task was to gather my breath and reel off a series of shlokas: for Snoop, for Paunchy and for myself. I prayed that Snoop hadn't been forced to take his clothes off. That Paunchy hadn't been mental enough to capture Snoop in the nude. And – most of all – that nobody had seen me in the corridor – not SP, not Eric, not Paunchy, not anyone. For if news got out that I had spotted SP and still not gone back to alert Paunchy, my life at St George's was as good as finished.

Our living room was pulsing with gruff laughter, the first sign of homely mirth for two months. My father was settled in a cane chair. Two of his friends, Sridhar uncle and Murali uncle – whom he had gone to college with – lounged on the leather sofa opposite him. These moustachioed men, sideburns greying and bellies well fed, had no qualms about making fun of my father. And he too didn't mind when they joked at his expense. Sometimes they drew from him such a free-spirited laugh I wished they would visit more often. Now, over tea and samosas, with smoke swirling and their tummies jiggling, they had lightened the mood once again.

My mother was nowhere to be seen.

'Elei Karthik,' my father went, stubbing out a half-cigarette into a brass ashtray, using far more force than was necessary. 'Why so late, da? Any problem?'

'No problem, Pa,' I said, eyeing the untouched samosas. 'Just got late in school.'

My father hid the cigarette packet behind the teapot. 'I saw it was 5:30 and was thinking … Umm … anyway … there are samosas in the kitchen. You should have them with ketchup.'

There was no reason for my father to be so fidgety. My mother and I knew he enjoyed a cigarette or two when his smoker friends came over. My father knew I knew this. He also knew that I knew my mother knew this. The only person who would have objected to his smoking was now safe in heaven. Still my father was flush with guilt, hesitant to meet my gaze.

'My, my,' said Murali uncle, his face obscured by a dense cloud of smoke. 'Back so late on a Friday evening, Karthik? Who's this pretty girl you've been flirting with, man?'

'Uncle …' I blushed and turned away.

'What da, Karthik? A chap like you will have girls lining up.'

'It's an all-boys school, uncle.'

'What is there in that? Don't tell me that has stopped any of you rascals from meeting up with girls after school. Even I studied in an all-boys school, silly fellow! I know this game.'

'No time, uncle,' I said, searching for a way to wriggle out.

'Ha, no time it seems. Which class are you in now? Sixth?'

'Seventh, uncle.'

'My, my. How time flies, Karthik. I remember cradling you in my arms when you were a teeny baby. Such a round football you were back then. And you, rascal, nearly broke my glasses!'

My father smacked his right thigh and chuckled at the memory.

'So your new school is all-boys, huh? Must be a madhouse.'

'Uh umm. Very strict school, Murali,' my father said. 'Their principal … I met him … one of those no-nonsense priests. All about old-school discipline. Doesn't take things lying down.'

'Hmm,' said Sridhar uncle, stubbing out his cigarette and taking a short sip from his teacup. 'But tell me, Subbu: why would any principal want to run a school by lying down, man?'

'Ah,' said Murali uncle. 'Maybe he just can't stand it.'

'But why not just sit pretty?'

'Because,' said Murali uncle, drawing out the second syllable into a singsong, 'sitting pretty is a pain in the backside.'

My father went 'oh god' – though he himself was a pun factory.

'Karthik,' said Sridhar uncle, seeing that I was slinking away. 'What's your favourite subject in school, man?'

'They are all interesting, uncle.'

'Look at this fellow. Such a diplomatic answer. Okay, let's try another way: what does Karthik want to be when he grows up?'

Two years ago, I would have swatted this question aside with 'astronaut' but, on hearing two boys say the same at a birthday party, I was determined to shift professions. 'Pilot' had worked well until a grumpy uncle made it known that my spectacles would render me ineligible. I had briefly moved to 'oceanographer' only to be deflated by a lady who had replied: 'That sounds so boring.' One time, on a whim, I had said 'postman' but everyone – including my dear mother – looked at me as if I had blown up their life savings. 'Mathematician' sounded cool but that was usually a prompt for a real-time puzzle. Every time I said I wasn't sure – which was, in fact, the unvarnished truth – it led to more questions. 'What is this, Karthik?' they would say. 'Surely something excites you?'

Sridhar uncle waited, a hint of mischief in his eyes, ready with a witty retort, irrespective of my response. It was a look so unsettling, so cocky, that it made me want to surprise him. And I blurted out the first thing that came into my head.

'I want to be a typist.'

I might as well have splashed a bucket of cold water on his face. Sridhar uncle set his teacup aside, picked up the pack of cigarettes and, eyebrows raised, turned to my father.

'Ah,' said Murali uncle, sitting upright in the sofa.

My father cleared his throat.

'Not going out to play cricket, Karthik?'

'Going, Pa.'

Sridhar uncle latched on to the change of topic.

'Batsman or bowler, Karthik?'

'Batsman, uncle. But I bowl now and then.'

'Ah, an all-rounder. I'm telling you, India needs an all-rounder soon. Poor old Kapil. The fellow finally got his world record. Now he better retire. He has become such a joke. Can you believe it? Kapil Dev of all people has been reduced to chasing records. What a fall. Anyway, you go play. We'll chat later.'

I scurried to the kitchen and headed straight for the samosas.

On Sunday night, after saying my prayers to Lord Ganesha and Lord Hanuman, I flipped a fifty-paisa coin. Heads: Paunchy was expelled from school; tails: he was temporarily suspended. Heads: Snoop had kept his uniform on; tails: he had been bullied into posing nude. Heads: I would be better off skipping school on Monday; tails: me staying away would only make my classmates suspicious. Best of three tosses for each scenario. Actually, best of five. No, just to be sure, best of seven.

On Monday morning, I burnt my thumb ironing my shirt, burnt my eyes with bath soap and my tongue too after biting into a green chilli at breakfast. Surely the universe was plotting my downfall.

Only when I walked into 7C did the strain somewhat ease. Nobody reacted on seeing me, and there was no sign of Paunchy or Snoop. Boys stood around and spoke in soft tones – as if in mourning.

'You won't believe what happened on Friday, Karthik,' Kulla whispered.

'What?'

'Paunchy, man. He has been thrown out of school.'

I couldn't stay quiet, of course, but I couldn't say too much.

'Are you serious?'

'Unbelievable, right? No idea what happened, man.'

'Oh!'

'Just can't believe it, Karthik.'

Everyone groped for an explanation. Musu suggested that Paunchy must have been caught scribbling graphic images on the toilet walls. No, said Metric, he must have started a big fight. Or the principal must have seen him bingoing someone.

By lunch break, Leo had made substantial progress.

'Went and spoke to some peons just now, dude,' he said, agitated. 'They are saying Eric might know what happened.'

Stephen shook his head, pressing a finger to his temple.

'Eric is a proper nutcase, dude. Never believe what he says.'

'I'm going to bribe him with twenty bucks, Stephen,' said Leo. 'We need to find out what the shit happened.'

'Mad or what? Don't waste any money on that idiot.'

'Actually, you know what? Eric probably knows something,' said Metric, eyes lighting up. 'I've seen him on some days after hockey practice in the evening. He sweeps the classrooms.'

'Oh. What the fuck was Paunchy doing in the classroom?'

Metric shrugged.

'I am only telling you what I have seen, man.'

'Have you seen Eric cleaning up the classrooms, Stephen?'

'Just cool the fuck down, Leo.'

'I can't understand anything, man,' Leo screamed, pulling his hair. 'I call Paunchy's number from the public booth and his dad tells me to get lost and never call again.'

'Why the hell did you call Paunchy? Gone mad or what?'

'I wanted to find out what the fuck happened.'

'Check in the canteen. Maybe Atiq knows something.'

'I already asked, dude. Atiq has the worst memory in the whole world. Says he didn't see Paunchy on Friday evening.'

'Then ask SP.'

'What? And get my ass kicked?'

'Then shut the fuck up for now.'

Nobody asked me for my views. Stephen and Leo likely assumed I wouldn't have any idea about a matter so weighty. Eric kept his mouth shut, even when tempted with twenty rupees. And none of the boys suspected Snoop's involvement.

Riding the bus back home, reviewing how things had turned out, I thanked Lord Ganesha for having mercy. I hadn't needed to take on Paunchy, hadn't ratted him out and yet, hadn't entirely abandoned Snoop. None among SP, Eric, Paunchy or Snoop had seen me in the corridor. And neither had anyone else.

What, though, had happened on Friday evening? Paunchy had had about three minutes in the classroom with Snoop – between when I left and when SP and Eric entered. Perhaps he had asked Snoop to strip off his clothes and, when he had resisted, forced him. Maybe that's why SP had rushed into 7C in a panic. I pictured the scene: Paunchy trying to undress Snoop, fondling him, unbuckling his belt and tugging at his underwear, only for a raging SP to wrench the two apart, wrestle a shell-shocked Paunchy to the ground, hammer the living daylights out of him and haul him by the ear to the principal's office. The principal would have battered Paunchy, then summoned his parents and lambasted them.

I was unsure what to make of the suspension. Paunchy was so easy to dislike, forever looking to target someone smaller and weaker. It was he who had made my first day at St George's so unmemorable: walking up, refusing my genial handshake, diverting my attention, stuffing my dick and squashing my balls. He had laughed as I bent double, and high-fived two boys as I struggled for balance. Now he was thrown out of school and nobody would have to put up with his rubbish.

Still, I couldn't help but kick myself for an opportunity missed. If only I had taken Paunchy on, or flung something at him, or rushed him with a sharp object. If only I could have signalled my disgust with an emphatic retaliation. Maybe he would have come to his senses. At the least, I would have shown Snoop that I was no weakling.

Now Paunchy was gone.

And so was the chance to redeem myself.

16

Cher

OUR MATHEMATICS TEACHER, FATHER JAMES, contracted jaundice in the middle of February, and was out of action for the rest of the term. Leo claimed Father James had faked an illness to realize a lifelong dream: a trip to the Vatican. Stephen dismissed Leo's theory as 'classic bullshit'. Father James, in Stephen's version, had renounced his priesthood and eloped to the Nicobar islands with 'sizzling Cynthia', who until recently taught the junior school. 'Why Nicobar Islands, dude?' asked Leo, as if that was the most curious part of this humbug. 'Because,' said Stephen, pausing for emphasis, 'nobody can locate it on a map.'

There was no clarity as to Father James' replacement. Maybe our Physics teacher, Brother Joseph, would step in? Or would it be our Geography teacher, Fax, who, as some recalled, had taught Mathematics many years ago?

'Fax knows absolutely nothing about Maths,' said Mangu.

'How does it matter?' went Ammonia. 'Ultimately we have to study everything on our own. Father James, Brother Joseph, Fax – no difference. A monkey can come and teach us for all I care.'

No monkey was forthcoming. On Monday morning late in February, with Metric leading Musu in a thrilling game of pen-fight, and most of us gearing up for yet another free Mathematics period, a bright red sari burst through the 7C entrance. Cluck, clatak, cluck, clatak – a pair of black sandals marched across the mosaic and smothered the classroom chatter. A delicate puff of lavender roused us from our seats, though we had no idea who this lady was and why she was standing at the head of the class, hugging a textbook. Perhaps she was about to make an announcement about After-School Dramatics. Or hand out fliers for Art classes. Or indeed teach Mathematics – though whether she was here for one class or for the rest of the term, we weren't sure. Neither was she in any hurry to spell out her purpose. She stood upright and took her time to sweep the length and breadth of the classroom with her large, expressive Winona Ryder eyes, studying our reactions, grading each of our manners. When a lock of hair dared to slip onto her forehead and inch towards her left eye, she swiftly banished it behind her ear.

'Good mor-ning, boys,' she said with a lilt.

'Good morning, cher.'

'Ah, the famous St George's cher. Short for teacher, is it not?'

'Yes, cher.'

'But it's only used for lady teachers, right?'

'Yes, cher.'

'And why is that?'

'It's always been that way, cher.'

'Ah. I better get used to it in the next few days.'

Stephen nudged Leo.

Leo mouthed an 'ooooh'.

'So anyway, my name is Tracy Rodrigues and I have been a Maths teacher at Holy Angels Convent for the last six years. Have any of you boys heard of that school?'

Stephen blushed, Leo and Metric giggled.

'Of course you have heard of it. My girls have told me all about you rascals. I have seen boys – in St George's uniform – climbing the Holy Angels compound wall!'

More embarrassment, more giggles.

'So anyway, I have been assigned to be your Maths teacher for the rest of the term. This is only temporary. I will be getting back to Holy Angels after your finals. Okay?'

'Yes, cher.'

'Alright then. Some rules to start off.'

She stretched out her right thumb.

'During class I expect you all to listen. You can take notes if you want but even if you don't, it's fine, as long as you listen.'

Up came the index finger to join the thumb.

'When I hand out homework I expect you to complete it on time. That goes without saying, of course.'

The middle finger popped out for instruction number three.

'Now … this is important. Every day, after school, I will stay back in the staffroom for half an hour. If you have any questions, doubts, concerns, anything, come and discuss them.'

'Yes, cher.'

'I repeat: I will stay back in the staffroom for half an hour after school every day. So, it's your chance to clarify whatever doubts you have. Don't come to me a week before the finals and say, 'Ma'am, I have not understood chapters 13, 14 and 15.' That would be madness. I won't have any time to explain.'

'Yes, cher.'

'Oh yes – cher. Did I say ma'am? See, it takes time to get used to. Anyway, does anyone have any questions so far?'

No hand went up.

'Questions, questions, questions,' she went, snapping her fingers three times, a snap for each aisle in the classroom.

Not a whisper.

'Alright.'

She set her textbook on the teacher's table, picked up a chalk piece and turned to the blackboard to write:

X is less than (<) Y
Y is older than (>) Z
A is colder than or as cold as (≤) B
C is as long as or longer than (≥) D

'These are what we call inequalities, boys. They can all be written out like equations and plotted on graphs. They work just like equations, except, instead of one final answer we have a range of values for x, y, z, a, b, c and d. Understood?'

'Yes, cher,' said a perky Pocket Rocket.

'It seems only this boy has understood. Everyone else asleep?'

'No, cher,' we roared.

'Let me try again: has everyone understood?'

'Yes, cher.'

'Good. Now let's get straight into a problem.'

$$3x - 1 > 5$$

Solve for x

'Now each of you may go about this in a slightly different way – and I am okay with any approach. Here is how I would do it:

$$\begin{array}{ll} 3x - 1 & > 5 \\ \quad +1 & +1 \\ 3x & > 6 \\ \overline{3} & \overline{3} \\ x & > 2 \end{array}$$

Double-underlining the answer, she swung around, only for her sari's pallu to threaten to slip from her shoulders and embarrass her in front of a room full of boys on her very first day at St George's. The pallu, though, stood no chance; she snuffed out its challenge by whipping it back over her shoulder.

'Any questions?'

No hand went up.

'Right then,' she said and swung around. 'Note this down ...'

Unlike Father James, Ms Rodrigues didn't bother with detailed explanations. She didn't start each class by lecturing us on how we ought to behave. Her mission was to straighten out problem after problem on the blackboard, the steps indented, her line graphs scarily straight and her answers double-underlined. She didn't call for volunteers to solve problems on the blackboard, didn't group boys into teams to face off in problem-solving contests.

Four days into her stint, having just solved a problem on Laws of Exponents, she swung around, straightened her sari, fidgeted with the shoulder of her blouse and fired off a question. Her tone suggested she was expecting us to slip up, so I stopped myself from raising my hand. The over-eager Pocket Rocket took a stab. 'Good try but wrong,' she said, erasing the hopeful smile from his face. Kulla went next. 'Wrong again,' she said and triumphantly turned to the board.

Such rabid efficiency was unlike anything we had seen from Father James. Had he received two wrong answers, he would have plunged into one of his trademark sermons. How easily we were distracted. How we refused to think through our responses. How, with barely a month for the finals, we were still taking our studies lightly. He would have gone on to invoke his childhood in rural Karnataka: a home without access to electricity, suffering through water crises, walking eight miles to school and back, preparing for exams in candlelight – all to be stuck with 'a bunch of irreparable wastrels with no fire in the belly'. So commonplace were these lectures I knew most bits by heart.

'So my question was ...' Ms Rodrigues said and went on to shatter Pocket Rocket's and Kulla's responses. She finished with an emphatic tick mark next to her answer, as if to make it clear that she alone would have the final say.

So striking was this move, Stephen went through the lunch break imitating her tick mark and the dainty swivel that had followed – her left foot slightly off the ground, her sari atwirl, the pallu arcing around – before she faced us and snapped her fingers three times, calling for questions.

Leo held a hand up, thumb out.

'You think all the chicks in Holy Angels start counting with their thumbs?'

'Never seen anyone count like that,' said Stephen. 'Looks so cool.'

Stephen and Leo weren't the only ones in Ms Rodrigues' thrall. One evening I saw Musu and Metric waiting outside the ladies' staffroom, notebooks in hand, as if to get their doubts cleared. The same Musu and Metric who had likely not asked any teacher any question anytime were now dying to make an impression.

Boys stopped scanning porn magazines in Mathematics class. No paper planes flew. This wasn't because of some sudden interest in Mathematics. Oh no. This was to avoid being shamed, for when Ms Rodrigues caught you daydreaming or chitchatting or, god forbid, giggling, she singled you out and – eyes enlarged and brows raised – ensured you felt lousy. Her signature punishment: to ask a difficult question and lock eyes with the errant boy when he muddled through his reply. She would then slowly walk to his desk, stand next to him with her arms folded, watch him squirm a little more before shutting him up with a categorical 'wrong'. Insults or canings were so prosaic in comparison. Here was a routine that left a mark on the entire class.

Ms Rodrigues was the best prepared among all our teachers. It was like she rehearsed her lecture multiple times before performing for us. She was not in the least fazed by a roomful of amped-up boys and carried herself with so much grace – her starched, vivid saris oozing confidence, her nose-ring adding zing to her smile.

I had been taught by some terrific women in Sacred Valley. Kavita aunty had made such a fine impression during English classes that we cried like teething babies the day she left – to relocate to America. We created a poster for Padmini aunty, our Art teacher: 'Best Teacher Ever'. Neither would have stood a chance in St George's. Boys would have hassled them during lectures, and some nutcases would have even dared to fling chalk at them when their backs were turned. It would have been the teachers, and not the students, who would have shed tears.

Ms Rodrigues was different. She knew when to shut us up and when to let things slide, when to lighten the mood and when to get serious. It may have been a matter of course for some boys to be distracted in class, to make fun of those who took notes and to be unfazed when punished, but hardly anyone in the last two rows tested Ms Rodrigues. To be the target of her piercing glare was to fall in her estimation, to let her down. What could be more humbling than that?

'So, Karthik,' Ms Rodrigues said in the staffroom one evening, after she had walked me through a Laws of Exponents problem.

'Yes, cher.'

'I have been going through all the unit test and mid-term exam answer sheets to get an idea of where everyone stands …'

I held my breath mid-inhale.

'… and I found your mid-term paper to be a strange one.'

'Cher?'

She touched a finger to her tongue and rifled through a register.

'You got forty on fifty in the unit test in September. Right?'

'Yes, cher.'

'And … let's see … sixty-two on hundred in the mid-terms?'

'Yes, cher.'

'What do you mean, "Yes, cher"? That's a steep drop, Karthik.'

'Cher … that was my worst exam. I was really tense and …'

'And what?'

'And I wasn't able to finish the paper.'

'Oh.'

Another finger lick. She flipped through a pile of answer papers.

'Let's see … Jagdish … Joseph … Karl … Ah… Karthik … I have been trying to make sense of this paper … '

'Cher …'

'Okay, so what do we have here. First section – you maxed. Ten correct answers out of ten. Great job. Everything neat and tidy.'

'Yes, cher.'

'Then you solved two problems in the second section. Both correct. Not that neat but that's fine. The steps were spot on.'

'Yes, cher.'

'You got problem thirteen wrong. Bad mistake, that. Then you started problem fourteen … and that's it. Nothing else.'

'Cher …'

'That's a really strange paper, Karthik.'

If only she knew ...

'Cher … I was very tense …'

'Still, Karthik. A student of your calibre shouldn't be getting sixty-two in such a straightforward paper.'

'Yes, cher. I should have done much better.'

'Is there anything I need to know?'

'Cher?'

'Did anything unusual happen during the exam?'

'No, cher. Nothing like that.'

'Hmm. I find that hard to believe.'

'Just ran out of time, cher.'

'I see. So let's get to the bottom of this.'

Elbows on the table, she rested her chin on her cupped palms.

'Why do you get tense?'

'I don't know, cher. I'm always making some silly mistakes.'

'Okay … what sort of mistakes?'

'Cher, basic things. Multiplication, substitution …'

'And you make these mistakes in all subjects?'

'Mostly Maths, cher.'

'Other subjects?'

'Not that many silly mistakes, cher. I make other mistakes.'

Her face lit up, her nose-ring glinted.

'So why do you think these silly mistakes are happening?'

'It's been happening for a while, cher.'

'But what is the reason?'

'Cher …'

'Do you know or not?'

'No, cher.'

'Hmm. You are not alone here, Karthik. This is a problem many students face. I once taught a girl whose parents were putting so much pressure on her that she was always tense before exams. Especially before Maths exams, because her parents thought anything less than a hundred per cent in Maths was a failure.'

I nodded furiously.

'Yes, I know. So my advice would be: forget the final answer.'

'Cher?'

'Yes, that is the best approach. You have to stop worrying if the final answer is correct or wrong.'

'How, cher?'

'With practice. Let's start today. I've given you six problems to solve for homework, right?

'Yes, cher.'

'Here's what you must do. I want you to solve each problem without doing the last step. No final answer. Okay? Just stop at the second-last step and move on to the next question. Then do the same thing for question two. And so on. Understood?'

'Yes, cher.'

'Good. Now don't worry too much. We will sort this out before the final exams. It's all about focus and confidence, Karthik.'

'Yes, cher.'

'Hurry along. See you tomorrow.'

'Thank you, cher.'

That evening, Mathematics homework was top priority. As odd as it was to abandon each solution at the penultimate step, I was grateful to be working to a plan. Ms Rodrigues knew what was bogging me down and that 'we' – as a team – could find a way. Unlike what my father had assumed, spur-of-the moment puzzles weren't the answer. To stop putting pressure on myself I had to nail down the approach and forget the result.

'Just looking at your handwriting tells me you are still in a rush, Karthik,' Ms Rodrigues said, reviewing my homework. 'You have to slow down. When done with a problem, close your eyes, take a deep breath, drink some water. Only then go to the next question.'

'Yes, cher.'

'And sometimes it helps to read each step aloud as you are writing it. It becomes easier to spot mistakes when you listen to yourself. Read slowly, concentrating on each line.'

'Yes, cher.'

'Try that today. I'll take a look tomorrow.'

I got back home, took a quick bath, said my prayers, and pored over my homework. My father was in the middle of a hectic period at work, and returned only after nine each night; so absorbed was he in official matters he had no time for our jaunts to Paragon Books. My mother, who had recently started work at a non-profit, came home around six. Once she got her 'All okay, K?' yell out of the way, she washed her face, said her prayers, cooked, ate, cleaned up and retired for the night, ready to wake up at five o'clock to prepare breakfast and lunch. Every few days she checked if I was on track with my homework and assignments. Mostly she acted as if I was all grown up and perfectly capable of taking care of myself.

This solitude turned into a blessing. Mathematics got less threatening with each problem-set. My fingers stopped trembling in the final stages of a solution. I wasn't over-keen to verify my answers. The slower I moved – taking deep breaths after each question, reading equations aloud – the more infrequent were my slip-ups. In a week's time, Ms Rodrigues reviewed my homework with a sprightly 'Good job!' in the margin.

'Well done, Karthik. Now it's important to keep this up. Okay? I don't want you rushing with any problem anymore.'

'Yes, cher.'

'How long did you take for these ten problems?'

'About an hour and a half, cher.'

'That's totally fine, okay? You will get faster in a week or so.'

'Yes, cher.'

'Good. And button up your shirt. This makes you look sloppy.'

'Cher …'

'The second button on your shirt, Karthik.'

'It broke, cher.'

'Uh ho. What is this?'

'Sorry, cher.'

'Got into a fight?'

'No, cher. Nothing like that.'

She reached for her handbag and whipped out a safety pin. 'This will work for now,' she said, waving the pin in front of my face. 'You can stitch up the button when you get home.'

I was about to extend my hand to accept the pin, but 'Let's see now,' she said and, crouching low, held the pin between her lips, jiggled my collar, clutched the plackets and set about the fastening operation. Her sharp breaths tickled my forehead and her lavender perfume floated up my nostrils. A trickle of sweat descended from her hairline to her left brow.

Irritated with my shirt's resistance, she tugged my collar and, in one panicky instant, pulled my quivering lips perilously close to her chin. 'Uffo,' she said, and tugged my collar once more.

I didn't know where to look. Scared she would sense my jitters, I closed my eyes and prayed that this operation be over at once, that someone switch off the electric current running in my head.

'So anyway, as I was saying,' she said, preoccupied with the pinning, 'you must continue to go slow with your homework.'

A bead of sweat clung to her left brow, and I feared that the globule was about to drop into her eye and blind her.

'Karthik?'

'Cher … yes, cher.'

'What "yes, cher"?' she said, folding my collar back into position.

'Cher … I'll time myself when I do homework.'

'Not yet. Not till I tell you.'

'Yes, cher. Whatever you say.'

Safety pin in place, she swung around, tucked the end of her pallu into the waist of her sari and returned to her seat.

My breathing slowed to a steadier tempo.

'Now I had something to ask you, Karthik.'

'Cher?'

'Why do you sit in the last bench? You're not that tall.'

'No reason, cher. Just happened like that.'

'Nobody told you to sit there?'

'No, cher.'

'You went and sat there yourself?'

'Yes, cher. On the first day itself.'

'I see. That's strange. But it's very good. Those boys could do with someone like you sitting there. It will help them focus.'

How I wish that had been the case, that we were living in a parallel universe where the last-benchers were focused through the year. How differently things would have turned out then. Paunchy would still be in school. My grandfather would still be alive.

'Yes, cher. They are all working hard.'

'No. They are not working hard enough, Karthik. Which is why I plan to conduct extra classes. One hour in the evening. Three days a week for two weeks.'

'That's great, cher.'

'Yes, it's important to do what I can. The rest is up to them.'

'Can I attend these classes, cher?'

'Don't be silly. It's only for boys who have failed in the unit test or mid-term. Not for the smart ones like you. What you need to do is to keep up your progress. Solve problems 21 to 30. Okay?'

'Yes, cher.'

'Now hurry along.'

'Thank you, cher.'

Stephen, Leo and twenty others stayed back after school, three days a week, for Ms Rodrigues' extra classes. As per Stephen's reports, Leo sat in the first bench most days. His eyes followed Ms Rodrigues like a puppy's would a biscuit, and his knees wobbled when she passed by his bench. One evening, Ms Rodrigues checked Leo's homework, then tilted forward to check on Stephen's notebook that lay on the desk behind. 'Her jugs were on Leo's face, man!' Stephen said the next day, shivering with excitement. 'The highway an inch from his eyes! How the heck did you keep a straight face, Leo?'

'Stop fantasizing, dude.'

'Surely your dick was rock hard?'

'Shut your gob, man. She's just slightly younger than my mom.'

'So? You ogle at older women all the time.'

'Those are porn stars, Stephen. Not teachers!'

'Oh. So why do you keep staring at her during class?'

'Please! I'm just paying attention to her lecture.'

'Even you don't believe that, Leo.'

'It's the truth, man. Absolute truth. She is the best teacher we have and she doesn't hit us. If all our teachers were like her, I would listen in every class.'

'Ah balls.'

'Seriously, dude.'

'You are just madly in love with her, Leo. Accept that.'

'Have you gone nuts? Even you listen to everything she says.'

'No, I don't.'

'Oh stop it, Stephen. You note everything down. That's what good teachers can do. They take charge and everyone listens.'

'Just wait till someone messes with her. She'd lose her shit.'

'Nobody will dare to overstep. She is too scary.'

'She's new to George's, man. Just wait for a few days.'

'She's different, Stephen. Nothing gets to her.'

'Pepsi bet?'

'You serious?'

'Ya.'

'You are planning to piss her off?'

'Are you taking the bet or not?'

'Sure. Pepsi bet.'

'Everyone has a breaking point, Leo. Everyone.'

'Hmm. Let's see about that.'

Thursday kicked off with a frenetic buzz around the final of the inter-house chess tournament. Boys analyzed the weaknesses of the finalists and potential game strategies. News from 7A was that Father Rosario had clobbered five boys for soaking up the classroom's rear with a spitting contest – where whoever spat the farthest was declared the winner. 'What next, donkeys?' Father Rosario had rumbled. 'Are you going to hold a pissing championship?'

Mathematics was the first period after the snack break. Ms Rodrigues strode in, erased the blackboard, wrote the date in the top-right corner and turned around.

'Any questions from yesterday's homework?'

Nobody raised a hand.

'Anyone who hasn't done the homework?'

Two hands went up.

'And what are your grand excuses, boys? Yes, Manish?'

'Cher, our football match finished really late yesterday.'

'Is that even a valid excuse, Manish?'

'Cher, it was nine o'clock when I went home and ...'

'Listen now. I don't care when you went home. Just because you are part of the football team doesn't mean you can skip homework.'

'Sorry, cher.'

'This is the last time I am going to put up with this.'

'Yes, cher. Sorry, cher.'

'Did you win?'

'Yes, cher. 2-1.'

'You have till 4:30 this evening. I'll be in the staffroom.'

'Yes, cher.'

'Now sit down. Yes, Stephen. What is your grand excuse? You didn't have a football match, did you?'

'No, cher.'

'So?'

'I didn't do the homework, cher.'

'That is the obvious bit, Einstein. The question is: why?'

'Forgot, cher.'

She shivered her head and widened her eyes.

'Cher … I forgot.'

She walked up to our bench, arms folded over her chest, the sandals' clickety-clacks slowing to a click … click … click. Between the clicks, an ominous silence.

'My dear Stephen. Every single boy in this classroom knows there is Maths homework every day of the week. Care to explain how you forgot?'

'Sorry, cher, but …'

'Continue. Yes, I'm waiting.'

'Just forgot, cher. Happens.'

Leo's face crumpled up. Metric raised his palms to his forehead. I moved away, distancing myself from Stephen. Ms Rodrigues tugged Stephen's right ear until his head tilted ninety degrees, then smacked him flush across his right cheek.

Phataak.

'Happens! Is that what you said? Happens?'

'Cher …'

'I stay back after school to help you boys get ready for the finals. I go home late three days a week. And this is what I get?'

'Cher … sorry.'

'Oh you sure will be sorry, mister. I go home late to my girls. I stay up to correct your extra assignments. Because I'm hoping you fools can improve. Because I don't want you to fail. And those extra classes … nobody pays me for staying back on three days. I do them because it is good for *you*. And what do I get in return? "Happens". Are you serious, Stephen? "Happens"?'

'Cher …'

'Do you even understand how important this final exam is?

'Yes, cher.'

'If you fail, you will be thrown out of school.'

'Yes, cher.'

'Now here is what is going to happen, Stephen. By 4:30 this evening, you will do the homework twice. You heard me? Twice.'

'Yes, cher.'

'And you will submit it in the staffroom.'

'Yes, cher.'

'In case it "happens" that you forget, don't enter my class ever again. Stay away.'

'Sorry, cher.'

'Gosh, such a massive waste of time. Okay boys, note down this problem. The heights of twelve students in a class are ...'

Stephen sat down, shell-shocked.

Leo turned around, aghast.

On the 25th of March, the last day of the academic year, our principal quoted Mahatma Gandhi and Matthew Arnold during the morning assembly. 'As Arnold said: life is not a having and a getting, but a being and a becoming.'

He went on to:

- remind us to stay away from all distractions in the next week,
- list the summer camps we could sign up for, and
- hand cash bonuses to the school's twenty-five peons, men who, he said, 'perform their tasks with utmost dedication'.

'Look at Eric,' said Stephen. 'Acting like he's won an Oscar.'

'Bastard,' hissed Leo. 'Dead sure that Eric knows why Paunchy was thrown out.'

'He probably wasn't there that evening, Leo.'

'Then why the fuck does he keep avoiding me, Stephen?'

'He must be sick and tired of your face.'

'I won't stop until I find out. I swear, I won't leave him alone.'

'You are wasting your time, dude.'

'I don't care, man. Someone needs to break his teeth.'

Whenever they analyzed Paunchy's expulsion, I was unsure how to behave. I stayed engaged but said nothing. Usually I nodded along, as if seeing both sides.

Ms Rodrigues went through her final Mathematics class by solving problems on Probability. She announced she would be in the staffroom all of next week in case we needed to clarify anything. 'If you have questions, come and meet me. Okay?'

'Yes, cher.'

'Do any of you have any questions now?'

Ammonia raised his hand.

'Go ahead.'

'Not a question, cher.'

'Okay?'

'Cher … on behalf of everyone … just want to thank you.'

'Oh! How touching. And a big thank you from my side too. I can now tell my girls at Holy Angels all about you rascals.'

Riotous laughter ripped around the room.

'Now one final thing,' she said and handed out our feedback forms. 'Be honest with your appraisals, boys. This is your chance to grade my performance. And remember: the feedback is anonymous. Don't go and write your names in there.'

I didn't read each line of the form, just filled in five on five for each question. Leo did the same. As did Stephen. And so perhaps did everyone else.

The last part of the form said: 'Additional comments/feedback.'

Stephen asked what I was going to write in there.

'It's optional, man.'

'I know. I think I'm going to fill in something.'

'What are you going to write?'

'You know any good poem?'

'A poem!'

'Why are you acting as if a bee stung your bum? Ya, a poem.'

'No way, Stephen. You can't fill a poem in there.'

'Why? I can fill in anything I want.'

'You'll be in trouble, dude.'

'You're such a waste of space, Karthik. Cram your ass off day and night and can't think of a single poem when you need to.'

'I know many poems, dude, but this is just …'

'Stephen. Karthik. Stop yakking now. Done with the forms?'

'Yes, cher.'

'Then come on, hand them over. No need to chatter away.'

'Sorry, cher.'

Ms Rodrigues wished us the best for our finals and, hugging the textbook and appraisal forms, marched towards the exit.

Stephen left the classroom to drink some water.

Leo turned around and tapped my desk.

'Karthik, listen now.'

'What?'

'Paunchy is leaving for New Zealand next week.'

'What?'

'Ya. His dad got a job there.'

'Whoa. So this is a permanent move?'

'Yup. It's great for him. The schools here won't take him anyway.'

'Good for him. It will be a fresh start.'

'Imagine, dude, New Zealand. Such a beautiful place.'

'Ya. Maybe he'll become a sheep farmer.'

Leo giggled, his body shaking.

'Or a medium-pace bowler. Dibbly-dobbly.'

'When does he leave, Leo?'

'That is what I was going to tell you, Karthik. They are leaving on Wednesday evening. I was telling Stephen that we should meet him before that. Anyway next week is fully study holidays. So maybe we'll see him on Monday or Tuesday.'

'Umm.'

'You'll come, no?'

'No way, Leo. I can't leave the house next week.'

'Dude, do you have any idea how far New Zealand is? You'll never see Paunchy after this. Just come and say bye.'

'No man. My parents won't allow me.'

'Tell them you're coming to school. For some Maths doubts.'

'Oh please.'

'You're such a frightened fool, Karthik.'

'I can't come, man.'

'Think about it.'

'No. I can't.'

'Jesus Christ.'

'Just wish Paunchy all the best from my side.'

'Oh fuck off, Karthik. If you want to wish him, come with us.'

'Okay, don't wish him.'

'You're such a mugpot, dude.'

'Okay. Whatever.'

17

Finals

A LITTLE AFTER SIX o'clock on Friday evening, two days before my finals, my father returned from work with a bottle of whisky and a box of sweets. I waited to hear the reason. A promotion? A raise? He set the goodies on the dining table and disappeared into the bedroom. Changed into a veshti and banian, he washed his face, lit a lamp in the puja room and chanted prayers. I had half a mind to open the box and gobble a sweet, but what if it was actually a gift for someone else?

'Karthik,' my father called out, a good half hour later.

'Pa?'

'Where did Tendulkar score his first test hundred?'

Something told me this was a trick question.

'You know or you don't know, Karthik?'

'Old Trafford. Against England. 1990.'

'Correct. Old Trafford is in which city?'

'Pa?'

'Are your ears working fine? Where is Old Trafford, Karthik?'

'Manchester, Pa.'

'Correct. So what if you can actually visit Manchester?'

'Pa?'

'There is good news from work, Karthik. I've been offered an overseas assignment. One year in Manchester. Starting in May.'

'One year?'

'Yes, but what is there in that? One year will fly by.'

'Umm.'

'And you know the best part? You and Amma can visit during your holidays. Our office is ten minutes from the cricket ground. Imagine! We can watch a match there.'

'Umm.'

'What umm gumm?'

'Super, Pa.'

'Is it not?'

'Yes, Pa.'

'Then why are you not excited?'

'I am, Pa. Very good news.'

'Here, take a sweet.'

'I'll take it later, Pa.'

'No later vater. Take one now.'

'Okay, Pa.'

The next few hours whooshed by. My mother dusted suitcases and hatched plans to prepare industrial quantities of pickles and masalas. She created a to-do list and stuck it to the fridge with a magnet.

1 Buy mini rice cooker
2 Dry clean sweaters, mufflers, scarves
3 Organize first aid kit
4 Buy 1 extra coffee filter

My father called his relatives to relay the news. He urged Savitri athai and Raju athimber to come to England and 'go sightseeing all over Europe'. Mr Chacko stopped by to pick up a spare key to their house. On hearing the news, he poured himself two fingers of whisky and recounted his trip to England four years ago. 'It was warm, warm, warm … then suddenly one day it would get all cold. Fully unpredictable, I tell you. But you know what? I used to listen to the BBC and they mostly got the forecasts right. Amazing Met department. And oh, everyone was going crazy about the World Cup. Football, football, football. Nothing else mattered.'

If only I could have been as upbeat as Mr Chacko, his laughter getting louder and cheerier with each sip. It was hard enough to come to grips with life without my grandfather. Now my father was going to be away for a full year. No one to play chess with, no one to accompany me to Paragon bookstore, no one to read newspaper headlines aloud. Who was going to introduce me to puzzles like the Monty Hall Problem? Or the Barber's Paradox?

I listed the upsides to his absence. There would be no headmasterly presence at home. I could watch as much cricket as I wished. I could read my comic books without anyone accusing me of wasting time. My mother was the least of my worries; an earnest apology was all it took to soften her down.

The weekend was full of distractions. My final exams ought to have been my number one priority but it was hard to overlook the panic over Leo and Stephen sending off Paunchy – what had he said? what had they inferred? – and a lingering worry about my father's overseas assignment. I was thankful that Paunchy was going far away, relieved I would perhaps never see him again, but I was conflicted about my father's trip, worried we would drift apart.

Monday morning arrived bright and cheerful, showing no regard for the anxiety that was ready to swallow me up. Standing in front of the life-size mirror, fretting over what to expect from Leo and Stephen, I examined a pimple on the tip of my nose. Chiku had said he drove these away by dabbing a cotton swab soaked in mouthwash, so I did the same and waited for the pimple to collapse. The stubborn zit was going nowhere. Another dab, still no luck: a clear sign that I was in for a rough day. The next five minutes, I searched for a lone black sock, which had somehow sneaked in among my mother's lingerie. Ten more minutes disappeared after I spilled a cup of hot Bournvita on myself and frantically cleaned the mess on the floor, then changed into a new pair of trousers before anyone noticed.

'Absolutely ridiculous,' my father said, shaking his head, but thankfully he was referring to a headline in the newspaper.

The signs were ominous when I missed the 8:05 bus. And by the time I reached school, the English Language exam was already underway.

'What is wrong with you, Karthik?' Father Rosario hollered, hurtling towards me from the head of the exam hall.

'Sorry, Father.'

'Care to explain this delay?'

'Father … there was an accident near Vellara Junction and …'

'Lies. Blatant lies.'

'Father …'

'Every single one of these boys has made it to the exam on time. And you are making up some grand story about an accident.'

'Father … I have never been late before and …'

'Stop it now.'

'Sorry Father.'

'I didn't expect this from you, Karthik. Not only do you come late, you have the temerity to lie to my face. This is appalling!'

'Sorry, Father.'

'I had high hopes for you, young man. I thought you would go far. But you are slipping at an alarming rate.'

'Sorry, Father.'

'Hurry up. You have already lost close to ten minutes.'

I made my way to my seat.

'Accident, it seems,' Mangu chuckled as I passed.

Baab covered his mouth to conceal a titter.

Leo and Stephen, though, paid me no heed, busy as they were filling in their answer papers. I asked Lord Ganesha if I needed to be worried. He commanded that I get on with the exam. I asked why He had made me miss my bus even though I had prayed for ten minutes this morning. There is a reason for everything, He assured me, but this was not the time for that analysis. Had He delayed me so that I would avoid Leo and Stephen before the exam? Lord Ganesha threw me a cold stare and pointed to the question paper in front of me.

Preoccupied with quizzing Lord Ganesha, I hurtled through the grammar section, wrote an angry letter to the local municipal council about the stray dog menace in our neighbourhood and knocked off three mid-size reading comprehensions – the last of which imagined a future where children would be taught exclusively by robots: a world where Father Rosario would lose his job, and where Musu would be suspended – maybe tasered – for peeking into Bugs' answers.

'Speedy Gonzales! There's still twenty minutes left, Karthik.'

'I'm done, Father.'

'Review your answers, young man. No point leaving so early.'

'Yes, Father.'

'But I must say: good work. I thought you'll run out of time.'

'Thanks, Father.'

Father Rosario tapped me on the head. I thanked Lord Ganesha for helping me make a resounding comeback.

During the break after the exam, I ran into Leo near the toilets.

'Hey?'

He let out a feeble smile while continuing to walk past.

'How did you do, Leo?'

'Okay, man.'

'Good stuff. All the best for the next one.'

'Thanks,' he said and turned away.

'Hey Leo … you guys met Paunchy?'

'Ya.'

'How is he doing?'

'Fine.'

'Must be really excited about New Zealand, no?'

'Ya,' he said, looking over me, refusing to make eye contact.

'Awesome. It will be perfect for him. Fresh start.'

'Ya.'

'Everything okay, Leo?'

Another 'ya' before he spun around and walked off.

Neither Leo nor Stephen asked for my notes. They didn't seek out important questions. As we walked into the exam hall, Stephen gave me a hesitant wave and turned away. No 'best of luck' even. Something was amiss but I couldn't work it out. If they were indeed pissed off, why hadn't they put me in my place yet? And if they didn't want to confront me in public, why had they not taken me to the volleyball court to administer a thrashing? A part of me took it that I was overthinking this. Given how crucial these exams were for both Stephen and Leo, they were obviously nervous. Especially with Mr Mohanraj taking it upon himself to ride his motorcycle to school and pick Stephen up after the English Literature paper.

Next morning, I sat with Snoop and brushed up on important definitions and formulae. I briefly considered telling him that Leo and Stephen had met with Paunchy but it felt cruel to spring this on him at this time. He had not said a word about that evening – even when we had been by ourselves, even when the opportunity presented. Now he was gearing up for the Physics exam, consulting his notes and revising his mnemonics.

'King Henry died by drinking chocolate milk,' he announced, and chortled on seeing my blank stare. 'It's a handy little trick, Karthik. Easy way to remember: kilo, hecto, deca, base, deci, centi, milli.' Three hours later, preparing for Biology, he introduced me to: 'Dumb kids prefer channa over fried green spinach.' Again, I was intrigued. 'Oh come on, man. Domain, kingdom, phylum, class, order, family, genus, species.'

The question papers turned out to be uncomplicated. I strolled through Physics and Biology; had little trouble with Kannada, Chemistry and Moral Science; and was relieved to be done with History & Civics and Geography. My memory didn't play tricks in the mornings and recalled definitions and diagrams accurately in the heat of the exam. Panic, for the most part, stayed away.

Mathematics, the last exam, was on Friday morning.

'All prepared, Karthik?'

'Yes, Pa.'

'Good. Stay calm. It's going to be fine.'

'Okay, Pa.'

'Have you prayed to Lord Ganesha?'

'Yes, Pa.'

'Good. Now listen.'

'Pa?'

Surely he was setting up for an impromptu quiz?

'When you are writing the exam, simply try and do the best you can. Okay? The final marks – we can worry about that later.'

I drew a deep breath.

'See … what I am saying is … sometimes we think too much about the result, Karthik. Take my case as an example. All these years I kept hoping for something to change at work. I worked hard, tried to keep my bosses happy, tried to make new connections in the office … but nothing much happened. Then, last year – around the time when Thatha had his first heart attack actually – I stopped worrying about promotions, pay hikes, overseas trips and what not and just put my mind to doing my best. See what happened? Just like that the overseas assignment has come.'

'Yes, Pa.'

'So what's the lesson here?'

'Pa?'

'We must only worry about doing our best work. The results will automatically follow. The Gita says the same thing, does it not?'

'Yes, Pa.'

'Your breakfast is getting cold, K,' my mother wailed.

'Just thought I'll tell you that, Karthik. Time to get going now.'

'Yes, Pa.'

'Oh. It's almost 7:45.'

'Yes, Pa. I'll be ready soon.'

I reached school at 8:40, twenty minutes before my exam. Enough time for a routine trip to the toilets.

Here's what they did:

- Pounced from behind,
- Socked my back,
- Dragged me into an enclosed lavatory,
- Latched the door,
- Grabbed my feet, and
- Held me upside down over the latrine.

Poleaxed.

Two fifty-paisa coins escaped my pockets and scampered around the wet toilet floor. My face dangled inches from the bowl, and my eyes zoomed in on gooey crap floating in the dark liquid. A godawful stench invaded my nostrils even as Leo set me straight with a mighty bingo, and then another. With fifteen minutes to go for the year's last exam, I was certain I was about to die.

Stephen thumped my back with his leather shoes. I thought of my parents, thought of Ms Rodrigues, wishing I could see them one last time. I thought of my favourite things: my mother's crisp dosas; the scent of rain on the parched earth; Banganapalli mangoes; the fountains at Bugle Rock Park; the view from atop Utility Building. I thought of my grandfather and was glad we would be reunited soon.

'Why the fuck did you lie, bastard?'

'I didn't, Leo … I didn't.'

'You said you didn't stay back the day Paunchy got caught.'

'I didn't … I swear … I didn't.'

'Fuck off. Paunchy told us everything.'

'I left, man. I left … I left before anything happened.'

'Why didn't you tell us that you were there?'

'I left. I promise. I left before …'

Stephen told Leo to 'shut the fuck up'. He then spoke, softly, decisively, his tone so steady and menacing that my teeth chattered.

'Stop acting like someone cut off your dick, Karthik.'

'I left, man. I swear to god, I left.'

'We know you left, idiot. Stop this broken tape!'

'I left before anything happened!'

'Okay, you left. Okay? I get it. But you know what? I can't believe you didn't see SP and Eric on your way out.'

More sobs, more wails.

'SP was in 7C one minute after you left, Karthik. Surely you saw them in 7A or 7B.'

'I don't know, man.'

'Did you or did you not see SP and Eric on your way out?'

'I left, I left.'

'You fucking sneaked to SP about Paunchy, didn't you?'

'No! I swear to god. I didn't.'

Stephen cuffed my forehead.

'Now cut this bullshit, asshole. Did you and Chhakka set Paunchy up?'

No words were forthcoming. Just loud, incoherent noises.

'Are you saying Paunchy lied to us?'

'I promise I left. God promise.'

'That's all you've been saying all this while, fucker.'

'I swear. I don't know …'

An electric bell went off, five minutes before the exam, signalling it was time to enter the hall.

Leo and Stephen led me to the granite basin outside the lavatory.

'Sorry … very sorry. I swear to god …'

'Stop this drama, Karthik,' Stephen said, teeth crunched.

I shut my eyes, exhausted.

'So now … how do you plan to make up for this shit?'

I didn't understand.

'Here's what's going to happen, Karthik,' Stephen said, massaging my shoulders.

'We know you get a hard on when you do Maths problems. So today you can answer both our papers.'

'What?'

'Answer Leo's paper first. Then do mine.'

'You want me to solve both your answer papers?'

'You forgot your brains at home or what?'

'How will I be …'

'Shut up. Let me repeat this for you one last time. You are going to answer both our papers today, Karthik. Both Leo's and mine.'

'I won't have time for my own paper, man.'

Stephen unloosened a stinging slap.

'Who cares about your paper, you fucking dick?'

'But …'

'Shut your bloody mouth.'

'I'll surely fail.'

Leo tugged my shirt so hard a button ripped off.

'Listen, bastard. You keep yakking like this and we'll lock you up here. You'll miss the exam. And when we tell everyone what a sneaky rat you are they'll finish you off.'

'Please man. Please … please …'

'You are going to write our papers or not?'

'Okay, okay, okay …'

'Just say: yes or no?'

'I'll d-d-do it. I'll do it.'

He shoved me against the basin.

The final bell went off. The exam was to begin in a minute.

Stephen and Leo picked up their bags and rushed off.

The exam hall's walls were lined with ageing Biblical prints. St Ignatius of Loyola and Immaculate Heart of Mary watched me suspiciously.

'Ad majorem, Dei gloriam,' said a banner engraving on the front wall, the lettered gilt in need of a gentle but firm polish. From the ceiling hung a giant chandelier, its safety guaranteed by the benediction of the Jesus figurine on the wooden cross on the back wall. The chandelier would not fall, the exam would not be cancelled, these things simply did not happen when I wanted them to.

A sense of feverishness hovered in the air, what with this being the last exam of the year. The medley of exchanges fused into one by the time they reached my ears. 'Off to Coorg this evening,' blended with 'the summer cricket camp is starting in …' Someone's request for an extra pen was drowned out by someone else's demand for a treat in the canteen. 'Jurassic Park releasing …' 'I'm going to Bombay …' 'Can't remember the damn proof …' 'She said that's not important, man…' 'Pie r square h …' 'Fucking hell, screwed big time.'

An array of folding desks awaited us, each labelled with a roll number. Stephen had settled into his seat, at a diagonal, behind mine. Leo sat to my left, and stretched out an arm to make sure he was at the perfect distance to exchange answer papers.

Ms Rodrigues handed out question papers. Her starched white sari was patterned with elephants, and her vermillion-red blouse patched with sweat from her armpits.

'Nothing for the first twenty minutes, okay?' hissed Leo. 'After that I'll exchange our papers and you can fill in my answers.'

'So I can work on my own paper for the first twenty minutes?'

'Do what you want, man. Who cares?'

This I hadn't expected: a chance to gather myself, to steady my breathing.

'Understood, Karthik?'

'How many questions should I answer for you?'

'Stop asking bullshit questions, man. Just make sure I pass.'

'Okay.'

'All the best, boys. I can see you are all excited about the summer holidays but let's not get ahead of ourselves. Okay?'

'Is everything clear, Karthik?'

'Mouth shut, Leo.'

'Sorry, cher.'

'Slow and steady, Karthik.'

'Yes, cher. Thank you, cher.'

'All the best, Stephen. Ready for the exam?'

Ms Rodrigues tapped his head with a pile of question papers.

'Always ready, cher.'

She blushed, hurrying along, a puff of vanilla in her wake.

I scanned the paper, assessing how best to utilize the two hours. It was critical I got through at least four questions in the first twenty minutes. Then I could bolt through Leo's and Stephen's papers in an hour, which would then leave me with forty minutes to ensure I didn't fail. This was going to be a furious battle against time. One tiny slip, and all three of us could sink. Worse: I could be expelled for cheating.

'Stay calm, boys. Always remember: haste makes waste.'

My eyes were on the first question:

> Anil and Jackie leave A and B towards B and A respectively and travel the same route. After they meet, Anil takes 5 hours to reach his destination while Jackie takes 8 hours. If Anil's speed is 48 km/hr, what is Jackie's speed?

I dashed through the steps even as my mind tried to piece together all that had happened over the last half an hour. Buoyed by my father's pep talk, I had walked into school aiming for a perfect score in Mathematics. I was determined to give him an ideal parting gift. Now I was on the brink of pouring kerosene over my future and setting it afire.

Three questions in, my bladder pulsed. My thighs pressed against each other. A bead of sweat trickled down my neck. The ambush at the lavatory had distracted me from my original purpose: to relieve myself. Now the onrush was unmanageable.

'Need to piss,' I whispered, hoping Leo would hear me.

'What?'

'I need to piss urgently.'

'Stop these stunts, fucker.'

'You guys didn't let me.'

'Shut upppp.'

'Want me to piss in my pants?'

'Jesus Christ.'

'I'm going now.'

'Try anything funny and I swear you're dead meat.'

I raised my hand.

'What is it, Karthik? All okay?'

'Cher … I need to go to the toilet.'

'Are you serious? Why didn't you to go before you came in?'

'Sorry, cher.'

'We're just fifteen minutes in, Karthik. What is this nonsense?'

'Cher …'

'Gosh. Run along. Such a criminal waste of time.'

'Sorry, cher.'

The toilets were deserted, wrapped in an eerie peace. Gurgling water magnified the quiet. Three crows sat atop partitioning walls and squawked with delight, mocking me for using a toilet when they could relieve themselves as and when they pleased – whether seated on a branch or a perch or gliding across the skies, aiming for a car top or a baldpate and cawing gaily at the sight of their ruin.

The piss stench taunted my nostrils, an odour I could have done without while fumbling with my zipper. So tortured was my bladder that it took a couple of seconds for the jet to surge forth. What a relief! However brief.

If only I knew how my bladder stayed so calm when the rest of me was falling apart. Three months ago, when stuck in a traffic jam, I had writhed in the passenger seat, certain I would wet my pants. 'Don't think about it, Karthik,' my father said. 'Add up the numbers that you see on number plates.' I had sat through a football final at

Sacred Valley, unwilling to leave for the toilets lest I miss a goal. My bladder had made me proud each time, calling forth a steadfastness that was buried deep within.

Bladder emptied, balance regained, my mind was on overdrive.

Option 1: I could riddle Stephen and Leo's papers with mistake after mistake, and ensure they both failed. Leo would have to repeat the year and Stephen would be thrown out of school. Their fate was in my hands. And I could teach them a lesson.

Option 2: I could tell Ms Rodrigues that I had a stomach upset and request for a re-exam. She would balk at first but then understand. The principal would take more convincing but I could contort my face, emit moans and maybe hold my stomach and retch. That would grant me a lifeline. Stephen and Leo would mostly fail again.

The first option was dangerous. The second was cowardly. Either way nothing was going to save me from the inevitable pummelling from Stephen and Leo. Whatever happened in this exam, my reputation at St George's was headed to the gutter.

I could run up to the chapel and ask the lord to help. But that would only eat up more time. So I sat on a ledge and prayed, first to Jesus, then to Lord Ganesha. I promised to give up fried lady's finger for six months, promised to stay away from the TV through the holidays. I would circle His shrine a hundred and eight times every Sunday, and pray for twenty minutes each morning and evening. I would never cheat in an exam, never utter a swear and never lie to my parents. I would never sleep through an alarm. And I would never, ever pleasure myself.

It was now 9:25.

The longer I was outside, the greater the chance of failure. It was up to the gods to guide me now. Passing the Pegasus fountain, I saw that the water was turned off. Was this a message from above? A squirrel rushed up a tree trunk, stopped halfway to its destination and eyed me upside down, like a swimmer ready to plunge into a backstroke. How was I to interpret this sign?

I re-entered the hall to find Ms Rodrigues frothing with rage.

'What in god's name were you thinking, Leo?'

'Cher ...'

'Do you even understand what you have done?'

'Cher, my answer sheet fell down and ...'

Smack: her right hand against his left cheek.

'Cher ...'

'Not only do you try to cheat, you come up with big, fat lies.'

'Cher ...'

She organized his blank answer papers, folded the sheets across the vertical, folded them across the horizontal, and ripped them. Once, then twice, the sharp creaks silencing the whispers.

'Cher ...'

'Your parents work hard. They send you to school. They hope you can make something of yourself. And what do they get in return? A flagrant cheat and a shameless liar.'

'Cher, I ...'

'Shut up, Leo. Shut your mouth. You know your problem? You think you can get away with anything. With absolutely anything. You think you're smart enough to bypass rules. But that's just nonsense. Because if you were smart enough, you won't be getting caught. You won't be standing here, begging.'

'Cher, what I'm saying is ...'

'I don't care what you're saying, Leo. Okay? There is a section in the school prospectus titled 'Misconduct'. You have obviously not read it. But I sure have. And it clearly says that in cases like this, my job is to report you to the principal.'

'Cher, cher ... please ...'

'Pack your bag and go to the front of the hall.'

'Cher ...'

'I said: pack your bag and go to the front of the hall now!'

Ms Rodrigues' waspish stare found me.

'Get back to your seat, Karthik, before someone else steals your answer paper.'

That's when I understood.

Leo had been busted exchanging papers. Rather than wait for me to get back, he had tried his luck when I was away. Madcap!

'All right, boys. Enough mumblings. Get back to your papers.'

I turned around to the row behind me, where Stephen looked like he had just spotted a ghost. Never had I seen him so rattled.

'Half an hour up, boys. Stay focused now. And don't try anything silly. You don't want to be thrown out, do you?'

Ms Rodrigues lugged her chair to the back of the hall, set it about five feet behind the last row and sat down. She made a show of crossing her legs and folded her arms, resolute.

'The best way to watch over you rascals is from behind your backs. Now let's see how many of you try to act funny.'

Stephen must have swivelled around.

'Turn back now, Stephen. Anyone who moves his head this way and that will immediately join Leo at the front of the hall.'

I turned to get a quick peek at Stephen.

'Which part of that instruction didn't you understand, Karthik?'

'Sorry, cher.'

'Less than an hour and a half left, boys. Make the most of it.'

A surge of electricity galvanized my senses. Just like that, the threats had vanished.

Leo stood at the head of the hall, hands behind his back, head bowed. A panicky Stephen was in Ms Rodrigues' crosshairs. Somehow, miraculously, the game had transformed.

Now there was nothing to hold me back. I was Diego Maradona at the Azteca Stadium, weaving past defender after defender, zigging and zagging along a delicate parabola, directing the ball as if it were stuck to his left boot, deceiving the goalkeeper with a delicate weave, tapping in the goal and punching his fist mid-leap. That much time had opened up in front of me. And so much freedom too. For I didn't have to mimic Stephen or Leo's handwriting, didn't have to write fours and sevens the way they did, didn't have to use a ballpoint. I could go cursive. Or keep my lettering straight. I could spend all eighty minutes writing in capital letters. With my left hand. And eyes closed. There was absolutely no reason to fret.

The question paper was all that mattered. I whizzed past a Simple Interest problem and dusted off a Profit-and-Loss calculation in four steps. The Compound Interest question offered no resistance. And the algebraic equations collapsed, like a line of dominos, as per my command. I attacked each question with a confidence I had rarely felt and each time I underlined an answer, I instinctively knew I was right.

At the end of question seventeen I heard the unmistakable sound of Stephen fidgeting. He must have been messing around with his divider or unscrewing and screwing his ballpoint pen. Knowing him, he would have bitten all his nails and spat out the fragments. Had Ms Rodrigues not been watching us from behind, I could have confirmed that he was indeed readying for failure.

Our principal, Father Menezes, marched into the hall, a chunky key-bunch jangling under his cassock with each assured stride.

He had a quick chat with Ms Rodrigues.

Then he turned to Leo.

'I heard you had some explanation for this stupidity?'

'Father, my answer sheet fell down and ...'

'Yes, I have heard that nonsense. Anything else?'

'Father, it was a mistake and ...'

'If it was a mistake, it sure was a costly one, young man.'

'Sorry Father but what I'm saying is ...'

'I perfectly understand what you are saying, Leo Pinto. And it's clear as crystal that you are lying through your teeth.'

'Father but ...'

'I've heard enough now. Follow me to my office.'

'Please Father ...'

'Enough. Follow me.'

Leo bowed his head and dragged his feet. His lips were pursed, his back in a stoop, his entire being covered in a film of defeat. Once he crossed the threshold he swung around. He first turned to Stephen, then to me – a fraction of a second when he betrayed both a softness and a burning rage.

And then he was gone.

'Final fifteen minutes, boys,' said Ms Rodrigues as she lugged her chair to the front of the hall. 'Time to get a move on.'

At last, there was no one breathing down Stephen's neck.

'Every dog has its day, Karthik.'

'I didn't do anything, okay?'

'Oh sure. Such an innocent child.'

'I had gone to piss, dude.'

'Screw that shit now. Just tell me: did you see SP before Paunchy got caught?'

'I already told you, man.'

'Just answer the fucking question, Karthik.'

'I left before anything happened.'

'Don't forget to review your answers, boys. And make sure to write your name and roll number in every answer sheet. They won't be corrected otherwise. It's very important to ...'

'So you didn't see SP that evening?'

'Shhh.'

'Just say yes or no, Karthik.'

Here was my big chance to come clean with the truth. 'To man up,' as Chiku loved to say. To bid Stephen an honest goodbye.

'Did you see SP or not?'

Perhaps Stephen would understand that my actions that evening were born out of a severe panic. Perhaps he would respect my directness and sympathize. Perhaps he would even forgive me.

'Answer the fucking question, Karthik!'

I turned around and looked him in the eye.

'Yes or no? Tell me now!'

'I didn't see him, Stephen.'

'You're absolutely sure?'

'I didn't see him.'

'Huh.'

It was time to start on question eighteen. But not before I noticed a pathetic smile break out on Stephen's face: a smile that conveyed either a loss of respect for me or a grudging admiration – for sticking to my story in spite of the threats and beatings. Surely he had expected me to crack. But here I was, coolly lying to his face.

He packed his geometry box and tossed it into his bag. Folding his answer sheets, he adjusted his hair, walked to the front of the hall and handed his papers to Ms Rodrigues. Watching him head for the exit, one might have assumed he had aced the exam. He crossed the threshold and made for the stairs, his black mop melting into the dark corridor.

I thought – and hoped – he would turn around.

But Stephen would not look back.

My classmates drained out of the hall. Afraid that Stephen and Leo would lie in wait, ready to gash my face with a steel divider, I made sure I was the last to leave. Downstairs, I peeked left and right, and left and right again, before gathering the courage to slip into the quadrangle.

Four boys played hand tennis in the middle of the driveway, forcing scooterists to swerve past them. A gardener tending to the nursery sneezed, then shouted at a peon for sweeping up dust.

I was about to sprint to my bus stop when Kulla approached.

'Leo is finished, man. The princi has called his parents.'

'Oh damn.'

'Only a moron will try and cheat in the finals, dude.'

'You saw Stephen?'

'He left. Rode off like a maniac.'

'You sure?'

'Hundred per cent. He nearly ran into a dog on his way out.'

'Oh.'

'Got to go now, Karthik. Happy holidays.'

'Same to you, man. See you on the day of the results.'

'Don't remind me of that now! Have fun.'

I entered the main corridor and passed the principal's office, its door half open, no sign of anyone inside. Further along, the field was swamped with boys playing cricket, football and hand tennis. A few sat under a giant peepul and snacked on burgers, samosas, apple cakes and Chocobars. A trio sprayed Pepsis on each other, ringing in the summer holidays.

Aakash, Tarun, and Nitin lounged on the pavilion steps.

'You guys got 20 for question six?'

'Ya. That was similar to the question in the additional problem-set. Cher had said that was important?'

'Oh ya. I knew I had seen that type of question somewhere.'

'Hey Karthik. How did you do, man?'

'Not too bad, I guess.'

'You got 20 for question six?'

'Ya. Pretty sure I got 20.'

'Question seven … I got 1600.'

'Perfect. Did you use a graph? I just solved it with the formula.'

'Me too. The graph would have taken time.'

'No, dude. The graph was easier. It took me two minutes.'

'Sure?'

'I'll solve it right now and show you.'

'Oh forget it, man. We all got 1600. That's all that matters.'

Barring the last question – for which I ran out of time – I had smashed the exam. Right royal smoked it. Nineteen correct answers. Ninety-five out of hundred. By far my best to date.

'I got two wrong, man,' said Aakash. 'Maybe I'll get some part-marks in each. So ninety-two or ninety-three. Damn. Should have maxed this.'

'Three wrong for me,' said Tarun. 'I'll get around eight-five.'

'Ya, I too got three wrong,' said Nitin. 'You, Karthik?'

'I didn't count, man. Not sure.'

'Stop woaling. You maxed it or what?'

'No, man. I'll get eighty or eight-five at best.'

'Anyway, I need to head out now,' said Aakash. 'Off to Bombay tomorrow. My cousin is going to teach me calculus. It's supposed to be really interesting.'

'Wow, that's awesome.'

'I'm also leaving, man,' said Tarun. 'Hey Karthik, do you want this samosa? I bought two and now I'm full.'

'Ya, sure. Thanks. I'm damn hungry.'

'Sure. Enjoy.'

I raised my hand to my mouth just as a kite swooped, snatched the entire samosa and delicately perched itself on the pavilion roof.

The three of them burst out laughing.

I stood frozen, startled by the aerial ambush, examining the distinct white scratch that the bird had left on my right palm.

18

Results

TWO DAYS BEFORE HE was to leave for England, with his suitcases packed – except for some 'little-little things' he had to sneak in on the morning of his flight – my father picked out a razor from his toilet kit, affixed a shiny new blade and matter-of-factly announced: 'Time to learn how to shave, Karthik.'

'Pa?'

'I'll be away for a whole year, Karthik. Best you learn now.'

'I don't have any hair on my face, Pa.'

'You will sometime. And there will be nobody to teach you.'

'Pa, is it not better …'

'Just listen to me, Karthik. I know what I'm doing. Okay?'

'Yes, Pa.'

I had assumed my first shave would have an elaborate set-up, with my father and I planning the event days in advance. Two grown-ups debating the pros and cons of razors before heading to the store to buy the chosen one. Perhaps he would pick an auspicious date and time for the deed? I had heard enough from Chiku about the importance of selecting a razor – like buying one's first cricket bat or tennis racquet – making sure it felt just right. 'You need a perfect match,' Chiku had said. 'You'll then stick to that brand all your life.'

My grandfather had stayed with his stainless-steel folding razor until the end, the deadly weapon going swichak when folded. My father used a silvery safety razor, its robust metal head and double-edged blade mowing his cheeks quietly.

I had no choice in the matter. My father squeezed out a blob of cream, dabbed it on my cheeks, handed me a wet brush and ordered me to scrub. 'Round and round first, then up and down. Correct. Round and round. Then up and down.'

He handed me a safety razor with a glinty 7 O'Clock blade nestled in its clamps.

'Start from below the sideburns and go down till your neck. Don't change direction through the stroke.'

'What if I cut myself, Pa?'

'Oh god. You won't cut yourself if you concentrate.'

The blade's keen edges barely grazed the surface of my cheek.

'Stop being so scared, Karthik. It's just a blade. Won't kill you.'

'But Pa, if I get cut …'

'Karthik! You're going to be thirteen soon. Please stop behaving like some frightened child. Hold the razor at a twenty-degree angle and slide it down.'

The next swipe was more ambitious. The blade attacked the teensy follicles and trapped flecks of hair in the metallic gaps.

'See, that's all. The key areas are below your chin. You know the best approach for that? Turn towards the top left corner of the mirror … ya, forty-five degrees … but keep looking at the mirror. Hmm. Now reverse the razor and swipe up. Ah. Again.

'Now to your neck. Top to down. Careful when you go over the Adam's apple. That's where most people cut themselves.

'Quick quick. You can't spend all day shaving.

'Good. The neck is done. Now fold your upper lip and carefully shave below your nose. Yaaaa. You know what that vertical groove is called, no? Correct. Philtrum. It was one of the questions on the *Quiz Time* TV show. Remember?'

'Pa … you think it will be okay if I keep a moustache like you?'

'Maybe when you are older, Karthik.'

'Pa, please.'

'Until you are out of school, get a clean shave. After that you can do what you want.'

'Okay, Pa.'

'Hmm. There's still some hair under the neck. Give me the razor. Umm. A bit here … lift your head … yes. Okay, all done. Now wash your face properly.

'Here … use this towel.

'And here's the best part,' he said, smacking a dose of Old Spice aftershave on my cheeks and neck.

'Burning, Pa!'

'Yes, it must burn. Feels good after that.

'Anyway, I'm leaving this razor, brush, cream and aftershave for you here. And there are a few extra blades in this drawer.'

'How do I fix the blade into the razor, Pa?'

'Don't worry, you'll figure it out. Or ask Chiku to help.'

'Okay, Pa.'

'Aha. All done. Looking shipshape, Karthik. Now you are truly in manly territory.'

He walked out of the bathroom.

I turned to the mirror.

There I saw a foamed-up version of myself with blood trickling down a cheek – like an atlas depiction of a railway track over a snow-capped mountain. The mirror was obviously telling me what lay in store over the next few months. My father was just a corridor away, but I was already feeling his absence.

A little before six o'clock on a Saturday morning, my father prepared to leave. He checked and rechecked the weight of his suitcases, sneaked in an extra pouch of holy ash, packed another Ganesha statuette to keep at his workplace and repeatedly counted the crisp notes in the money pouch hanging from his neck. He was so harried, he might as well have been preparing for a Mathematics exam.

'Leaving so early, Pa?'

'I want to be at the airport by seven, Karthik. Chacko was saying they re-routed traffic yesterday. Some road-laying.'

'Okay, Pa.'

'Study well, okay? We will speak on the phone every week.'

'Yes, Pa.'

'And always remember to pray. Morning and evening. That is what will help you when things are not going well.'

'Yes, Pa.'

He patted me on the back.

'Be a good boy. Take care of Amma.'

'Okay, Pa.'

Settled in the back seat of the taxi, he held an imaginary phone to his ear to signal he would call us when he reached. He offered me a thumbs up, then turned to my mother with his brows raised and head tilted, as if alluding to some secret. My mother nodded, murmuring a prayer, no doubt nervous that her husband was embarking on such a big journey on – of all days – a Saturday.

The taxi got smaller and smaller.

And then it disappeared.

Monday morning arrived sooner than I had reckoned. My uniform was wrinkled, my trousers linty, my belt buckle unpolished and my shoes uncared for. I was too nervous to set any of this right, preoccupied as I was with Stephen's results.

What if he had somehow, miraculously, cleared the exams? What if the school had decided to hold on to him solely for his sporting prowess?

Stephen's marks would decide everything. If he were handed a lifeline and promoted to the eighth standard, I was a goner. Finished. No question. I would be thrashed and locked up in foul lavatories. My uniform would be ravaged day in, day out. No Georgian would speak to me again. I would go through the next three years friendless, joyless and, worst of all, hopeless. So there was nothing ambiguous about my prayers now. Stephen had to fail. Lord Ganesha had to ensure that.

The trip to school took longer than usual what with several buses cancelled or rerouted. Waiting at the stop for half an hour I imagined my father cursing the bus drivers, the bus conductors, the city's transportation department, the lousy state of the government, the apathetic public, and the country at large. My grandfather would have asked him to stop overreacting and reminded him of the Emergency: 'You want your buses to be on time or you want your freedom?'

I walked through the school's main gate a little after ten. The chapel spire threatened to pierce the bloated blue sky. The sun baked the granite ledge around the Pegasus fountain and, in the nursery, a row of rose plants drooped from neglect.

The main corridor bubbled with chatter. Boys clustered near the notice board to check their results. Some high-fived each other, some wore pensive looks, calling to mind my first day at St George's: the buzz in the corridor, the scramble around the notice board, the square cork plank enclosed in a glass casing. How jittery I had been back then. How unprepared I was for what had followed.

Stephen and Leo were not to be seen. Relieved, I jostled the crowd and scanned the results. My eyes landed on Paunchy's name but they saw no marks against each subject. Just a final column with an N/A. Next, I checked Leo Pinto. Again, no marks but another

N/A. I scrolled down the list to hunt for Stephen Mohanraj. Too many heads blocked my view. I stood on tiptoe, bent under a sweaty armpit and twisted and turned in the swarm of warm bodies, until I chanced a tiny opening between two shoulders. Darting past Stephen's individual marks, I reached the final column. There it was, like a gash on a palm: FAIL in red block letters.

My heart skipped a beat. I rechecked the last column, only for the blood-red FAIL to stare back at me. Like those climactic movie scenes where a judge reads out a grave sentence, pounds his gavel on the table, adjusts his coat and walks off.

That was it, then: Stephen's life altered. Clobbered at home and banned from playing. Disqualified from most of the schools in Bangalore. His exploits at St George's – the championship-winning goals, the glorious sixes, the lethal free kicks, the athleticism, the jokes – all dwarfed by one towering reality: he had failed.

'Get out of the way, fool,' someone screamed.

I checked my own results. Ninety-two in English Language; ninety-five in Mathematics; the rest in the eighties. My best performance by a distance.

'You cracked it, dude. Brilliant stuff.'

Aakash found me as I wriggled out of the crowd.

'Thanks, man. Way higher than I expected.'

'Highest in Maths for sure. I knew you had killed it, bugger. Ms Rodrigues would have been so happy.'

'Ya, she was a major help. How did you do, Aakash?'

'Not bad, man,' he said with a delicate shrug. 'All nineties except English Lit and Kannada. I guess it's my lucky day.'

'That's just amazing, dude. Congrats.'

'Oh please, Karthik. It was a photo finish. Nitin and Tarun were damn close. And take it from me: you're going to be the one to watch out for next year. I can see you leaving us all far behind.'

'No chance, man.'

'Why do you look so sad, Karthik? You've done well.'

'I'm alright, man.'

'Okay. I better collect my report card from the princi's office before there's a long line outside. He seems free for now.'

'See you, Aakash. Enjoy the holidays'

'Bye. See you on the first day.'

Not much had changed in the principal's office. A lone tube light washed the room in a soft blue. The chandelier was polished sparkly clean. A framed 'Vitai Lampada', Sir Henry Newbolt's poem, hung from the back wall.

'Good morning, Father.'

I made sure to stand a good two feet away from his table.

'Good job, Karthik,' he said, scanning my report card. 'I see you have shown considerable improvement since the mid-terms.'

'Thank you, Father.'

'Truth be told, I was a bit worried about you. I didn't want those unruly boys to drag you down with them.'

I bowed my head.

'You heard what happened, didn't you? Fools ...'

'Yes, Father.'

'The sad part is we lost a terrific cricketer and footballer in Stephen. But really, I had no choice in the matter.'

'Yes, Father.'

'I hope they continue their schooling. Nothing worse than dropping out.'

'Yes, Father.'

'Anyway, you must continue to work hard. You will soon realize it's easier to improve than to stay consistent near the top.'

'I'll try my best, Father.'

'Good. See you in two weeks.'

I walked out of his office with my head held high. Strolling across the corridor, I scanned the field. The canteen at the far end had its shutters drawn. Boys sat on the pavilion steps and examined trump cards. A group played hand tennis on the basketball court. Nitin and Tarun stood near the long-jump pit, sharing peanuts from a newspaper cone.

I was about to walk towards them when I sensed a pat on my shoulder.

Looming over me was PK, the boy responsible for my cigarette puff, and two others, presumably from the tenth standard.

'What's going on, Karthik? Smashed the exams, huh?'

PK's face was as expressionless as ever, his mood unreadable.

'I did okay, man. And you guys?'

One of the boys wrenched the report card off my hand.

'Bugger has killed it. Ninety-five in Maths. Holy mother!'

'Oh. Einstein's long-lost great grandson.'

'No, no, even greater.'

'Thanks guys,' I said. 'Can I please have my report card back?'

'This chap has balls, man. That much you got to give him.'

'I'm in a bit of a hurry, man.'

'We'll think about returning your report card, dude,' PK deadpanned. 'But first tell us: what happened the day Paunchy was thrown out.'

I took a step back, expecting a bingo. Were they going to blackmail me with new information? Had they spoken to Snoop? Or had Eric said something damaging?

'Go on, Karthik?'

'I have told Stephen and Leo everything, man.'

'Lies.'

'I swear. I left before anything happened that day.'

'Listen, Karthik. If you don't tell us the truth now, we're going to squash your balls every day of the week. And we'll tell everyone about what a dirty sneak you are.'

'I left before anything happened, man.'

'More lies.'

'It's the truth.'

'Fucking bullshit.'

Standing upright, I stared into PK's hazel eyes. I held back blinks, to make it clear that I wasn't about to be cowed. I had no idea how to get my report card back, nor did I have a plan to convince them of my innocence. And I sure as hell didn't know how I would ward off their threats and beatings when school reopened. The one boy who could protect me from them was now thrown out of school.

But here is the thing. There was no panic eating me up, no regret for finding myself in another hole. Something told me I would find a way – or that the gods would provide an opening soon enough. As long as I didn't give in, I held the upper hand.

The mid-morning sun pricked my arms. I stood still, betraying no weakness. PK and friends were more powerful than me but they were the ones taking the risks. Eventually, they would try one stunt too many. And like Leo and Paunchy, fly off a cliff. My best chance was to do the opposite. I had to bear their blows and bide my time. I had to somehow wear them out. To win, I had to steadfastly endure.

Acknowledgements

This book owes its existence to:
Amma, who taught me how to read and write,
Appa, who knows how to tell a good joke,
Ganja, Paddy, Sloppy, Bandi, Saigo, Nanji, Perry … among other rascals,
SJBHS, Bangalore,
Rahul and Shruti, who believed,
Picador India,
Sanju, Chammu, and Peggy,
And Akila, who said, 'Write it.'